Unforgettable

To Mum & dad
with love
x

Unforgettable

Charlie
Maclean

Printed in Great Britain by Clays Ltd, St Ives plc

Edited by Janan Akkad
Set in Sabon
Typeset by Sinem Erkas

First Edition
Paperback
ISBN 978-0-99339-164-4

www.charliemaclean.co.uk

Any moment – however casual, ordinary
– is poised, full of gaping life

Fugitive Pieces, Ann Michaels

Near Sofia, Bulgaria

My mother, Madeleine

I once read that our earliest memories are the times in childhood we've experienced the most powerful and intense feelings. The instances of the greatest mental or physical distress, or both. Distress, our parents, if they'd been able, would have done anything to prevent.

It is only these occasions of heightened emotion that survive down the years with any kind of detail, as memories. Memories that, sometimes only once, flash before our eyes while we wait absentmindedly for the kettle to boil. Or we recall during lucid moments before falling asleep or after waking.

***

I must have been three years old at the time, as I'd begun to walk and she didn't survive to my fourth birthday.

Wandering carelessly along a supermarket aisle, the rows of shelves on either side towered above me, like shiny, brightly coloured buildings. Music was playing in the background, but it was indistinct

– only a warm buzzing sound to me.

I turned to look up at her, but she was gone. I spun around until I was facing in the opposite direction. She was not there. I blinked hard, my eyes stung and warm tears ran down my cheeks.

I trailed along the wide, seemingly endless aisles. At each turn expecting to see her, but instead finding unknown figures looming above me. I was alone, completely and utterly alone, for the first time in my short life. I brought my hands up to my face and screamed.

When I opened my eyes, a tall, beautiful, black-haired woman appeared from the farthest aisle. Running, her eyes were wide, darting wildly in every direction; it was her. She knelt before me and I threw myself into her arms. She lifted me close into her chest, delicately, but so quickly I missed a breath.

She kissed my face and whispered into my ear – I can hear her voice now – repeating the words again and again, "My son, I love you. Don't ever leave me. My son, I love you. Don't ever leave me. Alex, my son."

It was the first time I'd consciously experienced love – my heart was full, as if it would burst. I never wanted to leave this woman's arms; my mother's, or for that feeling to ever fade.

Madeleine Wright died three months later

Twenty-Six Years Later

Six months ago

Alex was waiting. Classical music drifted from Victoria underground station to the bus stop round the corner where he stood. After checking his watch, he glanced up and down the street, before beginning to pace back and forth along the pavement. He was wearing a dark blue City suit over a crumpled white shirt. He tugged again at his thin silk tie, with its wide red and blue school tie-like stripes.

A woman with long, dark brown hair was standing at the far end of the bus stop. She was wearing a bright red and green cotton dress with white specks, a small, faded, black leather biker-style jacket and long strappy black boots. She was reading aloud to herself from the bundle of papers, tied with a green treasury tag, she held in her left hand. Her right hand twirling her hair, which hung down over her face.

With one foot flat to the ground and the other held at a point, she was perfectly balanced. After a few moments, without looking up, she swapped feet gracefully, like a ballet dancer at rest. Her elegant posture and the curve of her leg reminded Alex of a beautiful swan.

Between them sat a hooded youth with large head-phones nodding along to some unknown sound. He was tapping continuously into his phone with his thumbs, oblivious to their presence.

Alex's eyes watched the woman speaking quietly to herself but he could only make out the occasional word. When she adjusted the handful of papers she was holding he saw the title page.

"I did love you once," he said aloud, but not directly to the mysterious woman, and stepped forward unconsciously.

"Indeed, my lord, you made me believe so," she said immediately in response, turning to him. Their eyes met for a moment.

Her head now upright, her long brown hair fell back and Alex could see her face for the first time. She had huge deep green eyes and full bee-stung lips. Closer now, Alex could see her dress was patterned by red roses with green thorns and its white specks were, in fact, skulls.

She looked down again, her attention returning to her script. Her hands around the pages, a large matt-red oblong-shaped ring on the index finger of her right hand, the fingers of her left hand bare.

"Rehearsal?" Alex asked.

"Audition," she replied.

"Well, based on the delivery of the one line I've heard, I'd definitely give you the part."

"Haha. Thank you," she said. "You know the play?"

"A little," Alex said. "When I was growing up I had to learn bits of Shakespeare by heart to earn my pocket money."

"No Shakespeare, no sherbet."

"Exactly."

"Why?"

"My dad had a thing about Shakespeare, still does. That and jazz."

"And you?" she said.

"When I was a kid, I hated it. It was just a bunch of strange words in a strange order, that occasionally sounded nice."

"And now?" she asked. "Isn't Shakespeare meant to contain *all human experience*?"

"Now it's not so bad, it makes a bit more sense to me," Alex said. "Now I've actually lived a bit, had some human experience."

"It must have been good for you, though."

"When I recited whatever passage it was, my dad would smile, which he didn't do that often," Alex said, pulling at his tie again. "I've always thought it was for him."

"I think you both got something out of it," the woman said. "It will have helped your reading, enhanced your memory and given you..."

"The ability to chat up beautiful actresses at bus stops?"

She rolled her eyes and smiled. Alex noticed the tiniest of dimples on each of her cheeks and that her nose was slightly uneven.

"Confidence," she said. "That's what I was going to say."

A bus appeared from round the corner and

approached their stop. Alex took a deep breath. The mysterious actress then looked away. He breathed out, *she wouldn't be leaving him yet.*

"You're playing Ophelia?"

"Hopefully."

"Yes, hopefully." Alex smiled. He brought his hand to his face to stifle a yawn. "Sorry. Excuse me."

"Late night?" she said. "*Antony and Cleopatra* was the Christmas play at theatre school, RADA. There's a good line in it about partying. 'Let's mock the midnight bell'?"

"More like the three in the morning bell."

"Must have been some party."

"Not really. I'm not sleeping well at the moment."

"Guilty conscience? That's always it in Shakespeare."

"You sure you're an actress and not a psychologist?" Alex asked. He looked down at his watch.

"What about you?" the actress asked.

"I've got an interview, somewhere near Vauxhall of all places," Alex said. "The law firm I work at is merging with a bigger, American, one. We're all being interviewed for new jobs, that look remarkably similar to our current ones."

"What will happen?"

"I'll either get a new job that looks remarkably similar to my current one," Alex replied, "or get made redundant."

"That's terrible."

"I guess so," Alex said, thinking about the two years of nights and weekends spent in the office becoming qualified. At the dinner the firm's partners held for him and the other trainees, while the other trainees had celebrated, instead, he'd felt relief.

He'd slipped away from the table and called his father's office. It was the first time he'd called him at work. When he'd got through to his father, there'd been a long pause at the end of the line. "Well done," was all his father had said before saying he had to get back to work.

Alex turned to the actress beside him. She hadn't returned to reading her script but was looking at him.

"Were you thinking about your interview?" she asked. Alex smiled and looked into her green eyes.

"I was thinking it must be great to act for a living," he said.

"You know a few lines of Shakespeare. They'll be looking for a Hamlet today," she replied.

"Come on, it must be fun to be someone else."

"You only get to play someone else for a few hours. And then you go back to being yourself."

Alex glanced along the street again for the bus.

"So, why are you a lawyer?" the actress asked Alex. "It doesn't sound like you like them very much."

"Neither did Shakespeare," Alex said. "'The first thing we do, let's kill all the lawyers' – *Henry VI*."

"Why didn't you study something else?"

"I applied to do a screenwriting degree first. But at the last minute I changed my mind, and my course."

"Why?"

"Law seemed the sensible choice. I thought it was what my father – he's a lawyer – wanted, too," Alex said. "I'm not so sure now."

"Why screenwriting anyway?"

"I love stories. The way a character starts in one place and ends up in another."

"Did you ever write anything?"

"Half a film script, in law lectures when I was meant to be taking notes. I still have it somewhere."

"What's the elevator pitch?"

"Cynical female American journalist, who writes romantic guides to cities of the world, falls for a handsome London sightseeing tour-bus guide, who also happens to be an aspiring singer-songwriter."

"What happens? Or am I going to have to wait until the movie comes out?"

"You might have to wait a long time."

"Quickly, tell me how it ends before my bus comes."

"They fall in love at first sight," Alex said.

"Obviously," she replied, rolling her eyes. "Then what, Spielberg?"

"It all blows up after a misunderstanding, they hate each other and it looks like they won't end up together."

"But they do, right?"

"All is lost, cue musician's mad dash to St Pancras station before gorgeous hack leaves for Paris and his life forever."

"I'd go and see it."

"Really?" Alex asked.

"You know – if nothing else were on," she said, smiling. "I'm not really into romantic comedies."

"I like to think of it as more of a drama, actually,"

Alex said.

"Does next summer's box office smash have a title yet?"

"Lovers' Guide to London."

"Nice. So he's her guide to the real London but also her heart. She makes him believe in himself and helps him write lyrics."

"What can I say? You understand my art."

Alex noticed she twirled her hair with her right hand again, as she'd done earlier. Perhaps she was nervous, or flirting with him – or it was just something she did – he wasn't sure, but it enchanted him.

"Why didn't you finish it? The script."

"I stopped writing."

"What did you do instead?"

"I read books about writing. Books about famous writers and their lives. Books about the travels of famous writers. Books by the lovers of famous writers about the famous writers. I even read a book about the pets of famous writers."

"That's a lot of reading."

"But not much writing. And if I wasn't reading, then I was shopping for great notebooks and pens."

"Stationary shopping is good for the soul."

"Then I thought a typewriter was what I needed."

"And was it?" she laughed, twirling her hair again.

"No. It was loud, it hurt my ears, after a few hours of typing, it hurt my hands too. You can't make changes. It's not practical or portable, either."

"I bet it looked amazing, though."

"It looked amazing and I looked ridiculous," Alex

said. "Then it was absolute silence. I thought that was the key. I stayed at home."

"Too quiet?"

"Yup. So, I went to cafés."

"Too noisy?"

"I'd drink too much coffee and get too wired to write," Alex replied. "I also liked doing the things I thought writers did."

"Hanging out in Parisian cafés?" she asked.

"Starbucks, Chalk Farm. I never did make it to Paris. There was a house party every weekend at the time," Alex said. "Now all my friends are turning thirty, it's all box sets and babies."

"Maybe they've grown up," she said. "I think I know why you never finished the script."

"Why?" Alex asked.

Another bus came round the corner. It was the number fifty, the bus Richard had told him to get – it was his bus. The actress looked from the bus to him. Alex looked away dismissively, glancing down at his watch but without registering the time.

"Are you sure that's not your bus?" she asked.

"I'm sure," Alex replied.

"Are we thinking the same thing?" she said.

Alex checked his watch again, this time noting the time, the interview was meant to be beginning at that moment.

"That we're both going to be late?" he said.

"That the music from the station is nice."

"Of course," Alex said, although at some point he'd stopped being conscious of the music. There were drums pounding and strings being played at a rapid pace. "Yes, it is."

"I prefer jazz, though, like your father, it sounds." She tilted her head back. "Live jazz I love especially – you never know where it's going to go, or where it's going to take you."

Alex was about to say something in response, but when he turned to look at her she was reading her script again, silently now.

"I've always thought it would be great to date an actress," Alex said.

The mysterious woman looked up at Alex. She smiled with her large lips, her dimples showing again.

"Really? Why's that?" she asked.

**

There was loud ringing near his left ear. Alex opened his eyes; there was just blackness with flashing white lines, like an old untuned TV screen he'd seen in films. He felt a cotton sheet against his face. Turning his head the light hit his eyes; brighter than it should be. Without seeing a clock, he knew he'd slept through his alarm, if he'd remembered to set one.

Without lifting his head from the pillow, he reached out with his left hand towards the vibrating phone which rested at the corner edge of the bed. When his shaky fingertips touched it, it slipped over the edge of the bed. He stretched his hand out and catching the phone in his hand, the momentum carried him over the edge of the bed and he tumbled onto the hard grey floor.

"Richard," Alex said, now lying on the floor beside the bed, spreadeagled.

He was dressed in a white shirt and beltless suit trousers from the previous day at work and the pub after with Richard.

"Yes, I'm getting up now. There's no need to shout," he continued. "I don't know why you bother, either."

Alex put the phone in his trouser pocket and pushed himself off the ground with both hands. He felt lightheaded and fell back onto the floor, banging his head. The phone in his pocket rang again.

"I haven't gone back to sleep," Alex said. "How am I meant to get ready with you calling me all the time?" He put down the phone.

Putting one hand on the floor and another on the side of the bed, Alex propelled himself upright. He stumbled across the modern-styled bedroom, one hand clasped to his aching head. Except for the bed and side table, the room was bare, with pale grey walls and a slate floor.

In the shower, Alex leaned against the wall, still unsteady on his feet. With the sensation of streaming water on his head, he imagined the neurons in his brain firing up one by one, reconnecting after being dulled by alcohol-induced sleep.

After hurriedly dressing, Alex walked through the empty corridor passing the open plan, kitchen lounge. Apart from the takeaway cartons on the floor in front of the sofa, the surfaces of the room were bare. Every morning he thought to himself it looked like someone had just moved out – it had been that way since Amy left. He descended the stairs.

He closed the front door of the flat behind him. Leaning back against it for a moment, he wished he could open it, climb back up the stairs and collapse onto his bed. The front of his head began throbbing and he remembered the countless rounds of Sambuca shots he'd insisted on ordering towards the end of the previous night. Richard had tried to stop him and he now regretted not listening to him, as usually was the case.

Alex stepped onto the cobbled Islington mews street. Richard told him the quickest way was the tube to King's Cross then Victoria line southbound, followed by a short bus ride. A taxi the whole route was Alex's preference but the journey would take longer due to the rush hour traffic, apparently.

The Angel underground station escalator lived up to its longest-escalator-in-Europe fame today, he thought as he tapped on the wall as he descended. Another image from the previous evening in his mind, he was kissing someone in the alleyway beside the pub – a tall, blonde trainee accountant called Sara, or was it Susie? He'd also kissed someone else earlier by the toilets, or had it also been her?

Alex straightened his tie and felt the limpness of his shirt collar. The little pockets underside empty of his metal collar bones; the thin, gold strips rounded at one end and pointed at the other which usually held his shirt collars straight. They'd been pocketed by a local builder the previous night after a lost arm wrestling bet, Alex trying to show off in front of a table of girls.

As he stepped off the last step of the escalator, Alex's phone rang. He pulled it from his pocket and glanced down at the unknown number. It went silent almost immediately as the mobile reception cut out and it went to voicemail. He guessed it was probably Mary from Bright Starts.

He thought social responsibility was something his law firm did so it could put a few shiny photos of its lawyers in overalls doing charity work into the annual brochure. To make them look less heartless and ruthless. However, he always attended the monthly presentations in the staff canteen. It was a break from the monotony of work and occasionally interesting, and always catered with great pastries.

Mary's charity recruited professionals from City professions to mentor secondary school children from deprived backgrounds in south-east London. Its target age was thirteen to sixteen – when it considered kids were most open to positive input and less susceptible to gangs and drugs.

While the social responsibility team dismantled the video projector screen in the interval, Alex had got talking to Mary. He'd been amazed at how the lives of young people could be changed by a few hours of mentoring a week. At the end, she'd caught him at the door and taken his phone number, given him the charity's number and made him promise to call her. He hadn't.

When Alex emerged from Victoria station, his headache had moved from the front of his head to the back and his shirt was damp with sweat; the train carriage had been packed full of people and the air conditioning out of order. He strode to the newspaper stall opposite the exit to buy a bottle of sparkling water. He opened it immediately. It sprayed over the front of his shirt and suit jacket. He took a long drink from the bottle.

There was a cool breeze and looking up, Alex noticed for the first time that it was a beautiful morning – bright and warm. He stopped on the pavement, commuters rushing past on either side of him. Tilting his head upwards in the direction of a sun, so golden in colour.

A familiar emptiness rose up inside Alex from his stomach to his chest. He could go weeks without feeling it but it would always return, sometimes only for a moment but often for hours, or even days, at a time. He gazed deeply into the strong sun, yearning for its seemingly eternal sunshine to fill the void inside him – to make him feel, for once, whole.

Someone brushed by Alex, and he looked down from the sky at the grey pavement in front of him. He began walking again, in the direction of the bus stop.

***

"Why's that?" she asked again. "Why have you always wanted to date an actress?"

The beautiful woman opposite Alex looked

expectantly at him.

"It's not like dating someone with a boring, normal job, is it?" Alex replied.

"It's not. It's hanging out with someone who never buys dinner because they're too poor, and who's never around because they have three jobs and…"

"It sounds like you're trying to put me off the idea."

"That's just the reality."

"I suppose I like the idea of testing her on her lines," Alex said.

"I'm sure your future imaginary actress girlfriend will find that helpful, perhaps even cute."

"Over the breakfast table," Alex continued. "Or better, in the bath. One of those roll-top ones with the taps in the middle so we'd be lying opposite each other, scripts in hand."

"You could give her a foot massage, too, while you were down there at the foot end," the actress replied. "In between scenes, obviously."

"Does the back door of a theatre have a special name?" Alex asked.

"No, it's just called the back door of the theatre," she replied, laughing.

"I'd surprise her with a huge bouquet of flowers every opening night at the theatre's back door."

Alex felt like taking off his jacket. The morning chill was now gone and the air was beginning to warm.

"You have a vivid imagination," she said, with a slight smile, flashing her dimples.

"You always wanted to act?" Alex asked.

"I wanted to be a dancer. I used to practice before school, after school, at weekends – I even used to practice in my dreams."

"That's dedication. What happened?"

"Fell off my bicycle, damaged my knee and after lots of scans and tears, I had to give up that dream – a tough thing at eleven."

She slipped off the biker jacket she was wearing. As she hung it over her bag, her thin lower right arm showing a hint of muscle.

"The dancing world is impossible to get into but acting is just as difficult – people only ever see the success stories.

"There can be huge highs but also crushing lows. That's combined with periods of financial hardship and unemployment," she said, with a small sigh. "Not all Londoners earn City lawyers' salaries."

She had such a serious expression on her face, Alex had to try and make her smile again.

"I understand that," he said finally.

"I know you were having fun, I was, too. I'm just nervous. I played Ophelia at school but haven't had a chance to prepare as much as I'd have wanted.

"Also, I just felt so tired just then. I was working till late last night and will be again after this audition."

"Jobs to pay the bills?" Alex asked.

"To *almost* pay the bills," she replied. "I have two jobs. Service jobs for the flexibility. I'm standing the whole time, which makes me so tired."

"Sounds like you're an actress in need of a foot massage," Alex said, but she continued to speak, seemingly to herself.

"I keep being in the final two for the roles I desperately want, then missing out."

"Sounds heart-breaking," Alex said. "How do you keep going?"

"I know it's what I really want to do, however hard it's been," she said, smiling again. "I'm going to keep going, at least for the next six months..."

"I'm sure it will happen for you."

"So what about this interview of yours?"

"I know I'm lucky to have my job," Alex said. "But I don't know if I really want it."

"Please don't say that in the interview."

"I won't. I promise," Alex said, laughing.

"I think you do know where you want to be," the actress said. Alex looked intently at her.

"Sitting by a swimming pool in Hollywood, writing film scripts – there's no shortage of actresses out there either."

"So we might be heading to the same destination then."

Alex went to check his watch but let his wrist drop without looking at it.

"So, let's get something straight then. Have you actually ever dated an actress?" she asked.

"No. I never meet any. I hang out with lawyers most of the time. My best friend, Richard, is an actuary, so all the girls he knows are into maths rather than Marlowe. Then there's only the ones that come into the Crown, our local pub. There's something else, though."

"What's that?"

"I don't mind paying for dinner and them being busy. I once dated – well, more than dated – an artist.

"But there are other definite downsides to being in a relationship with a creative person, far worse than those things."

"Such as?" the actress said, rolling her eyes.

"The big passionate rows, the shouting, the broken plates."

"The artistic temperament?"

"Exactly! They're all crazy. That's why I think a 'no artistic types of any kind rule' is only sensible. And definitely no acting types, I imagine they're the worst."

"They're the absolute worst," she replied. "Personally, I wouldn't dream of dating one. And I am one."

A more angular and darker red bus came round the corner, it was one of the older style ones. It was slowing down as it approached their stop. Now next to each other, almost touching, they looked at the bus and then each other, as if it was strange for the bus to have appeared at that moment and interrupted them. *This is it,* Alex thought.

Then the bus moved off without the doors opening. Alex and the actress looked at each other again and smiled.

"I thought that was it," she said. Alex looked at her. She continued. "My bus."

But as soon as Alex heard the low rumble of the bus engine of the new environmentally friendly buses, he knew she would be leaving.

"This really is me," she said.

"Break a leg, I think is the right thing to say," Alex said. "And I hope I didn't interrupt your preparation too much."

"It's helped me relax. Good luck for your interview! I hope you get the job," she said. "But if you don't then I'm sure that will be okay, too."

She turned, delicately. As she did, she stood on a loose lace that hung from her left boot, unbalanced, she was falling forward. The bus, which was getting louder and closer, didn't appear to be slowing down.

She fell towards the road and the oncoming bus, as it pulled into the bus stop. Alex stepped forward immediately and reached out for her. She was suddenly in his arms, her face so close he could feel her breath on his face and her heart pounding against his chest. Abruptly, and finally, the bus came to a stop in front of them.

She stepped away from him gently, he released her from his arms. "You caught me," she said quietly, her eyes glazed and with a faraway look.

She then smiled widely at him. It was not just her full lips that made her beautiful, wide smile so captivating. She smiled also with her eyes, in a way Alex had never seen before.

"Bye," she said, before turning and getting on the waiting bus in one flawless motion.

"I'm Alex," he called out after her. "What's your name?"

"Julia," she said, glancing back at him.

Alex opened his mouth but she'd already turned away. She tapped her Oyster card and made her way down into the bus. He could only stand and gaze after the beautiful, mysterious actress – Julia.

Chapter Two
Without Julia

As Alex stepped forward to follow Julia onto the bus, his phone began ringing – the interview he was now late for, he thought. He paused. The bus driver turned his head in his direction. Alex didn't move.

The driver turned back to face forwards and the doors shut with a mechanical hiss. Alex saw a flash of red and green of Julia's dress by the inside stairs of the bus, before a tall, dark-suited man obscured his view. The bus turned the corner and accelerated out of sight. *She was gone.*

Alex stood perfectly still. His phone, still in his jacket pocket, went silent. A smartly-dressed old lady came quickly round the corner before stopping beside Alex.

"Have I missed it?" she asked Alex, breathing deeply.

"Yes, I'm afraid so."

"I'm going to be late now."

"Me, too." Alex sighed.

"There'll be another along in a few minutes," she said quietly.

"I'm not so sure."

"You look like you've seen a ghost," she said.

"I hope not, an angel perhaps," Alex said and smiled. "I think I'm going to walk," he added after a few minutes.

He passed the Apollo theatre. He'd bumped into a mutual friend of Amy's outside there only a few weeks earlier. Amy had just had her first gallery show and quit giving facials and selling Mac products in Covent Garden – a job she'd had since art college. He was so happy to hear that. He also found out she'd got engaged. It had been a strange feeling to think of her life now.

Alex took out his phone to call the office for the exact address of the interview. While waiting for someone to pick up at the other end he smiled, imagining Julia sitting in an audition waiting room full of Ophelias, thumbing her script and twirling her hair as she'd done earlier.

He put his phone away, he now knew where he was going and they knew he was running late. He cursed himself. Why hadn't he asked for her number? The time had just passed so quickly. It would've been crazy for him to have got on a bus heading in the opposite direction to the one he needed, the wrong bus. But now, the bus she'd left on seemed like the right one.

* * *

"Mr Wright, may we call you Alex?"

"You may," Alex replied.

Alex sat back in his chair and ran his hands through his hair. He'd just shaken hands with the two management consultants sitting opposite him. He glanced around the room of the rented office, albeit a very upmarket one – he noticed the factory label was still on his chair.

One of the men explained what he already knew – that they were assisting in his law firm's restructure and conducting their assessments away from the firm's offices.

"We've been looking through your last few annual appraisals and have found a common theme."

"What's that?" Alex asked.

The two balding men had greeted him at the door of the small interview room in a polite but detached manner. Listened patiently, if passively, to his apology and explanation for being late before waving him towards the deceptively comfortable-looking seat in which he now sat. Both around the same height of 5'11" – slightly shorter than him – and wearing grey suits, they looked unremarkably similar. Alex discovered almost immediately, and much to his annoyance, that neither was a lawyer.

"What do *you* think it is?" the one on the right said.

Whatever the reasons given, Alex saw the merger for what it was: a highly successful, ambitious American law firm swallowing up an old English law firm, for its respected and solid – if not dynamic – reputation, as well as, its illustrious client list of the great and the good, or not so good as he'd found to be the case.

Alex leaned forward in his chair and breathed in deeply. He was remembering Julia's smile when he'd made her laugh for the first time. If only he'd asked for her number, he thought again. There was a cough.

He looked up to see the two men looking directly at him. Alex pulled at his tie, he found his shirt collar was damp again, he'd run the last half mile to the building. He looked at the room's window but it wasn't one that could be opened, the room was air conditioned – or meant to be.

"Would you like a glass of water?" one of the men asked.

"Yes. Thanks."

"Help yourself." The man indicated to his left.

Alex rose and crossed the room to the dispenser. He filled one of the tiny plastic cups and drank it in one go before returning to his seat.

"Gentlemen, if you speak to my clients and look at my case files, you'll see I do a decent job for the firm. And I'm sure I'll continue to do a decent job at Pinsent, Matthews, Young and…"

The two men opposite him glanced at each other.

"The new firm name. Brand. Hasn't been decided yet."

"At whatever you, or some advertising agency charging an obscene amount of money, decide to call the monster being created."

One of the men wrote something in a notebook open in front of him.

"We've analysed the statistics of all the non-partner

lawyers at the firm by experience, billing rate, number of hours billed," the other man said. "Then ranked the lawyers."

"You're going to be sacking people by spreadsheet?"

"It's not an exact science, and we've never done it with a law firm before, but we have confidence it's a robust methodology. The beauty is that it removes human judgement from the process. It removes the personal."

"And that's a good thing?" Alex asked.

"The partners have given it their full support."

"They would say that. They're never going to need to work again after this goes through."

The man wrote something down in his notebook again.

"I don't know if you guys understand how law firms work, but without clients, they're screwed. Practice law is a service industry. It's about building and maintaining relationships. It's about the personal," Alex said. "I happen to be good at that."

"And you've certainly shown that today," one of the men said in a flat tone.

"It's clear you've a good rapport with your team, the wider firm and, yes, with clients – and we've given this a numeric value," the other man said. "However, ultimately, your overall score is below the standard required for the new role for which you are being assessed."

Alex thought of his colleagues in other rooms in the building, sitting equally uncomfortably in their seats. Their suspicion the assessments were to get rid of the relatively expensive qualified lawyers before the merger appeared to be true. It was a Monday, though, and although he hadn't thought it was true, someone had once told him companies sack people on Fridays so as to cause as little fuss as possible.

Alex leaned forward in his chair, awaiting the interviewers' next question. He didn't think there was anything he could say that could save his job but he felt his manner so far had been abrupt – his father disliked bad manners intensely.

One of the men stood and took off his jacket before sitting down again.

"You're the kind of lawyer at the firm we're looking to help."

"Help?" Alex asked.

"We're offering very generous terms to employees who feel it's time for them to seek…"

"New challenges," the other man finished his sentence.

Alex sat back in his chair. He undid the top button of his shirt and loosened his tie.

"I'd been trying to work out which one of you is good cop and which is bad cop," he said, with a wry smile. "I realise now there's no good cop."

The room fell silent and the two interviewers shifted in their seats, glancing at each other.

"Please tell me about these new challenges," Alex said. "Where are they?"

"They're with other firms," the jacketless man said, after a long pause.

"I thought you were going to say that."

"Unless you want to fight for this job?" said the other.

It was at that moment that Alex knew he didn't want to fight for the job, his old job or the new one. He just wanted to get out of the room as quickly as possible.

"I think I'd rather you did call me Mr Wright after all, if you don't mind."

The next hour passed quickly, in a haze of statutory rights, contractual terms and non-disclosure clauses. Alex signed a seemingly endless series of papers. As a lawyer who wouldn't let a client sign a single document without him scrutinising every word of it, he barely glanced at the papers in front of him.

He desperately tried to concentrate but his mind kept returning to the mysterious brunette, Julia. Her deep green eyes and voluptuous lips, and the way she brushed the hair from her face when she'd looked up at him and responded to his line from *Hamlet*.

The two men opposite Alex seemed very sure of themselves now, back amongst their figures. They went about their work steadily and with the confidence of a team closing a deal. He understood that feeling well enough, he'd experienced it countless times in the course of his career.

"Generous terms?" Alex said. He lent forward in his chair. His attention had momentarily drifted to Julia again.

"Well, we can't get sued by lawyers, can we? Of course, they'll be a settlement of some kind."

Alex could not tell which one had spoken, they

both had their jackets off now.

"Settlement figure?"

"Based on your time at the firm and grade. As long as you abide by the clauses regarding non-contact with firm clients and not removing data from the office.

"It's one payment upfront and the rest when the merger is finalised in approximately six months."

Ten minutes later, Alex was putting his office entry fob on the desk in front of the men – the initials of the firm name printed on it in gold letters. From his wallet, he took out his identification pass and placed it beside the fob. The photo was from his first day at the firm. His face, with its eager, determined expression looking back at him.

***

Alex took a seat at the bar, as usual. He hadn't ever been in the Crown and Goose at this time. Two middle-aged men in shiny suits and gelled hair, were further down the bar, talking with two young women in grey pencil skirts – all with winter tans and from the local estate agent. He wondered if it had been late lunch drinks or an early finish. A table of students with their sticker-laden Apple Macs and bags of rolling tobacco drank their ciders casually. A handful of old men sat alone, drinking their pints of London Pride in small sips. Alex took out his phone and pressed to retrieve his voicemail.

"You're in early," the tall, fair-haired, Australian

bar manager said to Alex. "Did you get sacked or something?"

"Yes, I did actually."

He laughed and placed Alex's pint of beer in front of him, looking at Alex as if he was joking. Alex ordered a double whisky chaser. It came fast and he drunk it in one go before taking the first sip of his pint and then reaching for his wallet to pay.

"Thanks Tom," Alex said.

He rang Mary back. He explained what had happened and how sorry he was he wouldn't be able to help. She seemed to think it would be a good thing for his proposed mentee to see him set an example of resilience in the face of a setback in life. She was certainly more convinced than Alex that he would find a new job very soon. To every objection he raised, Mary seemed to have an answer. He even joked that she should consider an alternative career in law. His mouth dry and desperate to end the call, he reluctantly agreed go to the charity's headquarters the next day. He put down his phone on the bar.

"I got your message." Alex heard Richard's voice behind him. "Let you go early, did they?"

"No, they just, let me go," Alex replied, sighing.

"Your prayers came true then," Richard said.

Alex turned to look at Richard.

"What? Seriously?" Richard asked.

"Voluntary redundancy. But there wasn't much that was voluntary about it," Alex replied.

Richard looked up and down the bar, as if looking for someone to corroborate Alex's story. He turned back at Alex, now smiling.

"A minute ago you seemed upset."

"The morning wasn't all bad news."

"Okay. So there's a woman involved," Richard guessed. "Where did you meet her?"

"Actually, I kind of have you to thank for that."

"No surprise there."

"It all happened at the bus stop," Alex said. "We had an instant connection. It felt like we were inexplicably drawn across time and space to meet at that unlikely spot.'

"Who is this fellow dimensional traveller?"

"She's an actress."

When Richard didn't reply, Alex turned to see him looking down the bar at one of the bar staff, a petite blonde. The sounds of loud chatter filled the pub. A group of young teachers, with bags from the local school, had taken the booth in the corner. Three builders in yellow jackets, toolboxes on the floor beside them, were stood round the fruit machine by the exit.

The blonde woman returned to their end of the bar and put a pint in front of Richard. They shared a conspiratorial looking smile.

"Thanks, Ciara," he said.

"No worries."

Alex looked at Richard, whose eyes followed her down the other end of the bar where she began serving someone.

"Do you have to be Australian to work here?" Alex said.

"She's from New Zealand, you idiot," Richard said. "And she heard you."

"Oh no, is it like Americans and Canadians?"

Off the high street, the Crown and Goose was a local pub – you would only go there if you knew it, or had stumbled upon it. Alex and Richard came across it returning from a dinner party nearby, that had disappointingly and unexpectedly ended early due to a sick host. It was their first night out after Amy had left Alex.

They'd met two Swedish postgraduates studying at LSE after ordering what they'd intended to be a nightcap. It became the first of many rounds, followed by a series of late night bars and a nightclub, countless shots and hours of dancing. They'd watched the sunrise together by the canal in Camden. Afterwards, returning to Richard's flat and pairing off. She was the first woman Alex had slept with after Amy, her unbearable loss making him strangely lustful.

He sometimes thought of that night as he entered the pub. Something about the happenstance of it and the way that it'd flowed with a life of its own had made it so memorable. They'd had many great nights since that first but perhaps he and Richard returned because they hoped to experience the spontaneity of a night like that again, or recapture it in some way, however impossible that was.

"What's her name, again?" Alex asked.

Richard looked at him with a serious expression.

"She's new. That's all you need to know."

"Okay. I think I understand." Alex put up his

hands, palms towards Richard.

"I'm glad that's clear."

They drank their pints in silence, Alex in a determined manner and Richard in his usual measured way.

"Are they really allowed to let you go like that?" Richard asked.

"I never paid much attention during employment law lectures. But yes, they are," Alex said. "As long as they pay me off. Which they have."

"You can finish that bloody film script now," Richard said. "Or..." He trailed off.

"Richard, my life's falling apart and you're not even paying attention."

Richard was looking down the bar again at his blonde friend pouring one of the young builders a pint. Richard laughed, turning back to Alex.

"Why don't you go on holiday with the money?" Richard said.

"I don't want to go on holiday."

"You're a qualified lawyer. There must be plenty of jobs out there for you if you don't want a break."

"It's not that."

"What is it then?" Richard said. "You've met someone. This actress at the bus stop..."

"That's what I'm trying to say," Alex replied. "Never mind finding another job, I need to find her. I need to find Julia."

"And I need to get off home," Richard said, downing the last of his pint.

"You can't go," Alex said, his mouth and eyes open

wide.

"If you and Julia made such 'an instant connection' then why don't you just message her now – ask her out?"

"I don't have her number."

"So she wasn't 'inexplicably drawn across time and space' to give you her number."

"I forgot to ask her for it before she left."

"The one girl's phone number in London you really want and you forget to ask for it."

"Look, I'll buy the drinks tonight. You need to stay here and help me figure out a way to find her," Alex said. "And not get distracted by your new friend." They both looked down the bar at the blonde barmaid.

"Her name is Ciara. And another pint then, I suppose," Richard said, sitting back down beside Alex. "So, what do you know about this mysterious actress, except her name?"

"That's all I know."

"You know there are eight million people in London?" Richard said.

"Are you trying to say it's going to be hard, Richard?"

"It's going to be impossible, Alex."

"Impossible?"

"With the information you have, yes," Richard replied.

"If she's as amazing as you say she is, she's probably got a boyfriend anyway." Richard picked up his empty pint glass and put it down, turning his eyes back to Alex.

Ciara appeared in front of them again.

"Ciara, this is Alex."

"We meet properly," Ciara said. "I've heard a lot about you,"

"I'm a massive *Lord of the Rings* fan. Wonderful hills, New Zealand. Not like Australia, it's so dry there," Alex said. Richard glared at Alex. Ciara frowned, looking confused.

"Lovely to meet you, Ciara." Alex continued.

"Same again?" she asked, rolling her eyes at Richard.

"She definitely hates you now," Richard said to Alex, after Ciara had left them to get their drinks.

"Alex, I'm just being realistic about this Julia situation."

"I love it when you're realistic, Richard, it makes such a change," Alex said, sighing. "What about the internet? Facebook etc? Surely I'll find her there?"

"There will be hundreds, if not thousands of Julias in London, and she might not even be on there," Richard replied. "With no surname or any other details..."

"Thanks, Richard. I feel so much better about everything now."

"You should be concentrating on finding a new job anyway," Richard said, sighing. "What you really need to do is..."

"Is what?" Alex said, looking intently at Richard. Richard's eyes were drawn again to Ciara and he answered without looking at Alex.

"What you need to do is forget her."

"So, I lose my job, and the girl of my dreams, all in one day – is that what you're saying?"

"That's exactly what I'm saying," Richard said. "I crunch data all day and try to predict the future. The odds of you bumping into this particular Julia in this city are almost zero.

"You're more likely to get run over by a bus than to run into her again at a bus stop again, or indeed anywhere."

"I don't think I'm going to be able to forget her, Richard," Alex said, putting his elbows on the bar and his head in his hands.

"Why?"

"She's not the kind of girl you can easily forget," Alex said, before sitting upright again and taking a deep breath. "She's *unforgettable*."

Chapter Two

With Julia

Alex stepped onto the bus. His heart beating hard. He turned to get off but the door was already closing. He tapped his travel card and turned to the lower level of the bus, all the seats were taken. He scanned their faces but there was no Julia.

He began climbing the steep stairs to the top deck. The seats at the front rows were all full. He saw Julia at the back and the empty seat next to her. He made his way down the aisle towards her. She looked up at him with a surprised smile but didn't appear shocked – as if it was quite normal that he'd be there.

"I thought you were going towards Vauxhall," she said, cocking her head to one side.

"I thought I was, too," Alex said, slowly. "I got the address wrong." He indicated to the seat beside her. "Can I?"

"Of course," Julia said with a smile.

"The back row," Alex said, sitting down beside her. "It was where all the fun stuff used to happen, on school trips."

"I never went on any, so I'll have to take your word for it," Julia said. "What kind of fun did you have planned?"

The fabric of Julia's faded dress looked rumpled, like she'd picked it up off the back of a chair that morning. He could hear her long, black strappy boots pounding the London streets as she rushed between auditions, work shifts and home.

There was a thin ladder in her tights on her left leg, the one closest to him. His eyes traced the jagged line that emerged from the bottom of her dress on her thigh, narrowed at her knee before disappearing under the top of her boot. It was her only imperfection, and it wasn't hers.

"Richard would say 'the kind where no one gets hurt,'" Alex said.

"Who's Richard?"

"He's an old friend. My best friend, I guess. He looks out for me. Although I don't always deserve it."

"That's nice to have. You're lucky. Are you alike?"

"Opposites, but we're like brothers, in a way."

"Richard, the sensible big brother, it sounds like."

As the bus turned and accelerated forward they looked ahead into the bright sunlight. A man in black combat trousers and a green polo shirt with a London council emblem was tending to a patch of daffodils at the side of the road.

"So did your dad really make you learn Shakespeare for your pocket money?"

"The love sonnets first. Easier to learn than speeches from the plays. It was weird because although I knew what the words meant literally, I didn't really understand them. I was too young to know what love was

– romantic love, at least," Alex replied. "Strangely, they all seemed to me to be about my mother."

"Your mother?"

"She died when I was very young."

"What happened?"

"Cancer."

"I'm sorry."

"Thank you," Alex said, as he glanced away from Julia and out of the window. "It was a long time ago."

"I'm still sorry."

"Thanks."

"So, do you have a favourite?" Julia asked, smiling. "Shakespeare play."

"Well, at twelve, I loved all the blood and guts of *Macbeth*. At thirteen, the tragedy and comedy of *King Lear*. At fourteen, the politics of *Julius Caesar*. At fifteen, *Henry V* for honour and the valour."

"'We few, we happy few, we band of brothers,'" Julia said, in a dramatic tone. "Typical boy."

"Sixteen," Alex said.

"*Romeo and Juliet?*" Julia asked.

"'What's in a name? That which we call a rose, By any other name would smell as sweet,'" Alex exclaimed.

A large lady beside them in a green summer dress chuckled. "You got out of bed the right side today, didn't you, dear?"

"'The world's mine oyster, Which I with sword will open," Alex responded, with a smile directed at the lady.

"*Othello?*" Julia said.

"*The Merry Wives of Windsor*," Alex said. "I'm not crazy about *Othello*."

"Me, neither. I hate jealousy."

"Seventeen," Alex continued. "I liked the surrealness of *The Tempest*. I think Shakespeare must've been smoking something when he wrote it, perhaps it wasn't just tobacco Sir Walter Raleigh brought back from the new world."

"Eighteen?"

"*Hamlet*. Dark and complex – it's still my favourite."

"Wow. You were a precocious child," Julia said. "Did you ever play computer games?"

"My dad didn't really approve of computers, or TV, for that matter," Alex said. "So, what about your favourite play?"

"This is going to sound terrible, but I find Shakespeare a bit melodramatic. I'm more of an Ibsen fan. But if I had to choose, it would be *A Midsummer Night's Dream*. I love Bottom, he makes me laugh so much." She smiled to herself, while looking ahead, as if recalling a performance she'd seen.

Alex looked at Julia. He wanted her to look back at him, so he could feel the intensity of the gaze from her green eyes again. He wanted to ask her a question, so he could hear the clarity and weightlessness of her voice; listen for the delicate, exquisite pauses between her words. He wanted to make her laugh, so he could feel again her spirit in the air.

He looked at his watch. A panel of people would be waiting in a room for him somewhere behind them.

He pulled his phone from his pocket; he had a missed call and a voicemail. He knew he would have to get off the bus soon but felt strangely at ease.

"Do you have auditions every day?" Alex asked Julia.

"Depends. It's usually one or two a week. I have another tomorrow, though, in the West End, for Cabaret," Julia replied. "I hate open auditions, you can be waiting around all day."

"Open auditions?"

"Anyone can audition, whether they have an agent or not."

"Sounds like one of those TV talent shows," Alex said, looking at his watch again. "In case your stop is before mine," he added, "How many stops have I got left to ask for your number?"

"I'm sorry, Alex," Julia said, after a pause. "I'm kind of off men at the moment."

"Off men? As in, you're into women?" Alex asked, after a pause.

"Off relationships."

"Why?"

"I'm so busy with work and auditions, I barely have time to see my friends," Julia said. "Even if I gave you my number, I wouldn't have time to see you anyway – unless you started turning up to my auditions – and I'll have even less time if I get this part."

"Fair enough," Alex said. "I'm not going to beg for your number."

"Hang on a minute," Julia said. "What happened to your 'no actress' rule?"

"I was hoping you'd forgotten about that," Alex said. "Every rule has to have an exception, though, right?"

Julia was silent. The bus turned a corner and pulled suddenly up at a stop. Julia turned to Alex.

"My stop," Julia said, standing. "It was really nice meeting you and fun chatting. Oh and thank you for saving me from being flattened by a bus."

Alex's hand touched Julia's arm lightly. She looked down at him.

"Even though it means I don't get your number because you're too busy," Alex said. "I really hope you get the part. I mean that. I can see how much you want it."

"Thank you," Julia replied. She touched his shoulder and turned, taking a few steps towards the stairs.

"Julia, wait," Alex said, and she turned back to him. "How about I give you *my* number? Just in case an audition gets cancelled one day and you end up with some free time. "I know this great jazz bar."

"I'm sure you do."

Alex reached into all four of his jacket pockets in turn, becoming increasingly frantic, before looking up at Julia, empty handed. She put her hand into the depths of her bag, pulled out a pen and handed it to him. She held out the script in front of him with her other hand.

"Hurry."

Alex scrawled his number on the front page. Julia turned around and went quickly but gracefully down the aisle. When descending the stairs and almost out of sight, he thought she looked up at him for the briefest moment. But her hair had fallen over her face again and he couldn't be sure.

Out of the window, he saw her get off the bus and cross the street. She didn't look either way before stepping onto the road. Alex involuntarily held his breath. It wasn't until she'd made it safely across the road that he finally breathed out – *Julia*.

***

At the next stop, Alex rushed down the bus staircase, nearly tripping. He stepped off the bus, ran across the street and jumped on a bus headed in the opposite direction.

He listened to the two voicemails on his phone. The first was about his interview today and helpfully stated the full address of the assessment venue. The second was a long message from Mary from the mentoring charity. He deleted it. There was no way he'd have time to take on such a commitment with the hours he worked.

Alex remained looking out of the window to make sure he got off at the right place. The bus passed the stop where he'd met Julia earlier. He replayed the opening lines they'd exchanged and the moments of their encounter in his head, already feeling nostalgia for their meeting.

He took out his phone to call his office to let them know he was on his way. The moment he pressed the call button, the bus pulled up outside what Alex thought was the assessment venue. He immediately stood to leave the bus, his phone still in his hand.

As he stepped onto the pavement and slipped the phone into his suit pocket, the background picture appeared on the screen. A grainy photograph of a smiling woman sitting at a piano with a small, dark-haired boy in her arms.

Chapter Three

Without Julia

"What are you waiting for?" said the old lady beside Alex with a shopping basket.

He was standing in blue jeans and a crisply ironed work shirt at the bus stop round the corner from Victoria station. The crowd of people waiting there had initially remained roughly the same in number but had been steadily getting smaller. For almost two hours, Alex had been in the exact spot where he'd met Julia the previous day.

"A bus. The bus. My bus," he said, leaning in to view the poster on the inside of the bus stop. "The fifty-three."

They stood in silence for a minute until a bus arrived and she got on. Alex looked to his left and right, he was now alone.

At this time of day, he would usually have been at work for three hours already with a full day ahead involving client meetings, conference calls and drafting contracts. This would be followed by an evening of reading legal papers late into the night.

Alex looked up and spotted an internet café across the street. He crossed the road and entered. He was pointed towards computer number '4' where he inserted his work USB memory stick. While waiting for his file to print, he noticed the array of files saved to the desktop: CVs, tenancy agreements, immigration forms – even divorce documents, covered the screen.

A few minutes later, next door to the internet cafe, Alex was sat at the small wooden table by the window, at Cafe Concerto. His view, directly ahead, was of the bus stop. Glancing around he noticed the wallpaper of faded musical scores peeling at the room's corners. Beside the white mug of tea in front of him was a handful of loose printed pages. Across the top page in a typewriter style type, *An Original Screenplay by Alex Wright.*

Chapter Three
With Julia

Alex glanced up at its grand Victorian facade before entering the theatre – a short walk from Piccadilly Circus tube station. He was at the bottom of the wide, central red-carpeted staircase. At the top stood a short, balding young man with a clipboard. Beside him a large printed sign that read in bold black letters 'Open Audition'.

"What time does everything start?" Alex asked, when he'd got to the top of the stairs. He was in jeans and a white shirt.

"When the director feels like it," the man replied, with a brief glance at Alex.

"Where does everyone wait for the auditions?" Alex went on.

"You're here for the auditions?"

Alex put his hand to his forehead. "Yeah."

"Only female leads today, mate," the man said, now looking Alex up and down.

"Ah," Alex said. "I'm actually looking for Julia."

"Look, this is a professional audition," the man said, not looking at Alex this time.

"I really need to see her."

The man sighed and glanced down at the sheet of paper on the clipboard he held. "I've got at least a dozen Julias on this list. If it's that urgent," he continued, "why don't you call her?"

"I've lost my phone," Alex said. There was a beeping sound and he looked down to his jean pocket, the man's eyes followed his.

"I mean, she's lost *her* phone," Alex said. But the man was now looking ahead at the two women ascending the stairs. "Can I watch, at least?" he added.

"Open audition means anyone can audition, not anyone can watch," the man said, turning back to Alex. "That's a strict rule." He turned away and smiled in greeting at the first of the women up the stairs and now in front of him.

Alex stepped onto the stairs down towards the exit. Halfway down he glanced back, both women were now in front of the man and he was turning over the page in front of him. Alex spun round, went back up the stairs two at a time and almost broke into a run as he passed them, while trying to tread softly. He pushed open the first door he saw.

It was dark, ahead was the stage, beside him the back rows of seats. He slipped down deep into the closest, crimson velvet seat. Two men were in the front row, the only other people in the auditorium, their legs stretched out in front of them. Alex sat forward while still keeping his head low.

A piano began playing from beside the stage, out of view. The stage remained empty. A spotlight came on. From the side of the stage a high-heeled shoe, then a leg appeared, followed by a woman in a black slip, fishnet stockings and top hat.

The woman moved towards the lone chair in the middle of the stage in time to the music. The spotlight couldn't keep up with her, she outwitted it with each step. Alex couldn't see her face clearly, only the silhouette of her body, agile and slender but womanly in shape. He leaned further forward as she got closer to the centre of the stage.

The mysterious woman kicked out her leg and placed her foot on the chair. Turning to the front and pushing back her hat theatrically, the light fell upon her face. Alex caught his breath. He could see her huge green eyes, even from the distance he was away. Her face looked different with the bright red lipstick on her lips and dark mascara around her eyes. She sat down on the chair and began singing. *It was Julia.*

She looked into the crowd, pausing a split second when her eyes met his. Immediately, Alex doubted that she'd paused at all or even seen him. He tried, and failed, to catch her gaze as the performance continued.

"Bravo!" shouted the man in the front row, the director, Alex thought.

The piano was still playing but stopped as the director began to clap. He leaned over to the man next to him and spoke into his ear.

"Next," he shouted.

Julia exited the stage from the opposite side she'd entered. Alex's gaze following her until she was out of sight.

Chapter Four

Without Julia

"You write?" asked Marco, the tanned, stout cafe owner who'd just introduced himself, after appearing to Alex as if he might do so all week. He stood over Alex, looking down at the A4 lined, yellow legal pad in front of him with barely legible handwriting scrawled across it. "Or try to?" he added, smiling.

"When I'm not staring out of the window," Alex replied, putting down his pen and looking up. He was at the same table he'd spent the last four days during the cafe's opening hours, 7 a.m. to 4 p.m.

"Well, they say everyone has a book in them," Marco said.

"That's where it should stay for most people, I think someone else said," Alex said.

Marco laughed loudly, Alex glanced across at the counter and the woman he said was his wife, rolled her eyes.

"Is it comedy you're writing?" Marco asked, with a straight face.

"It's a film. A screenplay."

"You can't write at home? Cheaper, no?"

Alex followed Marco's eyes to the plate and three

mugs on the table around the pad.

"Gets me away from the TV."

Marco shrugged. "Well, good luck. Put some of your jokes in, everyone loves jokes."

Alex gathered up the pile of loose pages beside the pad. His phone beeped. It was a message from Richard, offering him dinner at his flat, carbonara – one of the only three dishes, all pasta-based, that Richard could cook. It sounded better than his empty flat and another cold dinner, as he'd eaten the last few evenings.

Leaving the cafe to walk to the underground station, he passed the bus stop and the old lady from earlier in the week.

"You still waiting for your bus?" she asked.

"I don't think it's ever going to come," Alex said.

***

"I've found her!" Alex cried.

"And I've found evidence of the Loch Ness Monster," Richard said.

Richard's laptop was open on the table in front of them. There were two empty bowls on the table and two empty bottles of beer. Richard was sitting back on the sofa, rubbing his stomach. Alex sat close to the computer screen.

"Forrester," he said. "Julia Forrester. *Hamlet*, check – he told me she'd been in a production. RADA, check – she went there, and did *Antony and Cleopatra*, check. Her height and date of birth seem about right," Alex said. "Everything matches."

"Sounds like everything matches," Richard said. "Let me see." He leaned forward and spun the laptop screen round to face him. The webpage had 'Talent Source Agency' across the top. 'No photo.'

"There's a number on here," Richard said, sliding Alex's phone across the table to him. Alex picked up his phone and dialled the number on the screen.

"I need to get in touch with Julia, Julia Forrester," Alex said. "No, I'm not a director. I'm not a casting agent. Theatre, no. TV, not exactly. Who am I? Well... I'm just a guy." He then held his hand over the microphone.

"I'm going to appeal to the romantic in him."

Alex continued speaking into the phone. "I met her... It wasn't in the street actually, it was at a bus stop."

He placed the phone on the sofa beside him and turned to Richard. "Guy hung up on me."

"Look," Richard said. "The internet browser wasn't pulling through images. I've tried another." He turned the laptop so Alex could see the screen. "You said she was blonde, right?"

"Brunette," Alex said, looking down at the screen. He closed the laptop, which had a blonde woman's face with blue eyes on the screen. He put his head in his hands. "Crown? We could just make last orders."

He got up off the sofa. Richard followed him up the stairs.

"Is your new friend working tonight?" Alex asked.

"If it wasn't for my new friend, there'd be no

free drinks, no after hours drinking, no..." Richard answered.

"Okay, I'm shutting up," Alex said, holding the door for Richard at the ground level exit of the basement flat.

"You can give up looking for this Julia now and start looking for a job."

Chapter Four
With Julia

Alex waited at the bottom of the theatre staircase for half an hour but no-one came down it – including Julia. The man with the clipboard could see him but seemed relaxed by his presence. He even smiled at Alex when he finally walked back up the staircase.

Before Alex had reached the top, the man said a single word, "Backdoor."

Alex left through the front door and followed the building round until he saw an unmarked black door. After a few minutes, a young, red-haired woman in purple leggings and a green jumper-dress came out of it, a gym bag slung over her shoulder.

"Hi," Alex said. "I'm looking for Julia. She had an audition…"

"Beautiful, brown hair, with the huge green eyes?" the woman asked.

"That's her."

"You've missed her. She had another audition to get to."

"Do you know where?"

"Sorry," she replied, before adjusting the bag on her shoulder and walking off.

When Alex entered the tube station, his phone beeped. He took it out and opened the message. It was from an unknown number.

A passion for Shakespeare, yes. You didn't mention a love of musical theatre too... J x

Alex stepped onto the descending escalator. Typed, and pressed send.

It's a new interest of mine... Drink? Alex x

***

"You're not playing it very cool, are you?" Richard said. "In fact, you're playing it the total opposite. You're playing it hot, if that's an expression?"

Richard and Alex were sitting in the Crown, at their usual spot at the bar.

"We made a real connection."

"What's all these games about then?"

"She's testing me."

"What's next? An assault course? An IQ test?" Richard said, and took a sip of his pint. "And anyway, how can you be so sure about her after a ten minute conversation? You don't even know her yet. To be sure about her you have to wait."

"And when you've waited, has it made you sure about someone?"

"Maybe not. But she's definitely waiting to be more sure about you," Richard said. "Love at first sight doesn't have a great record in terms of happy endings though, does it? *Romeo and Juliet?*"

"O fortune, fortune! All men call thee fickle...

Be fickle, fortune. For then, I hope, thou wilt not keep her long. But send her back," Alex said. He took a sip from his pint and stared into the rows of spirit bottles behind the bar, seeing his reflection in the mirrored glass behind.

"Back to the twenty-first century, please," Richard said. "So, how's the job search going?"

"It's going."

"Has it arrived anywhere? You've got a great CV, surely some law firm must want you?"

"I'm not convinced I want them."

Chapter Five

Without Julia

Alex sighed, despite it being early, Saturday tourists were already crowded around Camden underground station. He'd left Richard's for the station, having stayed over after a night at the Crown. Then, in front of him. *There she was.*

Wearing the same green and red dress as from the bus stop, she crossed Archway Road in the direction of the station entrance. Alex quickened his pace, realising she'd soon be inside the station and out of his sight.

"Julia!" Alex shouted, his voice barely audible over the passing bus engine's noise and clapping crowd that surrounded a green-haired man juggling flaming batons on the corner. He reached Archway Road as the traffic lights turned red. Glancing left at the two lanes of traffic and cyclists bearing down on him, he was surprised not to hear a horn as he ran across.

In the station, at entry barriers he tapped his Oyster card and began descending the escalator at pace on the left hand side. Halfway down he got a backpack in his face, a group spread across the escalator on the overtaking side. He saw Julia ahead step off the bottom of the escalator. She was disappearing out of view into a throng of people.

"Julia!"

Once at the bottom of the escalator, Alex paused. The tube line split at Camden Station into North and South lines. Julia could be heading to one of four possible platforms. At least every minute, trains arrived and departed. If he chose the wrong platform, he would lose her. But whichever platform he chose, if he waited any longer, *he'd definitely lose her.*

It was morning and she would likely be heading into London for work, not outwards towards home. And to central London and not the City, as most cafes there were shut at weekends. Southbound Northern Line, Kennington Branch – Alex guessed.

He ran, weaving in and around people, and jumping down the last steps to platform level. The platform then came into view along the tunnel ahead of him. He saw Julia step onto the carriage of a waiting tube train.

When he reached the platform, the carriage doors were closing. He could now see she was wearing large red headphones over her ears. The train began to pull away. Alex followed it along the platform.

He was level with Julia. She turned around and faced the doors. Finally, he saw her face. He stopped and stood motionless, heart beating hard. The train accelerated away from him. It wasn't her. *It wasn't Julia.*

Alex sat down on the nearest seat and watched the end of the last train carriage disappear into the black tunnel. He looked up, he was facing a billboard poster. It was advertising a dating website, with a picture of a couple sitting on a bench, overlooking a shiny London skyline. The slogan read *Now it's your turn to find someone amazing.*

Alex breathed out, smiled and leaned back in his seat.

"Not today."

Chapter Five

With Julia

Oliver's was the sign above its archway entrance. *Live performance at 8 p.m.*, said the website. Greenwich had taken Alex longer than he'd expected from north London. He hadn't been there since a school trip to the Royal Observatory.

If you want to see me, I'll be at Oliver's tonight. J x, Julia's response to his message had read. After Richard's words about his approach, Alex had looked up the venue rather than ask her for more details. He could be elusive too.

After handing over a fiver at the door, his wrist was stamped with a black O. The short staircase down opened up to a room of red walls, a green tiled floor, and a dozen or so round tables – a faint smell of incense in the air. All the tables were taken and there was a small crowd standing at the bar waiting to be served. He couldn't see Julia at any of the tables, or at the bar.

In the corner, a man with a ponytail sat in front of a piano, another in front of a small drum kit, two others held instruments; a double bass and a trumpet. Alex saw a small gap at the bar as a woman left with drinks. He slipped into it and looked up.

"You made it," Julia said from behind the bar in front of him. *She was working.* Alex smiled.

In the top left corner of her black polo shirt was a gold stitched Oliver's. She was in black leggings, a white apron around her waist with a bottle opener hanging off it. Her hair was up and a pencil held the bun loosely in place.

"Just passing," Alex said.

"Oh really?" Julia said. She looked to the door. There was a man in a brown suit, red cravat and slick back hair taking up most of the doorway. "You should probably order something," she added.

Alex saw there were no beers on draft – only bottles, wine or cocktails. He picked up the cocktail menu.

"What's good?" Alex asked.

"They're all good when I'm making them," Julia replied.

"An Old Fashioned, please."

Julia placed a tumbler on the bar before mixing the drink of whiskey, Bitters, a brown sugar cube and ice – and sliding it across towards Alex. He reached for his wallet. She waved her hand at him with a look.

The deep, low notes of a strummed double bass began, the other instruments joining in one by one. People took their seats, Alex sat on a bar stool. Julia, hands on her hips, looked across at the musicians. Alex leaned forward to speak. With a smile, she raised a finger to her lips, gesturing behind the bar to a small sign: 'Strictly no talking during performances.' Alex turned back to the room, all the heads were facing towards the band.

There was a rhythmic quality to the jazz music. Alex watched Julia. She began to twirl her hair, closing her eyes and moving to the music. The piece came to a gradual stop and Alex headed to the toilets. When he returned, the bar was lined with people.

"What time does this place close?" Alex asked the middle-aged couple sitting at the nearest round table.

"One a.m.," the lady said, turning to Alex.

"Thank you."

He had to research a law firm he was meeting early the next day. He stood, waiting for the bar to clear, stepping forward when the last person left to return to their seat. He looked at Julia, she looked directly back at him, smiling her wide smile and with her green eyes. As Alex opened his mouth to speak, there was a rhythmic rustle of a jazz drum beat, followed by the piano. He smiled back at her.

Walking up the stairs of the club, he recognised the instrumental the band was playing. He'd heard his father play it from a cassette tape on the kitchen stereo. It was Chet Baker's 'It's Always You'.

He took his phone from his pocket and typed a message and pressed send.

Dinner? Alex x

Chapter Six

Without Julia

Alex listened to the sounds of different alarm clocks going off in the flats around him. Then footsteps, running showers and baths, followed by various banging and clunking noises, as people left for work. Finally, the main front door of the building slammed shut for the last time. In that moment, knowing he didn't have to get on a packed tube train into the City and the law firm, Alex felt almost euphoric.

The feeling wouldn't last, it was fading quicker each day, and it was now Friday. With no more visits to Caffe Concerto, each morning he'd lain in bed till late. When he got restless, he'd move to the lounge to look for law jobs online, before switching between BBC and SKY News until he got hungry enough to go out.

Alex noticed how colourless the flat was. Without Amy's artwork, all the walls were bare and plain. He imagined her paintings in the empty spaces – all bright, abstracts oils on white canvases. Although the images weren't completely clear in his mind, he couldn't make out all the brush strokes of the works – he could still see the colours and shapes.

He'd loved watching Amy paint. Observing the ideas in her head – and that she'd discuss with him – come alive on the canvas in front of her; thoughts becoming physical images. It gave her a mystical aura, as if she had access to some special magic that only she could understand and control.

He also found it erotic to watch her in front of a canvas. Dressed in a white vest top, no bra, and faded black leggings with holes in them. At times, standing back and painting in broad thick strokes. Other times, very close up, making small precise strokes. She could be manically animated, pacing the room, or sat on the floor in front of a canvas, almost perfectly still, for many minutes at a time.

On Friday evenings, by the time he got home, Amy would already be back from Covent Garden. BBC Radio 6 would be playing loudly, after a kiss hello, paintbrush still in her hand, she would shoo him away. He'd pour himself a glass of wine from the open bottle she'd left on the floor, kick off his shoes before watching her at work from the sofa.

Eventually, she'd throw down the brush and declare she was going to kill herself. Alex would say they'd both be dead if they didn't eat soon. There'd be no food in the flat. Amy would need to change, he'd beg her not to. They'd row, she'd change anyway, and come out of the bedroom an hour later looking ridiculously sexy and they'd make love on the sofa.

It would then be too late to go out and they'd eat takeaway pizza from Papa John's and drink the constantly replaced bottle of champagne in the fridge

– *saved* for special occasions.

"Sometimes I dream a new shade of a colour. I wake with it in my mind and my eyes, it's real," Amy had said.

They were standing in the flat's lounge surrounded by half-packed boxes and her pictures stacked up against the wall in rows – a friend of hers waiting in a van outside.

"But when I try and mix it, the colour doesn't come. I can't get the right shade," she continued.

Alex listened silently.

"I have to give up. It was just a dream after all."

Alex hadn't seen her again. She'd picked up the last of her stuff while he was at work a few days later. When he'd got home that evening he found her keys on the mat below the letter box – no note.

***

Under the eyes were dark grey patches, around the mouth a thick, untidy beard covered patchily in white foam. Alex stood in front of the bathroom mirror in a pair of black underpants. He picked up the razor from the side of the sink and began hacking at his face.

After a few minutes he stopped, put down the razor and left the room. Having made a cup of tea – black, there was no milk – he sat at the kitchen table drinking it slowly. He saw his reflection in the shiny oven door, a half-shaved man, shaving foam still smeared across his face.

Alex rang the buzzer of Bright Starts's office. He was outside what appeared to be a converted schoolhouse. He'd walked from the Dalston Junction station through the market, passing stalls of cheap plastic phone cases and fake batteries. A man in a bloodied white apron had hauled a crate of raw meat past him from a white van. It was full of pigs' trotters and the smell in the warm air had made Alex retch.

He was dressed casually in jeans, a shirt and brown deck shoes, he'd got out a suit that morning but hadn't put it on – he'd told himself the boy would find it intimidating. In fact, he hadn't worn a suit since his last day at the firm, finding last minute excuses to postpone meetings with recruiters.

A tall man in his early twenties opened the front door to Alex and showed him through to a side room, where Mary and a boy were sitting.

The boy in front of him looked younger than fifteen. But was dressed much as Alex had imagined, in jeans and a hooded top. A flash of red hair under a baseball cap, which still had a sticker on the rim. He didn't seem particularly deprived, holding a shiny smartphone in his hand and wearing brand new looking trainers.

Alex then noticed the defeated look in his eyes and the way he let his shoulders hunch forward – like life had roughed him up already. He was lucky to have found Mary.

"Alex, this is William," Mary said. "William, this is Alex."

Alex put his hand out. Eventually, the boy gave him

a limp handshake with a soft clammy hand, barely making eye contact.

"Billy," the boy said, in a mumbled tone.

Success was based on the simple idea that young people have the best chance in life if they're supported by successful young adults, Mary explained. It was all about hard skills, soft skills, self-efficacy, long-term employability, career opportunities and professional networks leading to long term ambition.

Billy looked out of the window; his ambition at that moment appeared to be to get out of the room as soon as he possibly could, Alex thought. Alex felt the same, his mouth painfully dry and his hangover, rather than lifting, appeared to be settling in.

"It's once a month we meet, right?" Alex said, once Mary had finally stopped speaking.

"Once a week," Mary replied, with barely a pause. "It was in the email I sent you with all the details and responsibilities."

"Of course," Alex said. "The small print." He attempted to smile and force a chuckle. "I guess we're stuck with each other," he continued, looking at Billy and then Mary; both remained expressionless.

Mary explained the subsequent meetings could be held anywhere convenient to them, although not at Alex's home.

Mary left the room and, during a stilted but not unfriendly exchange, Alex and Billy arranged their next meeting: Café Nero by Nike Town on Oxford Street. When Mary returned she found them in silence, she must have seen these awkward scenes many times before.

"You can really help Billy," Mary said to Alex at the front door of the office, a few minutes later after Billy had left. "And don't think you won't get something out of this process too," she added.

"Well, I can help with his handshake, if nothing else."

"Sorry?"

"Nothing. It's not important."

"Do you remember what I said when I came to your office, about how important this age is for these kids, in terms of what direction their lives take?" Mary said, looking directly into Alex's eyes. "He's at that age. Don't waste his time." Her amiable manner had gone and there was a sternness in her tone.

"Or yours."

Mary's smile returned and she gave him a light pat on the back before closing the door.

The air outside was now even warmer, and Alex needed water. He crossed the road and began a route to the station that didn't go through the market.

The acrid smell of raw meat from the market still reached his nose. He went to bring his hand to his mouth but it was too late. He retched. He was sick on the pavement in front of him, specks of it covering his shoes.

Chapter Six

With Julia

"Tequila?" Julia said. She was standing at the bar and looking back at Alex. Her hair was down and ruffled. She could have looked formal in the little black dress she wore but had on her boots and black tights with a print of red lips, matching the colour of hers. A large shoulder bag was set down beside her. "I'll get the first round."

"Usually I have shots at the end, rather than the beginning of an evening, but why not?" he replied.

"Maybe it will be the beginning and the end, for once." Julia ordered and glanced back at Alex, giving him a wink. He smiled.

"Can I have a pint with that, too?"

Alex was wearing black ankle boots, black skinny jeans, a white fitted shirt and an old grey blazer. He looked at the two, full shot glasses on the bar. Slices of lemon on top and a salt shaker between them. Beside them his pint of beer and her gin and tonic.

"I don't like drinking alone," Julia said, lifting the salt shaker and giving Alex a look, her smile showing her dimples. She licked the side of her hand and applied the salt. Alex did the same. They clinked glasses and downed the shots. As Julia raised her shot glass to her mouth her right knee rose, her booted toe pointed to the ground, as at the bus stop.

Alex enjoyed the bitter acidic taste of the lemon after the sweetness of the tequila. From the sugary tequila and lemon juice, Julia's lips were now a wet, glossy bright red. *He needed to kiss her lips.*

***

"Are you always early?" Alex said.

"Are you always late?" Julia replied. Alex looked at her, unsure how to react.

She was leaning against the wall of Goodge Street tube station, looking down at her phone. Delays on the tube meant Alex arrived on time rather than early, as he'd planned. He'd stood in the train carriage, restless, even though there were empty seats.

"Don't worry. You're on time. I just finished work round the corner."

"Dinner?" Alex asked. "Or drink first?"

"Drink first."

They walked round the corner to the Fitzroy Tavern. He told her about its origin as London's first coffee house, The Hundred Marks. Then as the pub, the literary circle who'd drunk there in the '40s: writer Julian MacLaren-Ross, poet Dylan Thomas and artist Nina Hamnett, who'd impaled herself on the railings outside after a doomed love affair.

At the green door of the pub, its carpeted floor and wood panelling in front of them – Alex's phone rang. Julia looked at him with an open expression. He pulled out his phone and looked down at it. He glanced at Julia again and she nodded. He answered it but the line was dead.

"It was my dad's number," Alex said.

"You should call him back?" Julia said, smiling.

"You need a drink," Alex said.

"Call him. I don't mind at all."

Alex pushed the button on his phone to return the call.

"No answer," Alex said. "I'll try again later." He held the door open for Julia to pass through.

"How is your dad? You said he works too hard."

"He does," Alex said. "He's retiring, though."

"That's good then, right?"

"I'm not so sure," Alex said, as they approached the bar.

***

"So, did you get the part?" Alex asked. The barman had cleared away their shot glasses but they remained at the bar. It was a Sunday night and the pub was almost empty.

"Which one?" Julia replied. "Roxy, no. Ophelia, maybe."

"Only maybe?"

"I got a call-back. Which in acting speak means they want to see me again."

"That's great."

"More importantly," Julia asked, "did you get your

new / old job?"

"No. I didn't," Alex replied.

"I'm sorry," Julia said, with a concerned expression on her face. "To be honest, when we spoke, you didn't seem like you really wanted it."

"I guess they saw that, too."

"What are you going to do?" Julia asked; the concerned expression had returned.

"Actually, I've got an interview tomorrow afternoon," Alex said. "I'm not sure if I want this job, either, for different reasons."

"Tell me about it," Julia said, leaning forward. "The pros and cons."

"Okay, cons: the salary, it's a third of what I earn, or earned, I mean, until a week ago. No bonus, either; I could get up to twenty percent annual bonus at the firm. No career prospects, or virtually none, at the firm if..."

"But you don't want to be at the firm..."

"Okay, the pros," Alex said. "I'd be using and developing the skills I've already got, and helping vulnerable people.

"Also, at the end of the working day, I don't think I'd feel like it was a waste of time, which sometimes I've felt at the firm," he continued. "That's something, too, I guess."

"That's quite a big something, Alex."

"I'm still not sure," Alex said. "I mean, the money is really bad." He shook his head.

"Maybe you'd spend less money if you enjoyed what you do a bit more," Julia said. "No harm in going to the interview. So where is it?"

Alex explained it was a legal assistant role at a Citizens Advice Bureau, which gave free advice. They were now sitting at the bar on high stools. When he mentioned his redundancy pay-off, she advised him to keep it for something fun or useful, ideally both.

"I've got an embarrassing confession to make," Alex said.

"You're married?"

"No."

"You're a spy?"

"No. Technically, I'm still a lawyer for a little bit longer until my practice certificate expires."

"I give up."

"So, after you messaged me, I saved your number into my phone."

"What's strange about that?" Julia asked.

"I also wrote it on a Post-It note and stuck it to my fridge. And I wrote it down in a few other places," Alex said. "I had this irrational fear I was definitely going to get my phone stolen."

"That's not such an irrational fear in London," Julia said.

"And that I'd never see you again," Alex continued. Julia took a sip of her second gin and tonic; Alex had got their second round.

"How many women have made it onto your fridge?" Julia asked.

"Not many," Alex said.

"I feel honoured," Julia said. "Well, not many people get my number. It was sensible not to take any chances with it."

"Okay. Good. I'll stop being embarrassed."

"I mean, it's not like you got on the wrong bus to get it."

They walked to Mondelli's, just off Charlotte Street – Alex had read a good review in the *Evening Standard* the week before. It had a wooden floor, green walls, and tables set like a traditional Italian restaurant with red and white check tablecloths. It was quiet like the pub had been.

Strangely, an orange plastic lobster adorned one of the walls. They named the quirky addition Leonard when they sat down at their table – breaking a slight distance that had developed between them between the pub and the restaurant.

Over their shared starter of fried calamari, Alex squeezed a lemon. Julia gently took it from him, squeezing every drop from it and licking her wet fingers clean afterwards. He watched her fingers and lips as she made the licking and sucking sound.

Mondelli's was dimly lit. Alex and Julia noticed it didn't seem to be to enhance the mood, nor even to prevent diners from seeing their food, but was because most of the light bulbs overhead had blown and not been replaced.

"So is this where you bring all your first dates?" Julia asked.

"Where they can't see my face?" Alex replied, with a chuckle. "Yeah."

"That's not what I meant," Julia said, smiling. "You know, there's a sense of humour hiding that tortured screenwriter, isn't there?"

"First time here. The reviews were great. No mention of the ambient lighting, or Leonard, though."

The waiter appeared, picked up their plates and cleared their table – they watched him in silence. Julia took a sip from her wine glass. A drop of red wine spilled from the side of her mouth and ran down her cheek before falling onto her neck.

Alex wanted to pull her towards him, to kiss her neck, to taste her skin and the wine together. He breathed out.

"It feels surreal," Alex said.

"What does?" Julia said. She was twirling her hair with her left hand.

"This feeling."

"What feeling is that?"

"That you're not real," Alex said, putting his hands from his side onto the table.

"That I'm not real?" She moved her hand to pick up her wine glass again. Her hand brushed against his, he felt a charge – a shock.

"I mean we met," Alex said, "and now, a few days later, here we are having dinner."

"Isn't that just what people do all the time?" Julia said. Her face with a curious expression, her hand still twirling her hair, slower now. Her other hand rested on the table, the palm open slightly like a shell.

"But we didn't meet at a party, we met randomly in a public place," Alex said. "Doesn't that make it feel surreal that we're here now?"

"I hadn't thought so, but now that you say it," Julia

replied and laughed, "I'm worried this might all be in my imagination."

"We won't have to pay the bill. That would be the upside," Alex said. "The only upside, obviously."

The waiter was standing close by with a pair of smaller menus.

"Tell me more about this feeling," Julia said.

"It's the one you have when you're first getting to know someone. You have an amazing connection with them. But you're still strangers."

"Still strangers?"

"Yeah. You can say anything to them without feeling embarrassed or inhibited," Alex replied. "They're not truly real to you yet."

"How long does this 'stranger phase' last?"

"Usually, only one night."

"Only one night?" Julia said. She, seemingly unconsciously, rubbed her thumb gently on the white tablecloth. "So, if we meet again...?"

"We won't be strangers anymore. We'll care too much about each other's feelings, they'll be context and subtext," Alex said.

"While we're in this transient, momentary state of 'stranger-ness' we can still say whatever we want to each other."

Julia touched her lips with her fingers. Then rubbed the tablecloth again with her index finger, leaving a red smear. Alex tried to look away from Julia, but his eyes were drawn back to her almost instantly. She met his gaze directly with her own.

"You go first then," Julia said.

"If I ask you to do something," Alex said. "Will you do it?"

"Tell me first."

Alex had observed Julia as someone might a beautiful painting but it was a pure unfettered desire he felt now and the sense of wanting to possess her. There was a headiness in the air between them.

"What colour underwear are you wearing?"

"White," Julia said without hesitating.

"What kind?"

"French style."

"I want you to get up slowly and walk to the bathroom." Alex said. Julia was still looking directly at him. "With your every step I want you to imagine my gaze following your body and the way it moves." She now was looking down.

"In the bathroom, lift up your skirt and take off your knickers. Slide them off your bottom, down your legs and over your shoes." Alex continued. "Then fold them into your hand."

"What did you have in mind after that?" Julia asked, looking into his eyes again.

"Walk back in here and sit down opposite me."

"Then what?" Julia said. She leaned slightly forward, as if to dare him.

Alex leaned over the table until his head was level with Julia's. He whispered into her ear. Her face expressionless.

When they both leaned back into their seats, the waiter appeared and eagerly handed them dessert menus. They held them for a moment then both put them down without looking at them.

Julia rose from the table, placing her napkin delicately on her seat. Her face still expressionless, she glanced at Alex before she left the table.

The tables were very close together and she weaved her way towards the back of the restaurant. Alex's eyes followed the curves of her bottom moving in her dress. His appetite for her felt infinite. He could not imagine it ever being satisfied.

When she'd disappeared behind a door, he sat back in his chair and looked around the restaurant. But he couldn't think of anything else, only Julia in the other room. It was an exquisite pain to barely know her but to already feel her absence so acutely. *He could only wait.*

***

"I always know where to find you these days," Alex said, before sitting down next to Richard. Richard was where he'd expected to find him, in the Crown. He was sitting at the bar close to where Ciara was serving, staring intently at the large TV screen on the wall showing cricket.

"It's the sporting event of the year."

"I was thinking about something else being the reason you're always here..." Alex said. "When does this match end anyway? It looks like the same one that was going on last time I had a conversation with myself."

"It should end today."

"Great."

"But then there'll be another match. There's a series of matches in a test. This is Test cricket, remember?"

"I remember it tests my patience. As if cricket wasn't boring enough, they have to drag it out over days and days."

"Well, you better get used to it. It's not a usual series, either. It's the famous cricket biennial series between England and Australia: The Ashes. It's going to be on all summer."

"Well, my worst nightmare has come true then," Alex said. He took a seat beside Richard.

"You should take a holiday."

"And leave London?" Alex said.

"And Julia?" Richard asked, turning from the screen to face Alex for the first since he'd arrived. "Have you fallen for her already?"

Chapter Seven

Without Julia

"Dad, it's me," Alex said loudly twice, as he let himself in. He glanced at the bell, he wasn't even sure it still worked.

Alex had taken the train to Hampstead Heath, in the north of the city, from Dalston Junction, in the east. He'd passed the Flask pub and walked up the small hill to a 1920s modernist Arts and Crafts four storey block, nestled between the Victorian houses of the street. He'd slowly climbed the stairs to his father's flat, which took up the third floor.

Alex closed the black front door behind him. He made his way along the flat's single long corridor, with its cream-coloured walls, lined with doors. It led to a kitchen at the back overlooking a small lake and the Heath. He passed the first door, the music room; the piano was covered in piles of legal books and bundles. The rest of the flat appeared, with its 1970s minimalist style, in its usual tidy state.

Standing at the kitchen door, he saw his father where he almost always found him on his weekly weekend visits. Sitting at the narrow wooden table by the kitchen window, looking out onto the Heath.

Sometimes one of his jazz tapes would be playing. But often, he'd be sat in silence, as he was now, looking out to the ancient green land below, in apparent deep contemplation.

It had been the same since Alex was a child, but today his father didn't have the customary handful of paperwork files in front of him. The table was completely bare except for a white mug.

Alex touched the mug. It was half full. Cold.

"Another?" he asked. Alex stopped and observed his father more closely than usual.

His father turned his head slowly and looked up at him. Alex had told him about his redundancy over the phone but it was the first time he'd seen him since. His father nodded.

Alex lit the stove, the click of the lighter followed by the hushed sound of burning gas.

"What does Amy think you should do?" his father said.

"Amy?" Alex said.

"About your job. Or lack of one?"

"We're not really in touch anymore," Alex said. "I'm not sure she'd be a great source of career advice anyway."

Alex looked ahead, out of the floor to ceiling window panels that ran along the side of the kitchen, to the Heath. He then looked at his father.

"You remember we split up?"

"Of course, Alexander," his father replied. "I just thought you might still see her. I heard that was the modern thing."

"Thank goodness. I'm not sure I can cope with a senile father on top of losing my job."

"People seem to chop and change so much these days."

"I got chopped and changed, Dad."

"You make it sound rather dramatic."

"Well, it kind of was."

The kettle began to whistle, steam rising from it. Alex turned to the stove.

"She was so passionate about art – about life," Alex's father continued. "A woman to hang on to."

"Someone else is doing that now. She got engaged."

His father was again looking out of the kitchen windows; they gave a sense the room was outside.

"Oh well," his father said with a small sigh. "I really liked her."

"She really liked you too, Dad."

The quiet formality between them returned. Only once before, after his father had had more than his usual single brandy, had he asked Alex about his relationships, or commented on them.

Alex set down the tea mugs on the table and sat down opposite his father again. He glanced at the navy swimming trunks hanging on the radiator in the corner of the kitchen.

"How was the water?" Alex asked.

"Pleasant," his father replied. The same answer he got every time he asked, whatever the season, and even in the middle of winter. His father went swimming in the Hampstead ponds every day of the year and had done so for as long as Alex could remember.

Sitting together in silence at the small table, they drunk their tea. Both looking out across the Heath, at its great expanse of deep green grass, dark brown trees, and hills. A church spire became visible in the distance as the cloud that lay on the far parts of the Heath rose and faded into the dark blue sky.

Alex stood up and put their empty mugs in the sink.

"I'll see you out," his father said. Alex didn't protest.

"Tell me if you need anything, won't you?" his father said, reaching over and patting him awkwardly on the shoulder.

"Thanks, Dad," Alex replied.

When he walked home through a leafy Regent's Park, it was so quiet he could hear his own footsteps. He could feel a cool breeze as evening approached.

Alex went straight to the bathroom when he returned to his flat and ran a bath. He'd used the bath for the first time a week ago but now lay in it for at least an hour everyday.

In the kitchen, he opened the fridge and took out a bottle of Newcastle Brown Ale and switched on the black Roberts radio to a rock station.

Back in the bathroom, he stripped off his clothes, throwing them into the corner. He picked up the ale bottle again and stepped into the bath. He took a long drink and put the bottle on the right side of the bath. It joined a row of ten or so bottles that ran all the way to the taps at the other end.

Alex leaned slowly back into the tub, taking up its

full length. The opening cords of 'All These Things That I've Done' by The Killers came on the radio and he began singing. His voice echoing around the tiled bathroom.

Chapter Seven

With Julia

Alex looked at the silver face of his watch. The second hand was running slow. He adjusted it, with his other hand, against the clock on his phone and shook his left wrist twice quickly. His grandfather's 1950s automatic Rolex wound itself on the wearer's arm.

Julia appeared beside the table. It was the first time he'd looked away from the bathroom doorway since she'd left. Slowly she took her seat opposite him and, with a brief glance, took a long sip from her wine glass. Alex steadily refilled it, and then his own, holding the bottle above his glass until every last drop drained from it.

Julia reached down to her side. Something was in her hand. Alex caught a glimpse of white material between her fingers before her hand went into her bag.

They were looking directly into each other's eyes now. When the waiter approached their table, they looked up at him and then back to each other, both smiled.

"Do you want to order from the dessert menu?" the waiter asked. "Or perhaps coffee?"

Alex looked up at the ceiling and then back at Julia, stretching his hands across the table towards her. Julia looked back at him, her mouth very slightly open.

"Just the bill, please," she said to the waiter. Without breaking their gaze.

***

The black cab pulled up at the entrance to a row of mews houses, Alex pointed out his door. It was dark – there was only one streetlight on nearby. Alex opened Julia's door and paid the driver, while Julia walked ahead. She looked unsteady in her heeled boots on the uneven street. As she stumbled, he went after her and caught her arm.

Closing the front door, Alex leant back onto it with Julia in his arms. When he kissed her she bit his lip. She left his embrace, turned and sat on the step opposite him, pulling off her boots. She began to walk up the stairs.

"Do you have anything to drink?" Julia asked while Alex followed behind her.

"Champagne in the fridge. Scotch on the side table. Vodka in the freezer," Alex said.

"No gin?"

"No gin, I'm afraid."

"I guess champagne will have to do."

At the top of the stairs, Julia stopped and looked back at Alex, close behind. He took the last two stairs in one and brought his left hand up to the side of her face, the other round to her back and down to her bottom.

He could feel her naked skin under the thin black dress. He kissed her neck, smelt her skin. They kissed again, tentatively at first, then they were *at* each other with their hands and mouths.

Moving across to the middle of the room, Julia pushed Alex down onto the large, wide sofa. She climbed on top of him.

"Shall we go to the bed?" he asked, leaning forward.

"Who needs a bed?"

Alex smiled, he leant back again onto the sofa.

"Alex, this shirt," Julia said, holding his shirt collar in her hands. "Is it expensive?"

"It is," Alex replied. "London's finest, Savile Row."

There was a tearing sound and buttons flew across the room as Julia ripped open his shirt.

***

Alex blinked. He was looking at the ceiling. He turned his head slowly left on the pillow. An empty bottle of champagne and two glasses on the side table, on the rim of a glass a red lipstick mark. Turning his head slowly to the right, on the other side table, a bottle of Scotch open but with two-thirds full.

Unsteadily he rose and headed in the direction of the flat's kitchen. He yawned, stretching his arms above his head. When he passed by the lounge, a page, ripped from his notepad, was on the coffee table. He doubled back and went in.

'Alex' was written on the torn page in Julia's red lipstick. He paused, it was the first time he'd seen her handwriting. He reached down. He turned it over.

Thanks for dinner. J x

***

"You look like you've been mauled by a wild animal."

"At times last night," Alex said, "It felt like that." He was standing in the middle of the Crown.

"Can she be tamed?" Richard asked.

"I don't know," Alex replied. "But I want to keep trying."

"Well, for someone who looks like they've been beaten up and spent a sleepless night in a gutter," Richard said, "you seem remarkably happy."

Apart from Richard sitting at the bar, only a few tables were taken. Alex was still standing in front of him with a dazed expression.

"What really happened last night?" Richard said.

"Everything happened."

"Everything?" Richard asked. "Can you be more specific?"

Alex approached the bar and sat on a stool beside Richard.

"Julia happened," Alex said. "Is happening."

"I take it the date went well then."

"It wasn't a 'date', Richard. It was a meeting of minds. Souls even."

"Tongues too, it sounds like," Richard said. He

turned back to the TV screen. There was a crack and a ball was hit with a wooden bat. The camera panned out to a green field, a man running and catching the ball at the edge of the green field, the crowd cheered.

"Richard, have you heard of the Women's Institute?"

"My mum's a member. The Guildford Ladies, I think they're called," Richard replied, his eyes not leaving the screen.

"The Shoreditch Sisters, are Julia's lot," Alex said.

"I think you need to be a woman to join, Alex," Richard said, smiling to himself, his gaze still on the TV screen.

"I've offered to help out at a tea party they've organised on Saturday in East London. It's for old people."

"Doesn't really sound up your street."

"I don't know? I like parties, tea, old people," Alex said before closing his eyes.

"In that order," Richard said. "And you like Julia, it seems."

Alex put his arms on the bar and rested his head on top. "Is he okay?" Alex heard Ciara's voice above him.

"He's been struck down with something," Richard said.

"We do basic diagnostics as part of the radiography training," she said. "What are his symptoms?"

"Symptoms? Well, he's gazing into empty space, saying ridiculous things," Richard said. "Are you hungry?" Tapping Alex on his head.

"No."

"Loss of appetite," Richard continued.

"Ah… I see now," Ciara said, "a romantic condition. Well, there's no treatment for that."

Alex could hear Ciara and Richard chuckling to themselves above him but didn't have the energy to say anything. There was a cheer around him and applause from the TV. He lifted his head to see all the heads in the pub turned towards the wall mounted screen in the corner, except Richard and Ciara's heads turned to each other.

"Can you do me a favour?" Ciara said to Richard, as she moved off along the bar. "Explain to me the rules of this game. If it's on all summer, I'd like to have some idea of what's going on."

"On one condition," Richard replied "You support the home team, England. Deal?"

***

Camden Vice Bureau it read from across the road. 'Citizens', had faded so much it was barely visible and the 'A' and 'd' of "Advice" had gone completely from the blue and yellow sign above the shop front – only Bureau was intact. Alex's hand was on the entrance door.

He'd stood opposite for five minutes, after walking up and down Camden Road for ten. His morning was spent in LSE library, reading up on the latest housing, employment, wills and probate legislation – areas of law he hadn't advised on since pro bono work at law school.

The lady behind the front desk waved her hand. Alex stepped towards her. He then stepped back. A woman, from one of several chairs that lined either side of the entrance, rushed forward, an anxious expression on her face. Beyond her, the staff at the other three desks were deep in conversation with the clients sat in front of them.

"Are you here for the interview?" He heard a gentle voice behind him.

Alex turned around. Facing him, a middle-aged Asian man with a head of thick black hair flecked with grey, smartly styled. Dressed in black trousers and a white short-sleeved shirt, open at the neck. There was a pen in his top pocket and a cardboard tray of doughnuts in his arms.

"Raman," the man said, balancing the tray on one arm and offering Alex his hand.

"Alex." Alex shook his hand.

Raman walked between the desks – Alex following – stopping to offer the tray to staff and clients. They paused at the last desk where a large man sat, a client just leaving him.

"Take a break?" Raman said, with a smile.

"Whatever you say, chief," the man replied, with a boyish grin, standing up.

"All yours," Raman said, expressionless, to Alex. "Let's see how you get on and have a chat later."

Alex sat down behind the desk. He looked up; Raman was helping a woman with a pram wedged in the front door. Alex put his hands on his knees and took a deep breath. He stood.

"Who's next, please?" A frail, old lady – smartly dressed – raised her gloved hand and shuffled forward. In her other hand was a lead, at the end a small dog with a curly coat of hair, grey like its owner. Alex pulled the chair out and she lowered herself onto it, her hand on the desk for support. He brought his chair around the desk and sat beside her.

"Hi, I'm Alex. How can I help?"

"Mrs Jacobs," she replied. She looked at him closely. "You look like my grandson. He's got shorter hair, though."

She'd lost her husband that week. She was overwhelmed by grief, as well as all the paperwork she took out from her handbag and held before him in her shaking hand. They made a number of calls and filled out forms together. He saw her to the door when they'd finished.

"I'm so sorry, about you husband," Alex said. "Come back if you need anything, even if I'm not here someone can help."

"Thank you, I will," Mrs Jacobs said, patting his arm. "What's your favourite cake, dear?"

In the next two hours, Alex served a seemingly endless succession of people, until the seats by the door, suddenly and finally emptied. When he looked up from making his final case note, he saw Raman was standing by the desk watching him.

"Coffee?" Raman asked.

Raman gestured to some cushioned seats at the back of the office. It looked like the corner of a school staffroom. He made two coffees on a nearby side-board, and handed Alex a hot plastic cup. They sat.

"We're busy here."

"I can see that."

"Constant fire fighting, and the government cuts mean it can only get worse. We're an extension of social services a lot of the time too," Raman said. He took a sip from his cup and sat back in the low chair.

"So, why are you here?" he asked.

"I got made redundant," Alex replied.

"Lucky you – no doubt you were well rewarded," Raman said. "Why don't you go travelling? Or get a job at another firm?"

Alex sat back in his seat, feeling a wave of heaviness in his arms, unused to such an energetic day.

"I'm not sure I want to do either right now," Alex said, after a pause.

"Alex. I can see you'd be useful here," Raman said. "You have the knowledge and you seem very natural with people – especially the older folk."

Alex felt his heart beating faster and sweat on his forehead. "I've got the job?"

"Only if you can give me six months," Raman said, with a serious expression on his face. He lent forward, offering his hand to Alex. "Do I have your word?"

"*Dictum meum pactum*," Alex said, shaking Raman's hand.

Passing the Camden Image Gallery and the Grand Union pub on the way to Camden Station, Alex smiled to himself. He took out his phone and started typing a message to Julia.

Chapter Eight

Without Julia

"Let's get drunk."

"We can't afford to," Richard replied. "I have no money and you won't soon, either."

"I can afford to get drunk, which means we can," Alex said. "The blood money is now in my account."

"Which is where it should stay," said Richard.

"I think it's imperative we get drunk, Richard. I really do."

Ciara appeared in front of them with two pints. She set them down.

"Ciara, where have you been?" Alex said. "Has he been boring you with his cricket chat?"

"Actually, he's been teaching me the rules, it's such a complicated game," Ciara said. "He said it's going to take some time."

"I bet he did," Alex said. But looking up, he saw he'd lost Richard and Ciara's attention, they were now talking amongst themselves.

Cargo Ship Missing in the Bermuda Triangle read the headline of the newspaper on the bar; Alex leaned over it.

Richard finally turned to him.

"Have you heard about this missing boat?" Alex looked up at him. "Disappeared without a trace."

"Since when did you become so interested in the news?"

There was applause from the TV speakers and stirrings in the room as heads turned to look up at the screen.

"Are we even winning?" Alex asked.

"Actually, we are."

"I thought, when it came to cricket, we made it our business not to," Alex said.

"Well, that's been the case for a long time," Richard said. "Each summer begins full of optimism and hopeful expectation. Then, after repeated loss and humiliation, it ends in defeat, followed by a period of protracted analysis and introspection." Richard sighed, glancing across at Ciara. "Like my love life."

"Fuck's sake, Richard, brighten up. You're meant to be keeping my spirits up," Alex said, glancing at Ciara, who was looking at Richard. "This summer's started well though, right?" Richard sighed.

"How's your dad?"

"I saw him this afternoon," Alex replied.

"How is he?"

"Retired; as of last week."

"That came around quickly," Richard said. "What's he going to do?"

"I don't know," Alex replied. "Don't think he knows."

"A cruise? That's what people do."

"He hasn't said anything."

"I guess you didn't go on holiday much."

"We never went on holiday," Alex said. "But Dad would send me on all the school trips. Do you remember the Spanish exchange?

"So much for chicas and cervezas," Richard said. "Rained every day for a week in August, worst weather in a hundred years."

Alex turned to pick up his glass, it was gone – two new full pints had appeared on the bar in front of them like magic.

"Do you remember your dad taking us to Open Air Theatre in Regent's Park? I'd just turned sixteen and we'd got our GCSE exams results that day – both straight As," Richard said.

"I remember a theatre outing not exactly being the celebration we were hoping for," Alex said.

"Until he said we could drink wine."

"True."

"He was so into the production," Richard said. "I'd never seen your dad so excited about anything."

"He loves his Shakespeare."

"He'll have plenty of time for that now."

Alex felt an ache in his stomach. He hadn't eaten but had no appetite.

"I'm going to head off, Richard."

"I thought it was imperative we got drunk?"

"Tomorrow, maybe," Alex said, getting off the bar stool and crossing the pub. He took out his phone, looked at it, then put it away again. He hadn't called any friends in the past weeks, he didn't know how to explain what'd happened – he wasn't even sure himself – only Richard knew.

"Are you okay?" Richard said. He'd caught up with Alex at the pub door.

"I'm fine."

"I'm coming with you."

"You sure?" Alex said, glancing back towards the bar and Ciara.

Outside, they turned right down Delancey Street. Although parallel to Camden High Street, it was quiet – they walked in silence for a few minutes. Alex broke the silence.

"I was in my dad's study one school holiday, junior school. His study was kind of out of bounds when he wasn't around.

"There are bookshelves running along the whole of one side of the room. A huge volume of the *Complete Works of Shakespeare* was on the bottom shelf; still is. That afternoon, I was drawn to it.

"Sitting on the floor, I opened the worn red leather front cover. On the inside page on the aged paper, in my dad's angular writing, was a list."

"List of what?" Richard asked.

"Dates," Alex replied. "For each entry on the list, there was a date, a Shakespeare play, and a location. I worked out my dad was only thirteen when the list began."

"It was like a journal for him to record when he saw which play and where?" Richard said.

"The first entries had, after the date, play and location, a school name."

"School outings?"

"Exactly."

"The following ones had been written with a name, or names. Most I didn't recognise, but some I did – friends of my father, my godparents…"

"Who he saw the performance with. That makes sense."

Richard and Alex turned down another street, walking side by side.

"Then there was a series of entries. In fact, ten in total, which ended, *with M*. Like, *27th July 1978, Othello, Royal Court, with M*."

"Oh," Richard said. "For Madeleine – your mum?"

"Yes," Alex replied. "It can only be her because I've heard him talk about some of those performances."

"That's lovely."

"There are only two entries from the Regent's Park Theatre – following each other. The most recent was from when we went after exams."

"The other?"

"*12 August 1988*, A Midsummer Night's Dream, *Regent's Park Theatre (matinee), with M and A*."

"A – that's you, right? Madeleine and Alex."

"It's the last entry with her and the only one with all three of us," Alex said.

"All those years, he never went to see his beloved Shakespeare," Richard said.

"That summer, when Dad wasn't home, I'd pull the book from the shelf and sit with it in my lap. Staring at the list for hours, running my finger over that entry like it was a line from some sacred script. Saying it over, like it was a prayer."

"Alex," Richard said.

"I'd imagine that August day. My mother looking beautiful, like she does in all the photos. My father looking handsome and smiling, going to see one of his favourite plays. An ordinary family day out.

"On that date, that day, I would have been three years old. My mother got sick again not long after," Alex said. "I wondered if that could have been my father's last truly happy day."

"I don't know what to say," Richard said.

"After that summer, I forgot about the book, the entry – all of it. Until that day my dad took us there on exam results day.

"There was a moment during the play when I remembered: about the book; the list; the entry; and, the perfect day, as I'd imagined it. I looked across at him and I was certain he was thinking the same thing. About that day, but as it had actually been – with my mother and me."

They turned onto Parkway towards Camden underground station. There was a sound of a busker playing outside the station, it was Bob Marley's 'Redemption Song'.

"He was really proud of you that day," Richard said.

"You think?" Alex asked. Stopping in the street.

"Until the end of the performance," Richard said. "When you threw up red wine all over that couple in front of us, and yourself."

***

The letter lay on top of a pile of take away delivery menus, the flat's managing agency stamped on the envelope. Alex reached down and picked it up before closing the front door behind him. He sighed.

In the lounge, he picked up the TV remote and pointed it at the large screen hanging from the wall. An error message appeared under the Sky News Channel; his subscription had lapsed – he switched the TV off and threw the remote onto the sofa. He remained standing, very still. The silence seemed to settle on the room.

Below the TV screen, the long, wide, white book shelves still had gaps where Amy's big art books had been. He'd not bought new books to fill the shelves, or rearranged the ones left there. The absent books could have slotted back into the empty spaces.

Alex opened the letter, letting the envelope drop to the floor. The landlord was selling the flat, he had to move out by the end of the month. He got up and walked over to the fridge. Inside it was empty, except for a single bottle of beer.

With a satisfying fizz, the bottle top came off and hit the floor behind him, Alex tipped the bottle up and took a long drink. He felt light-headed, on an empty stomach, the alcohol hit his bloodstream almost immediately. But the buzz was short-lived and faded in seconds. He took out his phone. His finger hovered over his father's number, then Richard's – but even the thought suddenly seemed overwhelming.

Slumping down onto the sofa, Alex drained the bottle and put it down hard on the large coffee table in front of it. A crack appeared on the glass top. Lifting the bottle again, he brought it down harder, the crack grew and spread out.

He raised the bottle and brought it down again and again on the table, until the surface was shattered and his hand bled, glass shards stuck in the skin. He held the bottle overhead before hurling it at the wall. It smashed into hundreds of little green pieces.

Chapter Eight

With Julia

After crossing the road from Bethnal Green Station, Alex walked along Roman Road. The Victorian library, shrouded in the trees of the little park that surrounded it, on his right. The air was warming up, but heavy, humid – the sky full of dark, dense cloud.

A handmade sign in red and blue ink was attached to the park gates in a see-through plastic folder. The tube station's stairway had collapsed during an air raid during the Second World War. One hundred and seventy-five women and children had died. There was an image of a stairway that went up towards the sky – the proposed memorial – and a fundraising webpage below.

Alex could not imagine the fearful screams that must have filled the air so close to where he stood. He hugged his arms into himself, feeling the breeze across the park. Some dampness had got behind the plastic of the sign and the ink had run, the word 'hope' bled red and blue tears.

Alex crossed Commercial Road's wide expanse from a crowded north side. After turning down side street after side street, a huge church building appeared in front of him, the sign in the ground read – St Matthew's Hall. It towered over the street of run down Victorian houses on one side and squat, purpose-built blocks on the other.

Outside, small groups of elderly people were, slowly and cautiously, getting off minibuses of different sizes and various colours. A man in a wheelchair was lowered to the ground with a hydraulic hiss.

When Alex entered the large, wooden-floored hall, he heard a trumpet blast. On the left, a four-piece brass band was setting up: an older stout man in a tweed suit; two younger men with beards and wearing waistcoats; and a pale young woman with long blonde hair, in dungarees. To the right were twenty or so wooden tables and chairs. The tables made up with white table cloths, on top, cutlery and crockery for afternoon tea.

Dressed in a red and white polka-dot 1950s style dress and white serving apron over it, Julia leaned over a table of two old ladies, close by, to take their tea order. Alex approached the table but Julia then began making her way towards the line of trestle tables against the side of the hall. Tables laden with trays of cakes and sandwiches, and two silver urns with pouring taps. He changed angle.

"Julia." Julia looked round at him. There was a table between them. He went one way. She went the other. He went again, quicker this time – she let him catch her.

Alex held her, pulled her close, their lips touched for a second – she released herself from his embrace.

Walking off, leaving him standing there, only turning back with a smile when she'd reached the other side of the room.

"He's got a wild one there," one of the old ladies said to the other. He smiled at them.

"You must be Alex." Alex was greeted with a hand shake by a tall, mature lady with peroxide blonde hair, dressed in a black suit and a white frilly shirt – it was Bridget, the organiser. She directed him towards two men wearing overalls taking out more tables and chairs from a storage cupboard in the corner of the hall.

***

Alex put down a tray of washing up on a table and wiped his forehead. He'd barely spoken to Julia all afternoon, although they exchanged glances whenever she'd caught him looking at her across the room. An old man dropped his knife. Alex watched Julia fetch him a new one, and help steady his hand with hers as they cut into his cake. Alex tried to catch her eye again but she was onto serving someone else.

Laughter echoed around the packed church hall. Alex watched the faces of the old people break into grins and laughter. A few couples were now standing and dancing together, others swaying gently in their seats, to the swing music the band was playing. Bridget told him in a quiet moment, for some of them, today might be the first time they'd spoken to another person, in days, or even weeks.

***

Guests began to leave. Some walked to their waiting minibuses unaided, others with help from their carers. Leaving in a quieter manner than they'd arrived, tired now from the afternoon, but with smiles. Some of the volunteers started to leave too, Bridget thanking them and handing out leftover cake and biscuits in small bags. The band was packing up.

"I've never had tea out of a cup and saucer before. I think it tastes better," one of the young volunteers from the local school said on their way out.

Alex looked around the now almost empty hall but couldn't see Julia anywhere.

"Have you seen Julia?" he asked one of the female volunteers. She had a beehive hairstyle and a dress like Julia's, but in white and black.

"She took some boxes out," the young woman said, gesturing to the door at the back of the hall. It was made from the same wooden panelling as the walls and had an illuminated green fire exit sign above it.

Alex walked past the tables and went through the door into a narrow hallway. There was a black door at the end of it with a waist-high horizontal bar. It was swinging open and shut every few seconds.

He pushed at the door and it swung open violently as the wind took it, banging against the outside brick wall of the hall. When Alex stepped out, there was a low rumble above and he immediately looked up at the sky. Against a crimson sky were huge, dark grey clouds.

Tall, head-high piles of boxes were on one side, to the right a black iron railing, and the glass and steel skyscrapers of Canary Wharf on the horizon.

Julia was there in front of him. They were standing at the edge of the city, a burning sky behind them, its red orange streaks like flames: London on fire.

Julia had slung her apron over the railing. She was leaning back onto it. Her face angled upwards, catching the last rays of afternoon sun through the clouds. The wind playing with her hair. Shadows from the sunlight dancing at her feet as her dress swayed in the still strong breeze.

She didn't look over at Alex when he came out, although she must have sensed his presence and would've heard the slamming door. It was as if she already knew he would come to find her, like an actor on cue.

Alex was about to say something, but he paused, watching Julia for a few more moments, framing the image of her in his head. There was another rumble overhead, this time louder.

"When I look at you now, I think of this line from a J.D. Salinger short story I once read," Alex said.

Julia didn't look over at him but tipped her head still further back.

"What's the line, Alex?" she asked.

"'She wasn't doing a thing that I could see, except standing there, leaning on the balcony railing, holding the universe together.'"

It was then that Julia turned her head to look at Alex. The first flash of lightning lit up the sky above.

Followed by a loud bang and rattle of thunder, seconds later. Small drops of rain began to fall. *She stepped to him.*

"If you count the seconds between the lightning and thunder, you can tell how close the storm is," Alex said. *He stepped to her.*

His hands in her hair, her hands on his face. They kissed frantically as the storm broke above them with a deafening snap.

The rain now fell heavily. The sky behind Alex and Julia exploded into light, white fireworks against a red sky. Fierce thunder sounding almost immediately, shaking the very ground beneath them.

Four months ago

Chapter Nine

Without Julia

"We can't live like this," Alex said. His phone in one hand held to his ear, TV remote control in the other, pointed at the TV flicking through the channels. "No cable, no Freeview... Richard, are you still there? Alex threw down the phone and remote on the sofa.

Sitting down, he flipped open Richard's laptop on the coffee table in front of him – his own dropped during the move – he minimised a half completed job application and maximised the BBC News webpage. He leaned over to refresh the page. There were images from an earthquake in Indonesia.

***

"Never trust a man with a beard, my mam always said." Sal, or Big Sal, as everyone seemed to call her, including herself, loomed over Alex. She was wearing a black dress, slippers and a grubby grey apron, its original colour impossible to determine. She chuckled to herself. "Of course, my dad had a beard."

"Beards are in fashion now, Sal," Alex said, looking up at her from the battered Chesterfield by the door of

Nico's cafe – opposite Richard's flat. The faded green sofa looked odd amongst the plastic tables and chairs, as if put down for a moment on the way to being delivered somewhere else and forgotten.

"It's the East London look, Sal."

"It's the tramp look, love," Big Sal said. "You look like you've wandered in off the street." She shuffled back down the cafe, passing the seaside mural that covered the surface of one of the walls.

When Alex had asked Sal who Nico had been, she'd shrugged, saying she'd bought the lease off an alcoholic called Spiros ten years previously. She dismissed as crazy, Alex's suggestion that she could rename the cafe after herself.

Alex picked up the styrofoam cup with its thin plastic lid that Sal had left on the table in front of him. From the silver urn behind the counter – topped up with heaped spoons of powder from a large tin – even with specks of loose ash from Sal's cigarette in it, it was the best tea he'd ever tasted.

"Bacon sarnie?" Big Sal shouted back at him. Alex shook his head. "You don't eat." She sighed. "And he eats too bloody much." Fondly patting a stocky man in a fluorescent builder's jacket she passed. The man nodding in acknowledgement.

***

"Bastard machine." Alex pressed the button to pay the £1.88 surcharge, a few seconds later and he had £500 in bank notes in his hand – his maximum daily withdrawal limit. He was standing at the cash machine in the wall of the newsagent's a few doors down from Nico's café, and conveniently next to the betting shop.

Entering the red framed door of the betting shop, he was immediately drawn to the row of Roulette machines along one side; flashing bright colours frenetically in lines and shapes.

He quickly fed two twenty pound notes into the Roulette machine in front of him, it's money slot opening with an electronic growl when his hand came close. As it ate up the bank notes a cash register noise sounded over the loop of constant repetitive music emitting from it. He fed it more notes.

Until a few weeks before, he'd never been into a betting shop. Ten pounds in a poker night at university was the most he'd ever gambled, and lost.

The nearest TV screen was showing the greyhound racing, in the corner of the screen the time in digits. Every minute of his day had previously been recorded on an electronic billing sheet against a client. He'd lost £100 in ten minutes.

He ran his finger down one of the newspaper columns pinned to the wall, it had the race meeting location, race times and the horses entered for each race – with their racing colours, form, weight and handicap.

He'd called his father's mobile phone that morning but the line was dead, his father also never answered the landline. An envelope, containing a neatly folded piece of yellow, legal drafting paper had arrived on the doormat soon after in the morning post. In a very short tidily written note his father explained that his mobile phone had broken and he'd decided he no longer needed one. *Alex needed to go.*

His finger stopped moving down the race cards and hovered over one of the horses, Rambo's Arrow – in the 5 p.m. at Doncaster.

He placed the remaining money from his wallet on the betting counter before returning fifty pounds to his wallet. Slipping the betting slip into his pocket, he hurried for the door.

***

'93 Paxton & Whitfield' read the gold letters on the black shopfront, appearing above Alex when he turned the corner of Jermyn Street. The same lettering on the bags he remembered his father arriving home with on Friday evenings. Cheeses of all sizes and shapes, filled the window.

"Do you know the name?" the young blonde woman behind the counter said, smiling, in a white apron and cap.

"It smells of old socks," Alex said.

"Probably French."

"Actually, I think it was English, weird name."

"Stinking Bishop, perhaps?" she replied. "It's made with rotting pears, the bishops."

"Ah. That's it," Alex said. She took a thin round cheese from a fridge behind the counter and began wrapping it.

"Any Port or brandy with that?" she said, when the cheese was wrapped, pulling three bottles of each down from the shelf and placing them quickly but carefully in a row on the counter. "It takes a strong spirit to go with a strong cheese," she added, smiling again.

"Boys drink claret. Men drink port. But those who aspire to be heroes drink brandy."

"So what do you drink?" she asked.

"Well, I'll take this one for my dad." Alex placed his fingers on top of one of the brandy bottles.

***

Descending the escalator inside Chancery Lane tube station, he was standing near a thin, greying couple both wearing comfortable khaki trousers, walking boots and fleece tops.

"Smells like death down here," the man said in an American accent to the woman beside him, who Alex assumed; was his wife.

"Well, it's an old country," she replied, in the same accent.

"The death is in the bag," Alex said, glancing at the couple. "Cheese. Blue cheese."

"He's got some cheese in the box," the man said, turning to his wife and smiling. He turned back to Alex. "You know, young man, in the US, unpasteurised cheese is illegal."

"Illegal," his wife, repeated. "It's true."

"But we live in San Francisco," the man said.

118

"We've got a guy."

"What, like a dealer?"

"We just like to call him our 'cheese guy'," his wife replied.

"If I was in your predicament," Alex said, "I would have certainly have a 'guy' too."

The rank odour of the cheese was becoming stronger the lower they got and the warmer the air. It was too much. At the bottom of the escalator, Alex turned around and took the other escalator back up and left the station by the north west exit. He'd occasionally walked an hour home from the city and it was only half an hour further to his father's.

***

Alex opened the front door and shouted for his father. He didn't hear the usual response of "Alex". His arm ached from carrying the bag. He put it down.

Alex stepped inside the music room, the piano still covered in legal books. A cream material-covered two-seater sofa on one side, an analogue television in the corner. His father didn't use the TV so he hadn't, either – even the Queen's speech on Christmas day they'd listened to on the radio in the kitchen. His dad loved the cinema, though. Sunday afternoons, growing up, were spent at the Phoenix Cinema in Finchley, watching movies. Afterwards, always pizza and ice cream, or gelato which his father preferred.

Alex sat on the low cushioned piano seat. Amongst the books piled up above him was a silver-framed black and white photo. His mother was wearing an elegant, white wide-brimmed hat, and his father in coat and tails. His mother, a stranger, and in a way his father, too – he had an expression on his face Alex had never seen.

He opened the piano lid, resting his fingers on the ivory-coloured keys without pressing down. As well as teaching with it, his mother had often played it herself, too – according to his father. He closed the lid slowly and silently.

***

Alex put the kettle on the stove and lent against the work surface. An intermittent firing in the background from the ancient boiler, the only sound, like a sick patient slipping in and out of consciousness before an inevitable death. There was no milk in the fridge.

He switched on the radio. It was the end of the news, the sports round-up. A male announcer announced the day's race results, the winners, in a monotone. Alex took a deep breath.

"Five p.m., Doncaster, Rambo's Arrow," the voice said.

He took out his wallet, opened the credit card pocket where he'd been keeping betting slips. It was empty. There was sweat on his forehead, his heart was racing; he took another deep breath. He blew out. He felt inside his trouser pocket, then the other – only to find them empty. The only winning bet of the week... He sighed.

He sighed again. He took out his phone to call Billy, he couldn't face their meeting in an hour. He pressed the number, then cancelled the call before the dialling started. He took the kettle off the stove and left the kitchen for the front door.

"Dad." Opening the door he found his father on the threshold. Keys in one hand and a pint of milk in the other, the denim on his father's left knee was torn and there was dried blood.

"What happened to your knee?" Alex asked.

"Nothing," his father replied. "Leaves on the pavement. I'm going to call the council."

"Sounds like you should be suing the council," Alex said, still standing in the doorway. He raised his hand to his forehead.

"I should have been more careful," Alex's father said, "are you going to let me in?"

"Sorry," Alex said, stepping out of the way. "I've got to go but I'll see you soon, okay?"

His father passed him and Alex watched him walk down the corridor towards the kitchen, his shoulders very slightly hunched. He forgot his father was nearly seventy.

＊

"It wasn't for the view was it?" Alex said. A pair of black Doc Martin boots attached to a pair of legs with tights passed. "You chose this place." He was standing at the barred street-facing window of

Richard's basement flat.

"It was for the cheap rent," Richard replied, sat on the sofa, still in his work suit. "There're some great pubs in Camden, too."

"We only ever go to one pub, Richard," Alex said. "And currently, there's no chance of us going anywhere else."

"I don't hear you complaining about Ciara's free pints."

Alex and Richard surveyed the tiny room; boxes were stacked on every surface, carpet only visible on the paths between the front door, sofa and kitchen. When Alex's landlord had threatened to evict him, leaving his possessions in the street, Richard had hired a van and collected Alex and all his stuff from his mews flat.

"I'm getting claustrophobic," Richard said.

"Let's go," Alex said and began up the stairs, Richard behind him. When they were at street level, Alex added. "Actually, we'll need to do something about the flat. For my belated moving in party."

"What party?" Richard asked, turning back to look at Alex, who was now grinning. "Let's have one when you move out," Richard added.

When they walked into the Crown, the first thing Richard did was look over for Ciara. It was quiet and they approached their usual spot at the bar.

"You really do like her, don't you?" Alex said.

"Shut up before she overhears," Richard said.

Ciara appeared with a pint in each hand, and smile. Without saying anything, she put the drinks down in front of them before going to serve down the other end of the bar. Richard gazed after her.

"I'm trying to play it cool for the first time in my life."

"I can see that," Alex said, smiling.

"You're love life isn't exactly going anywhere at the moment is it?" Richard said.

Alex looked down at the pint in front of him. He picked it up and put it back down again on the bar without taking a drink. Richard glanced at him.

"Something wrong with it?" he said. "Or you?"

"You know, Richard, until a few months ago, I was going somewhere – in a direction," Alex said. "I'm not so sure now it was the right one but... I mean – I never thought I'd be crashing on a sofa in some dingy shithole in Camden."

"Thanks."

"You know what I mean."

"Again, thanks." Richard said. "Look, you ungrateful bastard, you can stay as long it takes until you get on your feet."

"I'm going to cook for us, I promise," Alex said. "Tomorrow, definitely tomorrow." Richard rolled his eyes.

"So tell me about this Billy kid. I hope you've been a bit more positive around him."

Chapter Nine

With Julia

"How many weddings have you actually been to?" Julia asked.

"I've lost count," Alex replied.

They turned off the motorway in Alex's father's 1980s maroon Saab hatchback he kept parked in the street outside his flat. It only had a cassette tape player and Alex had forgotten his iPod lead. Julia was rifling through various tapes from the open glove compartment before choosing one.

Alex heard the mechanical clink of a tape in the stereo as they drove briskly down the Gloucestershire country road. A crackling and winding sound was followed by the opening of Fleetwood Mac's 'Everywhere', the sound from the original speakers of the car surprisingly clear.

"You like Fleetwood Mac?" Alex asked.

"Who doesn't?" Julia said.

Alex noticed her phone vibrating; she glanced at it without picking it up.

"You must have a rough idea, Alex," Julia said. "About the number of weddings."

"You remember," Julia said. "I'll count."

"Is my conversation really that bad?" Alex said.

Julia reached into her canvas handbag and took out an old envelope. She was wearing a yellow cotton summer dress covered in black palm tree silhouettes. She kicked off her yellow flip flops and drew up her knees to her chest, her bare feet resting on the seat. Alex was beside her in faded blue jeans and grey T-shirt. Julia turned down the music.

"My first," Alex sighed. "Cousin Jenny to Simon. Then after university, there was Alex and Lizzy, Michael and Claire, Dave and Emma, Dave and Anna."

"Same Dave?"

"Different Dave. Then there was Hannah and James, Will and Catherine, Joanna and John, Matt and Susie, Iain and Georgina – castle in Scotland, amazing. Then, Emily and Sam, Becky and Darren, Laura and John, Gavin and Jackie, Dan and Mia – great name, Biblical, I think. Simon and Kate, very London – Hackney Town Hall. Adam and Jan, very *not* London – rural church, reception on a village green. Roger and Helen. Helen and Jamie."

"Same Helen?"

"Same Helen – first in Vienna, second in Vegas. Then, Riaz and Claudia, the reception in an art deco theatre in Cornwall, beautiful. Ed and Daisy – he owns a cider brewery, hazy. But there's photographic proof I was on the dance floor. Matt and Rachel's wedding was special, barn on Essex-Suffolk borders, Beatles tribute band. Garrett and Stephen's in Dublin."

"That's a lot of weddings," Julia said, tilting her head back and blowing air out of her mouth.

"Who else? Let me think…"

"More?"

"Lucan and Sheila in Spain, Lucy and Jack's in France, Matt and Maria in Shropshire, Dom and Emma in Portugal, Nick and Charlotte, in the Seychelles – on the beach, my favourite so far. Who else? Phillippa and Nic, Rory and Becky. Damian and Claire – God rest her soul."

"She died?"

"She did, too young. She was a beautiful person." He looked out of the window.

"You done?"

"No. Saul and Aki, Tom and Becca. Paul and Joanna."

"Today will be number thirty-six, you realise?" Julia said, looking down at the notebook on her lap.

"I'm not sure how I've found the time."

Alex stopped the car, they were at a junction on the country road – two possible turnings ahead.

"Do you think it's strange you've been to all these weddings," Julia said. "Never your own?"

"I've always enjoyed other people's birthdays more than my own," Alex replied.

Clunk. The cassette tape came to an end, he hadn't noticed the song finishing. Julia picked up her phone. Alex looked out of the window. The green fields flashed by on either side of the road as they continued to rush down country lanes in silence.

"All these weddings," Julia said. "You must have

some wedding dos and don'ts."

"I suppose so," Alex said.

"Do I get to hear them?" Julia replied.

"Okay..." Alex paused. "Do get there the night before, to avoid stress and traffic. Do stay in the reception venue, to minimise distance from dancefloor to bed. Do book the following Monday off work so that you can recover, that's become more important in recent years. Oh, and lastly, don't forget the wine carafe."

"Wine carafe?"

The air was now warming. Julia shifted her position and opened the window. The wind blew her hair, she reached into her handbag and pulled out some large black sunglasses and put them on.

"It must have been about half way through that list I discovered the perfect wedding present," Alex said. He tapped the steering wheel unconsciously for emphasis.

"It's something people wouldn't buy for themselves, when they see one they want one but they always forget to buy one. It's way more interesting than some silver spoons from the wedding list. It's impossible to really tell how expensive it is. And, as the giver of the wine carafe, it kind of bestows upon you an air of sophistication." Alex grinned cheekily.

"Wow, is all I have to say." Julia laughed.

South Lodge, in blue letters read the large white sign fixed to the huge oak tree at the turn off. They followed the narrow, tree-lined winding driveway for some minutes. The sun was hot and there was a slight breeze. The driveway got wider and wider until a huge country house appeared in front of them.

"Are we staying here?" Julia asked.

"All the rooms were booked," Alex replied. "There are some rooms in the grounds that used to be stables, I managed to get one of those."

When they pulled up in front of the house, Alex opened his door and sat back in the car seat and closed his eyes. As the sunlight fell on his face and he smiled, thinking about a whole day and night ahead with Julia at his side.

"Alex, you realise then," Julia said, as she opened her door, "technically, we haven't followed any of your tips, your 'dos'."

"Look behind your seat," Alex said.

Julia peered over her shoulder. In the foot space was a bag with a neatly wrapped white box inside, tied with a white ribbon.

"There's a card in there for you to sign, too."

"You do seem to know what you're doing." Julia turned to face forward and stretched her legs. "So, what about 'don'ts'."

"I don't know – don't get too drunk, don't get in a fight. Don't hurt yourself."

A very old but beautiful lady, in a tweed skirt and cream blouse appeared from the edge of the driveway and walked across the grass. She looked familiar. Pausing in front of their car, she looked directly at them. Alex looked back at her and their eyes met. She smiled at him.

Alex turned to Julia. But she was out of the car

already, making her way round to his side of the car. Stuttering bursts of Metronomy's 'The Look' could be heard in the background – the sound of a band doing some kind of sound check. Still wearing her big sunglasses, Julia moved to the music beside him.

She pulled Alex out of the car by his arm and they danced together, until the band stopped completely a minute or so later.

***

Alex sat on the bed while Julia walked around the room, opening and closing cupboards and drawers. Although early, they'd managed to check into their room, a short walk from the main house.

"Do you like the room?" Alex asked. He was sitting up on the bed, he'd taken his shoes and socks off.

"The sexy man in the middle of it isn't bad," Julia replied.

"Breakfast?" Alex asked, picking up the bottle of champagne from the ice bucket on the bedside table, beside it two croissants and pain au chocolats.

"Why not?" Julia replied. Alex popped the cork and filled the two glass flutes. Julia had her back to him and was looking out of the window onto the grounds, her muscular calves tightened as she stood on her toes. It was the first time they'd shared a hotel room.

Alex stood up from the bed and reached for Julia's waist but she moved away, out of his reach.

"I want you," Alex said.

Julia began to giggle, then opened her mouth and laughed. She let herself fall onto the bed and rolled around laughing. She stopped and looked up at Alex, with a serious expression.

"I want you," she said, blowing him a kiss with just her lips, then laughing again and laying out flat on the bed – arms outstretched.

Alex climbed onto the bed. Julia sat up. He pulled her close into him. They were sitting opposite each other, Julia's legs inside his and his around her. He pulled her in closer. Their faces almost touching, Alex could feel her breathing. He looked into Julia's green eyes, she blinked, her eyes narrowed very slightly; as if asking a question.

Closing his eyes, Alex tilted his head moving slowly forward to Julia's, his closed lips to hers. When he felt her wide lips on his, he opened his mouth which opened her mouth. Its warmth and taste sending an electric charge through his body, every cell pulsing with a craving for her. Their mouths coming together over and over again, their tongues playing with each other tenderly.

"I want a shower," Julia said, when they finally came apart.

"We've got plenty of time," Alex said.

"You would say that." Julia laughed.

She left Alex's arms, and got off the bed. Standing beside the bed, Julia pulled the yellow dress she was wearing over the top of her head. She let it drop from her hand. She was standing in a white bra, and thin white knickers – a dark patch of hair just visible underneath.

Alex lent forward and reached for her. She pushed him away.

"I'm going for a shower now." Julia reached her hand behind her back. Still not used to seeing her body, Alex looked on intently, desperate to absorb every inch, every detail. Taking off her bra, Julia's breasts moved as they came free.

As she pulled down her knickers, a strip of short dark hair below her belly button was revealed. Putting her hands on her hips and posing, her serious expression melted into a seductive smile. Alex reached to take her hand, but she pushed him away again with her hand.

"Are you going to make me beg?" Alex asked.

"I'm going to make you wait," Julia replied and turned.

Alex watched her walk naked towards the bathroom, the curves of her firm but shapely bottom rising and falling with each step.

***

"Stay still," Julia said with a stern tone.

"Put your hands down," Julia said. "And lean back."

She was standing beside the bed, a white towel wrapped around her body, drying her hair with a smaller towel.

Alex laid back on the bed and put his arms to his side. Julia threw the small towel onto the chair by the bed and unwrapped the towel around her body, letting it drop to her feet.

She climbed onto the bed, naked. Her long brown hair was hanging down, still damp, clinging to her chest – the tips of her nipples showing through. She put her knees down on either side of his head.

Alex looked up from between Julia's legs at her smooth stomach and her swaying breasts above him. He breathed in her smell. He moved to her. He reached her. She put her hand on his head. He lent up to reach her again, purposefully; Julia looked down at him.

"Julia, I need you, I…"

Julia brought her finger up to her mouth.

"Shush," she said, lowering herself onto Alex's face. She rocked back and forth above him, after a few minutes beginning to sigh. Slow, quiet sighs at first, gradually building into longer and louder ones. Alex reached up to her breasts and cupped them, her nipples now hard under his thumbs – she didn't resist.

Julia's sighs became quicker and quicker, shorter and shorter, as she moved rhythmically in a circular motion. Alex felt a small shudder above him and her muscles around his face relax.

Julia reached for the table, picking up one of the glasses of champagne. Alex stopped and shifted under her. She moved back so she was sitting on his chest, and looked down at him.

"Wow, you taste so fucking good." Alex took a deep breath.

"Then, why did you stop?" Julia asked.

"But I thought..."

"You're not finished yet."

Alex opened his mouth to speak again.

"Shut up, Alex," Julia said, slapping him with her free hand.

Alex's face stung. Julia's stern expression turned to a smile at his shocked face. He wanted her to hit him again. She lowered herself down onto his face again.

After some minutes, a series of moans came from above Alex, rising and falling in sound. Then a long low moan, followed by a short high-pitched cry. Julia pulled away from Alex, suddenly. The champagne flute falling from her hand and there was a clear, sharp sound of breaking glass beside the bed.

Julia climbed off him and the bed. With his hand, Alex wiped his wet mouth and chin, dripping with her, before glancing down to the floor by the bed. The broken flute hadn't shattered, it was broken at the neck into two distinct pieces.

"Julia," he said, but she didn't look back before entering the bathroom.

* * *

Alex moved off the bed. The bathroom door was open. He could see Julia standing in front of the mirror, her back to him. The silk dressing gown she'd slipped on had short sleeves and went to the back of her knees. A slender calf visible and showing a hint of muscle, her weight on one foot. He stepped towards the bathroom door. She was brushing her teeth. Her hair wild and unbrushed.

He stood in the doorway looking at her reflection. Her gown was open at the front, her pert breasts exposed, nipples still hard from minutes earlier. He had a rush of blood below. He stepped inside and directly behind her, looking at her in the mirror over her shoulder. Julia caught his eyes in the reflection. She stopped brushing and smiled at his reflection.

"Oh, hello," she said.

Alex remained expressionless. He reached up to her smooth neck with both his hands, running them through her hair, collecting it in his left hand. He leaned close and kissed her neck; it smelt bitter-sweet, her perfume mixed with sweat.

With his right hand, Alex pulled the thin dressing gown to one side to reveal Julia's naked bottom. He remained silent as he unbuttoned his trousers and freed himself. He brushed against her bottom.

Julia took the toothbrush from her mouth. Bent over the sink to put it down beside it and stayed down, her weight shifting onto both feet, her hands stretching out in front of her. She took a step wider and parted her legs, turning her heels outwards – making a high pitched sound on the tiled floor.

Alex's head was now beside hers, she whispered something in his ear. He pulled her hair tighter in his left hand, like a fist. Julia sighed breathily as she yielded to him. Bending over further, raising her bottom, opening herself to him.

Alex was gently rubbing himself on her then pulling away, teasing her until she was panting deeply and hungrily; straining to open herself wider to him.

"Are you going to make me beg?" Julia said, breathily. He finally entered her. "Alex," she said, sighing with her whole body.

Sweat ran from their bodies as their breathing grew heavier. Alex paused. He tore Julia's gown from her body, dropping it to the floor. Plunging desperately inside her again, even deeper than before, she banged her fist on the surface. Their breathing growing louder and louder, and simultaneous, as if they were taking one breath. She ran the taps to drown out the sound.

"Don't stop," she said, over and over again.

Julia screamed. And Alex held her close into him; her body, now limp, shuddering in his arms, his head now beside hers.

When he finally looked up into the mirror at their faces, for a moment, he forgot which one was his.

***

"Do I look okay?" Julia asked Alex, from the step of a vintage red Routemaster London bus. She was wearing a bright red figure-hugging dress, in her hand a white vintage-looking clutch bag, and on her head a white wide brim hat.

"It's embarrassing," Alex replied. Julia looked at him with a confused expression.

"It's embarrassing," Alex said, "when your girl-friend is so beautiful there's a serious danger she'll upstage the bride." And Julia's face broke into one of her glorious smiles.

He was wearing his father's morning suit, it had been his granddad's, too, and was over fifty years old but in great condition and fitted Alex perfectly.

They climbed the stairs to the top of the bus. As they sat down, Julia slid her hand under her bottom to sweep her dress to the front – a perfunctory act, she did with such grace. Alex was at the back of a bus with Julia, again, as they'd been a few months before. He was about to point this out to her, but she was complimenting the woman in front of them on her fascinator, which was made of peacock feathers.

Alex and Julia were handed folded cream cards by an usher when they entered the church a few minutes later. Alex glanced at the order of service he held, it had the religious ceremony and a mixture of hymns and readings.

"Bride or groom?" another usher asked them. Julia looked at Alex.

"I'm both." Alex shrugged, he glanced at Julia. "Let's go groom, I think Hilda's got more friends." The usher gestured to the right.

The inside of the church looked medieval – the walls of, seemingly, ancient stone. The ceiling had a central wooden beam and others across it, like ribs.

"So, how many of the women here have you slept with?" Julia said as they both looked around the full church, all the guests having now been shown their seats.

"Including the bride?" Alex asked.

"No?" Julia looked at him.

"No," Alex replied. "But her sister? Poppy. Yes.

She's married now – last summer, I think."

"It wasn't on the list, was it?" Julia asked.

"I guess that wedding invite must've got lost in the post."

***

Alex and Julia stood together amongst the guests on the lawn, the country house in the background – the reception in full swing. They were handed Pimms in jam jars with striped straws from a passing tray. A tall, broad, fair-haired young man, Alex remembered to be the bride's younger brother, approached them.

"You're an absolutely stunning addition to the day," he said to Julia.

"Thanks," she said. "I came with the marquee."

"Ha, brilliant, cracking sense of humour, too," he said. "I'm Toby, brother of the bride."

"Julia."

"Who do you know?" Toby asked.

"No one – except you now. And Alex," Julia said, putting her arm on Alex's shoulder. The man turned his face to Alex.

"A brother, too?" Toby asked, offering his hand.

"Boyfriend, actually," Alex said. Toby shook his hand with an iron tight grip – Alex remembered he played rugby for England under 21s.

"I must mingle or I'll be in terrible trouble with my sister, and Mummy."

Alex and Julia rolled their eyes at each other as they watched Toby wander off, shouting someone's name in greeting.

Julia got out a Chinese fan from her clutch bag and began to fan herself slowly. It had a white background and black branches with red blossom flowers – that matched her red dress and nails. The band began to play.

They turned as a guest, also dressed in a morning suit, tripped and became tangled in the guy ropes of the marquee. He freed himself and wandered waveringly into the marquee.

"All this drinking in the sun must have gone to his head," Alex said.

"I think it might be going to mine, too," Julia said.

Alex went to the long serving table nearby and returned with a large glass of water. Julia drunk it in one, delicately but quickly. A man in a top hat emerged from the house and marched onto the lawn, banging a brass gong with a wooden stick – the so-called wedding breakfast was announced.

Alex ran his finger down the list of tables and names on the large printed page, pinned to a board and propped on an easel at the marquee entrance. The inside of the vast marquee, decorated with white flowers and large round tables, all fully laid with cutlery, bottles of wine and water.

"I'm sorry we're not together," Alex said to Julia. "I did ask. I think you're in the groom's Aunt Lizzy's seat."

"Where's she sitting?"

"She's laying, in a hospital bed in France, broke her femur skiing last week in Chamonix," Alex said.

"We should send her flowers," Julia said, with a mischievous grin.

"We probably should," Alex said, with a smile.

"Don't worry. I'll be absolutely fine," Julia said.

"Okay, but if you get bored – so I can rescue you – promise to give me a sign?"

"Promise," Julia said, with a wink. She turned and headed in the direction of her table.

Alex called out to her. "Julia, what will it be? The sign? Your fan?"

"I'll be flirting with the good looking men at the table." Julia replied.

***

Alex sat down in his seat at large round table, it was now full. He introduced himself to the men either side of him as people began picking up their bread rolls and pouring each other wine. Alex recognised the man around the table as the cousin of the groom who'd done one of the number of readings, Shakespeare's Sonnet 116.

"I enjoyed your reading," Alex said to him when he passed Alex the sparkling water he'd asked for.

"He was good, wasn't he?" said a blonde woman beside him.

"Thank you," he said, offering his hand to Alex. "Felix. And my wife, Emma."

"Hello," Emma said.

"I've heard that poem read at three weddings so far this summer," Felix said. "Still don't have the foggiest what it's really about."

"Do you still have it on you?" Alex asked. "The reading."

Felix reached into his jacket pocket and handed a folded piece of paper to Alex. Alex opened up the page in front of him. Conversations around the table came to an end, or at least paused, and he felt their eyes on him.

"'Let not the marriage of true minds admit impediments,'" Alex read aloud. "What Shakespeare is saying here is that nothing should get in the way of Charlie and Hilda getting married, simply – they're a great match.

"'Love is not love which alters when it alteration finds,'" Alex continued. "Now what he's saying is, that love isn't really love if you stop loving the other person when circumstances change, if one of you gets fat or loses their job – real love transcends all that.

"'Or bends with the remover to remove' – or when one of you goes away, to war, or even just a business trip.

"'O no; it is an ever-fixed mark, That looks on tempests, and is never shaken'. This bit means real love doesn't get blown away and the storms of life are observed by the love; essentially, love has its ups and downs but endures.

"'It is the star to every wandering bark, whose worth's unknown, although his height be taken,' means, this kind of love is like a guiding star to everyone; he's evoking the universal here. Essentially, you can see how amazing it is but cannot truly measure it – it's immeasurable," Alex said, gesturing with his hand. "And it goes on like that."

"Wait. You can't stop there, my good man," Felix said. "We're on the edge of our seats."

Alex looked up. He saw that he now had the attention of the whole table.

"'Love's not Time's fool, though rosy lips and cheeks Within his bending sickle's compass come' – love cannot escape time completely, it evolves.

"'Love alters not with his brief hours and weeks, But bears it out even to the edge of doom' – however, it does not change materially over time and will be there on the last day of existence. Shakespeare gets quite dramatic here, even by his lofty standards.

"The last line, so simple, so poetic and so very beautiful," Alex took a sip from his wine glass.

"'If this be error and upon me proved' – if everything I've been saying isn't true, then prove it, because, 'I never writ, nor no man ever loved'. If it's not true, then no man has ever loved."

"Bravo!" Felix exclaimed, "I'll enjoy it infinitely more at the next wedding now I know what the bloody hell the Bard was on about."

***

"Who's the woman in the red?" The man next to Alex, who'd introduced himself as James, asked the man on his other side. Alex turned and saw they were referring to Julia.

"I don't know, but she's an absolute beauty," the

other man replied. Alex smiled.

"She's going out with a friend of the groom apparently. Lawyer, just been made redundant, poor fellow."

"Shame."

Alex was unsure whether he was saying it was shame that Julia had a boyfriend, or that he'd been made redundant.

He looked up and saw Julia approaching. He eased his chair back and pulled her down onto his lap as she passed.

"I wasn't looking for you," she said, smiling. "I was looking for the ladies."

She gave him a brief kiss and wandered off. Alex's eyes followed her all the way out of the marquee.

"Red, anyone?" Alex said, lifting the nearest bottle of red wine. After filling glasses, he filled his own almost to the top.

"So you must be Alex," said the guest next to James who'd enquired after Julia. "I'm Ben."

"I'm the unemployed lawyer," Alex said.

"Sorry, I didn't realise," the man said, with a sheepish look.

"Don't worry about it," Alex said. "It's lucky she's not with me for my money."

He emptied his wine glass and filled it up again to the top.

Ben looked awkwardly at James, as if looking for guidance, unsure of what to say; or to witness to what he'd just heard.

"How's it going?" James said, turning back to Alex

with an earnest expression on his face.

"People give daytime TV a bad name, but it's actually not that bad," Alex replied. James looked at Alex, with a concerned look, unsure if he was joking or not. "I've got another job now." Alex added.

"Good for you," James said, with a firm smile.

There was a banging of glass on cutlery and the speeches began. After the groom and the best man, the father of the bride provided a chronological account of Hilda's life. Alex smiled and laughed when the others around him did, but he couldn't take his eyes off Julia across the room. Finally, to a few knowing groans, Toby, the bride's brother, stood and announced he wanted to say a few words.

A couple at the nearby table looked restless. He'd seen them smoke at the reception on the lawn earlier and recognised the feeling.

"Cigarette?" Alex mouthed to the couple, making a smoking gesture with his hand and indicating to the nearest exit flap in the marquee.

Outside, cigarettes were handed out with conspiratorial looks in the warm evening air.

"Would you like one?"

"Thank you but I just came out for some fresh air," Alex said, with a wink. He looked down and noticed she had rolling tobacco in her hand. "You know what, I'll take one of those." She handed him a pouch of tobacco and cigarette papers.

It was strange how his hands remembered the sensation of rolling, even though he hadn't rolled a cigarette, or smoked, for two years.

"So this is where the cool kids are hanging out." Alex heard Julia behind him and turned. The man nearest offered her an open packet of Marlboro Lights. She deftly took one out and he lit it for her attentively, after which she took delicate drags.

Alex lifted the cigarette he was rolling to his mouth. Julia looked directly at him for the first time. Her eyes opening wider and mouth falling slightly open, he could tell she was thinking about the hotel room earlier; his mouth between her legs. He licked the length of the glue side of the paper. Her eyes widened further. She licked her lips, unconsciously, moving her weight onto one foot, and took a deep breath. The cigarette in her hand had burned down to the filter.

Alex sealed the roll-up between his fingers and took the offered light. He took the cigarette smoke deep into his lungs and breathed out slowly. He felt dizzy and took a step back, feeling the gravel path underfoot. A man appeared at the door, a boyfriend of one of the women. "He's wrapping up," the man said, and they followed him inside like naughty teenagers.

***

When The Artic Monkey's 'I Bet You Look Good On the Dancefloor' came to an end, the dancefloor was full, and Alex and Julia were arm in arm.

"Let's get some air." Julia pulled Alex out of the marquee doors into a beautiful night. The sky was clear and the stars were out.

There was a man asleep on one of the benches outside. Jacketless, in his white shirt, he lay curled up using his hands as a pillow.

"Someone's had a good night," Alex said.

"I think it's Johnny," Julia said. "The best man."

"Our revels are now ended," Alex told him.

"Huh?" the man said, stirring.

"Party's over," Julia said. "Everyone's going to bed."

"I'm fine here," the man replied, then jumped to his feet and staggered off in the direction of the main house. They watched the light from inside swallow him up as he entered.

Julia shivered and Alex put his jacket over her shoulders and his arm around her. They walked back towards the converted stables and their room.

"That woman from this morning, in the driveway, I never saw her at the wedding," Alex said.

"I don't remember her."

Chapter Ten

Without Julia

"Who do you support?" Billy asked Alex. They were looking out of the window of Camden Starbucks onto the high street.

"Politics?" Alex asked. Billy gave him a look. "Football?" Alex continued.

"Er. Yeah." Billy replied.

"Oh right. Like a team?" Alex said, shaking his head. "I haven't got one,"

"That's weird," Billy said. "For a bloke."

"Isn't that being unfair to people who aren't interested in football," Alex said, "and to women football fans?" Billy grunted.

"You're originally from north London, Billy. So that's Tottenham Hotspur, right?"

"Are you blind?" Billy said, pointing to the badge on his shirt. Alex looked at the faded red shirt Billy was wearing; the badge said 'Arsenal Football Club'.

Billy took a sip of his hot chocolate, both his hands around the huge white mug.

"Are you married?"

"No."

"Girlfriend?"

"No."

"Divorced?"

"No."

"Gay?"

"No."

"Kids?"

"No."

"But you're old," Billy said. "That's so weird."

"I'm twenty-nine, not forty-nine."

"My cousins all had kids by the time they'd left school," Billy said. "Well, they left school because they had kids."

"I seem old to you because you're a kid but I'm definitely not old," Alex said. "And I've had girlfriends. I just don't have one right now."

"Where do they go?" Billy took a sip from his mug.

"I keep losing them."

Billy spat out a mouthful of hot chocolate.

"I've never met anyone like you."

Alex took a sip of the coffee in front of him and took a deep breath.

"Neither have I."

Billy spat out another mouthful of hot chocolate, giggling loudly. The people at the nearest table looked over.

"Remind me again what I'm meant to be doing," Alex asked.

"Inspiring, motivating and instilling aspiration and confidence," Billy said, doing a good impression of Mary from Bright Starts.

"You have a good memory, Billy," Alex said. "I'm

going to try something," He turned to Billy and put out his hand. "Shake my hand."

"You're not meant to touch me," Billy said.

"I don't want to touch you. I want to teach you to shake hands like a man."

"Isn't that being unfair to women hand shakers?" Billy asked, a smile spreading across his face. Alex still waiting, hand outstretched.

"My uncle, he was an ex-boxer. My hand used to ache for days after he shook it," Billy said, before he straightened his posture and, finally, shook Alex's hand.

"Can I have another hot chocolate?"

"Actually, we need to go."

"Where?" Billy asked. Alex pointed out of the window towards Parliament Hill in the distance. "Is that a joke? I'm knackered from football training."

"It's a nice walk."

"I don't like walks."

"Everyone likes walks."

Billy took a last long sip of his drink before pushing the mug aside and resting his arms on the table, sighing. When Alex stood, Billy appeared to drag himself upright.

"It will make sense when we get there," Alex said.

***

When Alex reached the top of Parliament Hill, Billy was trailing behind him, eyes looking down at his phone. The mist that had been there earlier when he'd crossed to Camden had lifted to reveal a clear view of London's skyline.

There was a metal sign at waist height facing back towards central London. It had the outlines and names of all London's major buildings and landmarks inscribed on it: St Paul's Cathedral, the Gherkin, the BT Tower and, the Shard; which cut the city in two. Billy caught up with Alex and stood beside him in front of the sign.

"At this spot I always ask myself the same thing," Alex said.

"What are we doing here?" Billy said, not appearing to have heard Alex.

"Sometimes I think that," Alex said. "But what I mean to say is, sometimes we can be too close to our lives. It can be helpful to step back."

"Like seeing the bigger picture, my nan would say," Billy said. He put away his phone and finally looked up.

"Exactly."

Waiting for Billy earlier, Alex remembered asking him during their last meeting about school. He'd said the teachers were okay, he didn't mention any friends which Alex thought was strange.

"When you're growing up, your world seems so small, and it kind of is. When stuff happens, especially bad stuff, it seems like a massive deal and the feelings that come with that can be overwhelming," Alex said. "So sometimes, as your nan would say, you need to step back and look at the bigger picture."

"Perspective."

"Spot on. You won't be at school forever. Soon you'll be able to hang out with whoever you want."

"Seems like forever till then," Billy said, sighing.

Alex's phone rang, he switched it to silent. A moment later, his phone pulsed in his pocket; the caller leaving a voicemail.

"Until then, look at it this way," Alex said. "In those computer games you play, you can't control the other characters, can you?"

"No."

"But you get to control yourself, right? Your moves, actions and reactions to things."

"Of course. I'm the hero."

"So don't worry about other people's actions so much and focus on yours. Be the hero in your life, I guess."

"Be the hero in my life," Billy said, repeating the words to himself a number of times.

He joined Alex who had moved to sit on a nearby bench, looking out across the city.

"I can see where I live. In one of those things," he said, pointing to some high-rise towers in the distance. "I wish my mum and me lived somewhere round here, though."

"My mum and I," Alex said, finally. "You're the subject of the sentence. Do you want to try again?"

"You vexing me about my grammar?" Billy said, looking disbelieving. "You're not my teacher."

"Okay, I'll shut up. But I'll tell you something grammar is good for, other than for school work and jobs."

"What?" Billy said, with a flat tone.

"Girls."

"Girls like grammar?" Billy asked, looking confused.

"Not grammar per se, but girls like boys who can express themselves, and good grammar helps."

"What does 'per se' mean?"

"'In or of itself' – it's Latin."

"What? As in the Romans?"

"It's useful."

"For sounding like a dickhead?"

"There was a rhyme at school: 'Latin is a dead language, dead as dead can be, Latin killed the Romans, and now it's killing me'."

Billy giggled to himself again.

"Can we go now?" he said finally, when he'd calmed down.

Alex nodded and they began descending the hill on the tarmac path, side by side this time. Billy began tapping into his phone again. He stopped walking.

"My battery died," he said, staring accusingly at his phone before putting it slowly into his pocket.

At the bottom of the hill, they turned to look back up at the top together before heading towards Camden station.

"Apart from the walk, that was all right," Billy said.

"I'll see you next week," Alex said. "And I'll try to get married in the meantime, or at least get a girlfriend."

"You'll be lucky with that on your face," Billy said.

Alex was about to reply but the boy had already jumped the ticket barrier. To the sounds of beeping, he disappeared though the lift's sliding doors. Alex brought his hand to his face and touched his beard, surprised at Billy's comment.

He took out his phone, pressing message recall. In a formal tone, his father thanked him for the cheese and brandy he'd left. He said he'd been delighted by the gift. Alex breathed in, it was the first voicemail message his father had ever left him.

Chapter Ten

With Julia

"So, how long have you got?" Julia asked.

She stood in front of Alex's bedroom mirror getting dressed for work. It was 6 a.m. and her shift at the cafe started in an hour. He was leaving with her; he would open the office as he had Raman's keys on him, and work on some training guides for the charity's volunteers. Alex lay on the bed dressed, but without his shoes on.

"A little while," Alex said.

"Where are you going to go?" Julia said.

"Richard has a sofa. I'm sure I could stay there for a bit."

"What about your father's?"

"I wouldn't know how to ask him," Alex said, almost to himself rather than in response to Julia. "Julia, I just remembered, I'm meant to be meeting Richard tonight and we're going to see Annie Hall at Screen on the Green." Alex took his phone out from his pocket. "I'll cancel Richard."

"Don't cancel Richard. I don't want him to think I've stolen you away. And you've been neglecting him," Julia said. She was now sitting on the bed in front of the mirror, brushing her hair, her back to Alex. "I'll meet Dan later, I've been neglecting him. He's really keen to catch up."

"Is he?" Alex said. "Okay. But I'll miss you tonight."

"Well, miss me down the pub with Richard. You'll see me tomorrow."

"Feels like a long time to wait."

"But that's a nice feeling, right?"

Julia put her hairbrush into her bag. She turned to Alex behind her.

"Let's go."

At the front door, Alex held Julia's coat for her to put her arms into.

"I'd like to be able to watch you get ready every morning," he said to Julia, as he closed the front door behind him.

"Are you asking if you can move in?" Julia laughed. "You know my flatmate is moving out next month to live with her boyfriend?"

"I didn't," Alex replied.

* * *

"You seem brighter than when I last saw you," Alex's father said to him.

They were sitting in his father's kitchen. The sky over the Heath was overcast, and it seemed to creep into the room, bathing it in half darkness.

"I got a job," Alex said.

"That was quick. Well done," his father said,

sitting forward, eyes widened. "Magic circle?"

"Not exactly."

"Top fifty? There are some great medium sized firms doing very interesting work."

"Actually, it's a slight change in direction."

"Change in direction?"

"I'm working at the Citizens Advice Bureau in Camden."

"Are they paying you?"

"Of course," Alex said. "The work is actually quite challenging." Looking at his father's facial expression, which had changed from interest to concern, he added, "It's a six month contract, so I'm not tied in for life."

"What about that expensive flat of yours?"

"I'm moving out."

Alex's father breathed in deeply and sat back in his chair.

"Well, at least you're not spending your money down the pub, or worse."

"Julia said the same thing. She said to save it while I work out what I want to do next, longer term."

"Julia?" his father said.

Alex reached up and pulled the cord for the light, which hung above the kitchen table.

"That's kind of my other news," Alex replied.

"Well, Julia sounds like a sensible woman."

"She's an actress."

"Really?" his father said, standing.

"I'll make the tea, Dad."

Alex stood up as his father sat back down. After

putting on the kettle, he pulled some tea bags from the old metal tin beside the stove.

He was about to ask his father about his retirement but he seemed to anticipate his question – even though he was looking out of the window and not at Alex.

"Quiet," his father said. "It's been very quiet."

Alex followed his father's gaze out of the window and into the gloomy Heath.

***

"Hello, stranger," Richard said, when Alex walked into the Crown in his suit. "How was your first week?"

"More stressful than you'd think."

"How so?"

"If I gave incorrect advice to a client before then, worst case scenario they lose a deal – now they lose their house."

"But you're enjoying it?"

"I think so," Alex replied. "This one woman, Mrs Jacobs, comes in every day. Husband's just died, no children nearby or support network; only her dog for company – she didn't even know how to pay a bill when she came in during my interview shift. I wanted to give her a hug."

"Did you?"

"No. But when I told Raman afterwards, he said that if it felt appropriate to the circumstances then it was fine to do so."

"Raman?"

"The manager. He wanted to be a barrister but had to give up his studies to support his sick parents."

"Well, I guess at least Mrs Jacobs has her dog," Richard said.

"She's struggling to look after herself at the moment, let alone the dog."

Richard pushed Alex's pint of beer towards him.

"Alex Wright has found his social conscience again," he said, holding his pint up to make a toast. "Cheers to that."

Chapter Eleven

Without Julia

"How was Hilda and Charlie's wedding yesterday?" Richard asked.

"I don't remember," Alex replied, from the sofa at Richard's.

"What?" Richard said, sitting back in the armchair opposite him. "What *do* you remember?"

"I remember them getting married. The church bit, the vows, etc. Someone sang 'Ave Maria' while the organist played along quite badly."

"After that?" Richard asked.

"The champagne reception on the lawn of this big house. I thought I'd got into a fight at one point but I'd tripped on the guy ropes of the marquee."

"Then?"

"At the wedding breakfast I didn't know anyone on my table," Alex said. "So there was no alternative but to drink through it."

"I'm almost too scared to ask," Richard said. He was now sitting forward in the chair. "But what happened next?"

"That's it." Alex sighed.

"What do you mean, that's it?"

"That's all I remember until I woke up in my hotel room the next morning. On top of the bed covers, still in my suit – I even had my shoes on."

"Why did you get so drunk?"

"Well, I drank on the train there to get over my hangover from the night before. Then, almost by accident, I kept going."

"Kept going?"

"I drank before the ceremony and after it. In fact, the only time I didn't drink was in the church, and that was because I'd left my hip flask in the hotel room."

Alex was lying flat on the sofa in jeans and a T-shirt, barefoot, only half his face visible.

"Didn't you ask anyone this morning what you got up to?"

"I checked out as soon as I woke up, walked two miles to the local station and got the first train back to London," Alex said. "I had to leave before breakfast. I couldn't let anyone from the wedding see me like this, Richard."

"Like what?"

Alex lifted his head from the sofa to reveal the other half of his face. The whole of his cheek was red and covered in dried blood, up until just under his eye.

"Nasty," Richard said, with a concerned expression. He got up and perched on the sofa next to Alex, looking closely at Alex's face.

"I think I've still got some of the gravel path in my face."

"Does it hurt?"

"Not really."

"You know why that is?" Richard said. "You're still drunk."

Richard took out his phone and typed into it. A few seconds later it beeped and he rose. "Let's go."

"Where?" Alex asked. He was now curled up on the sofa. He'd made a half hearted attempt to pull the duvet, over himself.

"The Crown."

"The one time I can't face a drink and you want to go to the pub," Alex said, but he was rising from the sofa. "I guess a Guinness might settle the stomach."

"Where are you going?" Richard said, looking confused. Alex was heading towards the bathroom, not the front door.

"To the..." Alex said. He stumbled quickly into the bathroom, knelt down beside the toilet bowl and threw up repeatedly into it, his throat becoming sorer each time.

"Look at the state of you." Richard was standing at the bathroom door.

***

Alex lay on a bar top of the Crown. His head rested on top of a handful of beer towels. Out of the corner of his eye, he could see a petite lady in a cleaning smock shuffling around the room quickly and methodically. Richard and Ciara were speaking above him.

"'Oh, that men should put an enemy in their

160

mouths to steal away their brains,'" Alex said.

"Your brain definitely got stolen last night," Richard said.

"Alex, are you okay?" Ciara said.

"Just ignore him," Richard said, before Alex could answer. "He's still drunk."

Ciara put some clear liquid on a cotton wool pad and dabbed at Alex's face. He winced as it stung and tried to move away from it.

"Do you want me to hold him down?" Richard said, pretending to do so. "Frankenstein's monster, he's alive!"

Alex didn't have the energy to respond.

"This might hurt a little bit." With a pair of tweezers, Ciara began to pick out gravel fragments from his face. She said something to Richard about her sister visiting from New Zealand. The metal of the tweezers in his cheek; Alex felt light-headed from the pain and smell of antiseptic in his nostrils.

**

Daylight stung Alex's eyes; the lounge curtains wide open above him. From its stillness, he sensed the flat was empty. His last memory was leaving the pub and Richard helping Ciara set up for the day. He'd taken the painkillers Ciara had given him with a slug from a half empty bottle of red wine he'd found by the sink in the flat's kitchen.

Alex looked down at Richard's closed laptop. The pink Post-It note stuck to the top read: *Open me,* in Richard's neat handwriting. Alex lifted the lid to reveal another.

Yes, it's Monday – you slept through Sunday! Find a job, loser! it read. Richard had drawn a smiley face below his writing. Alex flicked the Post-It onto the floor.

***

When backing a horse there was sometimes a communal feeling in the betting shop, even though others in the room would invariably be wanting different horses to win the race. But, although next to each other, strangely, playing the roulette machines was a solitary experience. Also, with horse racing there was a certain mysticism, a feeling anything could happen, with the machines only a cold, hard efficiency.

Alex was the first and only customer, or 'punter' – as Anne-Marie called them – of the day. Standing in front of the roulette machine, feeding bank notes into it – fifteen 'twenties' and five 'tens'. For weeks he'd withdrawn his daily limit without checking his balance. Today he'd found he had insufficient funds, £350 was the maximum he could take out.

He'd fallen asleep reading about the Monte Carlo staking system, essentially just doubling up he realised. He staked £50 on Black, his first bet, and lost. He doubled up and lost a further £100. Clicking the stake button until all £200 worth of electronic chips were stacked up on the black square icon, reduced his 'bank' balance to zero – matching his actual bank balance, he thought. He pressed Spin.

On the screen, they were spinning, the roulette wheel in one direction, the ball in the other. He felt the urge to turn away but couldn't. The ball slowed, jumping and tumbling on the screen in and out of the coloured pockets: black, red, black, red, black.

The ball slowed further and fell into a black pocket, but still vibrating within it. The screen seemed frozen. The ball then popped out of the black pocket. Alex blinked as it hung in the pixelated air. It was sucked into the pocket next to it, a red pocket.

Alex instantly turned away, looking out across the betting shop, as if someone could, or would, help him. The sound of a cash register. He glanced back at the screen, it was flashing 'Enter Cash to Play'.

"I more than fancy her to go the distance," Bob, one of the regular punters, was saying to anyone who would listen, about a horse and an upcoming race – as if canvassing support in an electoral campaign. Alex wasn't really listening. He just wanted to get away as fast as he could from the machine in front of him, that place, that street.

Outside, his legs and arms felt heavy and he sat down on a wooden bench along the street, in the direction of Regent's Park. He looked up, above Camden, murky grey clouds covered the entire sky – he couldn't see one glimmer of sunshine or a single patch of blue.

***

A key in the door lock above him, Richard was descending the stairs. Alex lay perfectly still on the sofa, the lights off and the curtains drawn. The TV was off and the only noise, an easy listening track from Swanky's Barbers upstairs playing pop music.

"Have you moved from that sofa today?" Richard asked, as he lowered himself slowly down into the armchair opposite Alex.

Since waking, Alex hadn't left the flat and barely moved from his spot on the sofa all day. He'd been daydreaming that if he stayed completely still, motionless, for long enough, then he would disappear.

"Alex?"

"I went out," Alex said, in a barely audible tone.

"Where did you go?" Richard asked, in the tone of someone talking to a child.

"I didn't get as far as I wanted."

"You can stay here as long as you want, Alex, but, you know, not forever," Richard said. He went to the window and opened the curtains fully. Alex closed his eyes, the light still burnt his eyes but he tried not to move.

"Not forever." Alex repeated Richard's words.

"One day, I might want to bring someone back."

"What, like a woman?"

"Yes. Like a woman. Like a girlfriend."

"Oh really?" Alex said, looking out of the small lounge window onto the pavement of Camden Road. Watching the procession of different shoes – different lives, he thought – as people rushed to and from the station.

"You're hardly a pulling machine these days," Richard said.

Swanky's laugh was audible from upstairs, the radio station was between songs.

"Sorry," Alex said, he spoke louder this time. "For being mean. I…"

"Stop apologising, it worries me," Richard said. "Drink?"

"I don't have any money."

"What do you mean?"

"It's all gone."

"What about all your redundancy money?" Richard said, looking at Alex with an incredulous expression. Alex stared down at the floor for a long time before looking up at him.

"I just mean until tomorrow. I… withdrew my daily limit."

"I thought you didn't get far today." When Alex didn't answer, Richard continued. "I'll buy the drinks for a change."

"Unless you-know-who is working."

Alex took out some clean jeans and trainers from one of the boxes and changed into them in the lounge.

***

"Have you thought about buying a flat?" Richard asked, as he and Alex walked along the street.

"Have you thought about buying a ticket to space on Virgin Galactic?" Alex replied.

"You must have some savings?" Richard said.

"With your redundancy money, a pretty decent sum, I bet."

"I spent what I earned, mostly."

"What about investments?"

"Investments," Alex said, stopping in the street. Richard carried on and then turned. "I do have one investment." Alex continued.

"Stocks and shares?" Richard asked, when Alex'd caught up with him.

"No."

"You've never told me about this."

"To be honest, I'd completely forgotten about it."

"What is it?"

Alex and Richard entered a busy Crown, their usual spot at the bar was taken and they drifted to an empty table along one of the walls.

"I met this guy in a pub."

"Stories that begin that way never end well."

"It was a client lunch that turned into a client dinner, and, in the end, a client breakfast."

"So after the client lunch, but in between the dinner and the breakfast the next day, we're in a pub in Marylebone and I get talking to this random guy," Alex said. "And he tells me about this opportunity."

"That was too good to be true?"

"Yes."

"Did he also say you had to act fast?"

"He did," Alex said. "Look, Richard, I know how it must sound now."

Richard sighed, he looked over at the bar, there was no sign of Ciara. He looked back at Alex.

"So what was it you bought off this guy? A car you have in a lock up somewhere? A Fabergé egg?"

"A house."

"A house?!"

"A majestic villa mansion with rustic charm, was how he described it. Looked really nice from the photos."

"Where is this villa mansion with rustic charm of which you speak?"

"Bulgaria, somewhere near Sofia, apparently."

"Apparently?"

"I haven't actually been there."

"How much did you pay for this house, sorry, villa mansion, in Bulgaria, somewhere near Sofia, apparently?"

"Ten grand. All my savings."

"You bought a house in Bulgaria for £10,000 off a guy in a pub?" Richard asked. "And it slipped your mind?"

"It was a couple of years ago now," Alex said.

Ciara appeared and placed two pints in front of them. Richard rolled his eyes while indicating to Alex beside him, she smiled before leaving to serve a customer. Richard, unusually, took a long drink of his pint.

"Did you get a receipt?" Richard asked. "Is there at least some form of legal contract of ownership?"

"I suppose it wasn't the usual conveyancing process."

"No shit, Sherlock," Richard said, placing his head in his hands. "I take it you didn't see a floor plan?"

"He showed me some photos on this ancient mobile phone, they were a bit grainy."

"You can't trust an estate agent's photos at the best of times. Go on."

"It was all done in ten minutes. He gave me his bank details, I transferred him the money there and then. I gave him my business card and some paperwork arrived in the post a few weeks later."

"In Bulgarian?"

"I couldn't understand a word of it but the cleaner from the office at the time was Bulgarian and she looked it over, said it seemed okay."

Richard put his head in his hands.

"So the guy, – the seller – he was Bulgarian, at least?"

"Latvian, I think. But that's close to Bulgaria, I'm pretty sure. He told me Bulgaria was going to be the next French Riviera."

"When did he foresee that happening?"

"He said it might take a couple of years."

"Couple of decades, maybe."

"He also said it was going to join the Euro."

"Has it?"

"Last time I checked it still had its own currency."

Alex and Richard both took drinks from their pints.

"I remember his exact words when we shook hands on the deal: 'the price is so low it can only go up,'" Alex said.

"At least you've made some money on it?"

"Actually, it was a while ago, but I read Bulgaria

is one of the only property markets in Europe to have gone down in the last few years," Alex said, "it's worth less than I paid for it."

"That's impressive, considering what it cost, I guess," Richard said. "Who on earth would buy it anyway?"

"Some idiot in a pub is probably my only hope," Alex said.

A mouthful of beer came out of Richard's mouth as he laughed to himself.

"Just as well you don't need the money," he managed to say after a few seconds.

Alex's mouth felt dry, he took a sip of his beer but choked, his throat tightening.

"For someone moderately clever, you're bloody stupid sometimes," Richard said.

Alex was about to reply but sighed instead.

"Why aren't you answering back?" Richard asked when Alex didn't respond after a minute or so.

"Because you're right about everything. I'm stupid, a stupid idiot," Alex said. Richard looked at him with an expression of concern mixed with confusion.

"Alex, you don't seem yourself. You've obviously had some kind of career burnout, and that's nothing to be ashamed of," he said, breathing out. "Maybe you should talk to someone about your feelings."

"I don't really feel anything." Alex said, looking down at the table.

"The main thing is, you're having a nice relaxing break now." Richard smiled. "And the best bit." Alex looked up from the table.

"You have all that money sitting in your bank account for a rainy day."

Chapter Eleven

With Julia

A horizontal strip of light blue appeared on the skyline when Alex and Julia stepped onto Queen's Road from Brighton station. Straight ahead in front and all the way down the hill, past the shops and bars that lined the sides of the road, was the sea.

"To the sea," Julia cried.

The morning sun hit Alex's face as he caught a glimpse of their reflections in a shop window, he smiled. Julia in an emerald green dress, her big sunglasses, a tan leather belt and matching small tan satchel on her shoulder. A long gold necklace hung from her neck with a fox-shaped pendant at its end. He was beside her in faded black jeans, white T-shirt, biker jacket and red Ray-Ban Wayfarers.

They walked purposefully down the hill into the cool breeze coming up from the seafront. Passing the clocktower and down through the underpass to sea level, Julia ran the short distance onto the pebble beach – Alex following.

She slipped on the loose stones, Alex reached her just in time. He steadied her in his arms, holding her close – the sweet smell of the Prosecco they'd drunk on the train on her breath.

"I love the seaside," Julia said. "It makes me feel so peaceful and yet so wild at the same time." She wriggled from his grasp and ran free across the beach towards the frothing sea.

***

They climbed the stairs up to the Palace Pier and stepped onto its wooden-beamed floor. After walking past the food stalls, they entered the central arcade halls, the smell of candyfloss in the air. From the cacophony of noises and relentless bright flashing lights, they emerged at the pier's end – in front of them: a rollercoaster that went over water, a ghost train, dodgems. Julia dragged Alex onto the nearest ride, made up of giant spinning tea cups on a giant rotating tea tray.

Walking back towards the promenade along the side of the pier, they stopped in front of a sign, '£10 for ten minutes' it read – they looked up. Painted colourfully across the side of the traditional Romany caravan was a woman, her hands open around a crystal ball full of whirling smoke, above it, 'Fortune Teller'.

"You want to do it?" Alex asked Julia, beside him.

"Not really," Julia replied. "It's silly."

"Don't you wonder what would have happened if I hadn't got on that bus with you?" Alex said, turning to her.

"We'd probably have never met again, be with

172

different people. Our lives would be different, doesn't mean we'd be unhappy."

"You really think that?"

"I know what my friend, Dan, would say."

"What would Dan, the great thinker, say?"

"That the human belief in the mystical is just an extension of our psychology, nothing more."

"Maybe he's right but I can't help thinking there was something fated about the way we met."

"Whether how we met was fate or not, doesn't make it any more or less special. What matters is that we're happy."

"I suppose you're right."

"'It is not in the stars to hold our destiny, but in ourselves' – isn't that the line from Shakespeare?"

"*Julius Caesar.*"

Alex took the few steps to the side of the pier, leant over the railing and looked out to sea. A windsurfer beyond the pier was twisting and turning in the water, struggling to find the wind, its direction constantly changing.

Julia's arms slipped under his from behind and around his chest. She nestled her head by his neck.

"You promised me fish and chips," he heard her say. He turned within her arms, pulled her towards him and embraced her.

"Okay. Let's go, darling. I think the place we used to go is this way," Alex said after a few moments. They started down the pier again towards the promenade, hand in hand.

"You used to come here on holiday with your

dad?" Julia asked.

"Each summer, just for the weekend. We didn't go abroad when I was growing up," Alex replied. "I can't really imagine my dad lying on a beach, although there are photos of him and my mother on a beach somewhere from before I was born."

The sun was beginning to set over the Brighton rooftops.

"You called me darling just now," Julia said. "I can't remember when you started doing it, but I like it."

***

"I hope you're going to share that," said Katie, one of the volunteers, standing over him.

Opening the round metal Quality Street tin to reveal a white-iced carrot cake, Alex smiled. At the firm, he'd forgotten the names of the clients who'd sent him Fortnum & Mason hampers, particularly at Christmas, but he wouldn't forget this gift.

"You must be busy. I should be getting on," Mrs Jacobs said. She was sitting in front of him.

"You can't stay and have a cup of tea? We'll all have some cake," Alex said, glancing at Katie, with a smile.

"I'm going to see the stone mason. I want to make sure everything is right and proper for Stanley," she replied.

When Mrs Jacobs had left, Alex signalled to Raman with a drinking motion. Raman waved his hand away. Alex passed Diana, the office manager, a packet of her cigarettes, Pall Mall Blue, in her hand.

"Can I?" he asked.

"You don't smoke, do you?"

Diana led the way to the fire exit at the back, alarm deactivated long ago, apparently, handle worn where it'd been opened many times. She sat on the low wall opposite. Alex imagined her in the same spot, counselling past, present and future student volunteers through break-ups and exam pressure with her calm manner, sound advice and her tactile pats. "Better out than in," he'd witnessed her saying to more than one.

Alex leaned forward and she lit his cigarette, carefully and with the attention he'd seen her make the tea, followed by hers, with the same flame – her delicate manner slightly at odds with her size.

"You remember what to do next?" Diana said, smiling and taking a puff of her cigarette.

As Alex leaned back against the wall, he had a sick feeling inside. He looked down the alleyway.

"Might never happen. Unless it has, in which case you can't do anything about it," Diana said. Alex turned back to her.

"I wish it were that simple, Di."

"Things are as simple as we make them, dear."

Alex blew the smoke upwards out of his mouth.

"Do you miss it?" Di asked, her eyes widened.

"Smoking? Not really."

"No, silly, being a lawyer. Don't you miss doing the big deals and all that."

Alex looked down at the brown liquid in the

cracked mug he held. "The coffee was better."

Diana laughed heavily, ending in a cough.

"We'd better go in," Alex said.

"I spoke to Mrs Jacobs on her way out," Di said. "She's going into a nursing home next weekend, early signs of dementia. She has to give up her dog. She's so upset."

"She didn't mention that to me, and I saw her for half an hour. Her memory really must be going."

"I just wish we knew someone who could help," Di said, sighing. "She lost her husband and now she's going to lose her dog."

**

Alex closed the door of his father's flat. He didn't shout his usual greeting. There was something in the quiet stillness the flat contained that he didn't want to break.

Pulling off his shoes – damp from his walk over the Heath – he put his hand on the window ledge to steady himself. He felt a layer of dust. When he took his hand off, he looked at his dusty fingers before brushing his hand on the side of his trousers. He picked up the supermarket carrier bag beside him and walked down the corridor.

Alex sat across from his father at the kitchen table. The windows shook every few seconds, a strong wind blowing around outside.

"You're quiet," Alex and his father said at the same time, after a long pause. They both laughed. The laughs didn't last long, but they were real.

"How's that lovely girlfriend of yours you're hiding away?" his father asked.

"Still lovely," Alex replied. "She's working today."

Alex and his father sat silently. The wind continued to shake the windows.

"I should go," Alex said eventually. His father opened his mouth slightly then closed it, remaining silent.

At the kitchen door, Alex turned back to his father.

"Dad, is the cleaner on holiday?" he asked.

"She was having trouble on the stairs, she said she could find someone else," his father replied. "Now I have the time. Seems silly to have someone in."

"Okay." Alex said, stopping to look at his father.

"You forgot your bag," his father said, holding up the carrier bag Alex had brought.

"I picked up some things for you in case you hadn't been out."

"You didn't have to."

"Dad," Alex said, "can I borrow your kitchen tomorrow?"

"As long as I'm not going to regret not having a cleaner anymore."

As he walked to the station, Alex tried to think what had been different in the kitchen – something was missing. The spot on the radiator where his father's swimming trunks were always hanging out to dry, had been bare.

**

"I'm a bit nervous about meeting your friends, especially as you've known them so long," Alex said.

Alex and Julia entered Hampstead Heath from up the hill, after meeting at Hampstead Heath tube station minutes earlier. Alex was carrying some carrier bags of bottles and a Tupperware box under his arm, Julia, a covered salad bowl and a large French breadstick.

"That's sweet, but you don't need to be," Julia replied. "I'm more worried about you meeting them. They're a little eccentric."

Alex spotted a couple sitting on a large tartan picnic blanket with a wicker hamper beside them. The woman stood and waved vigorously in their direction.

"There they are," Julia said, and waved back.

Julia introduced them to Alex when they arrived.

"Hi," Alex said, kissing Zara on each cheek and shaking Max's hand firmly.

Zara was petite with long, straight blonde hair, and Max was tall, stocky with shiny black combed back hair. They were both wearing pale cream chino trousers, Max in a pale blue shirt and Zara a white one, a pair of Ray-Bans hanging from each of their shirts.

Alex put the shopping bags and the box down beside him.

"What did you bring, Alex?" Julia asked.

"Prosecco for you, ciders for me. Pimms for everyone."

"Great, but I mean in the Tupperware."

Alex peeled open the box and revealed perfectly shaped yellow shells.

"Behold, the boyfriend can bake!" Zara said, "Madeleines!"

"They look great," Max said.

Zara winked at Alex.

"Did you buy them?" Julia asked.

"I made them."

"Don't you need a special dish for the shape?"

"There's one at my dad's."

***

"This drink needs fucking ice. If someone brings me ice, I swear I will suck them off," Zara said, holding up her drink in the air.

At that moment, a middle-aged couple walked by with two young kids in tow, and the man smiled. The woman glanced in their direction with an expression of contempt. Zara descended into fits of laughter.

"Zara! You can't say things like that," Julia said.

"I bloody well can," Zara said. "I'll say it again, and louder this time." She stood up.

"Sit down." Julia pulled Zara down beside her and between her and Alex. "I need you here next to me, you lunatic."

"Alex Wright," Zara said. "So are you Mr Right for our beloved Julia?" Looking Alex up and down before looking at her drink again, she frowned.

"I need fags," Max said, standing up. "I'll get ice,

too. I haven't had a blow job since my birthday."

"I'll go with him," Alex said, standing.

"Your boyfriend is an absolute hero for offering to go with my brute of a fiancé."

"Boyfriend? He's still on trial," Julia said.

"Okay, your lover then, sounds so much more fun," Zara said, laughing hysterically.

"No Dan? I thought you said he was coming," Alex said as he got to his feet.

"He had to cover for another doctor at the hospital at the last minute. He was really upset to miss today," Julia said.

"Oh. That's a shame," Alex said.

"You almost sounded like you meant that," Max said.

"Poor Dan. All the nurses love him but he loves someone else," Zara said. "He's like Willy Boldwood in Tess."

"What do you mean?" Alex asked.

"She's just talking rubbish," Max said. "Let's go." Taking Alex's arm gently. The couple with children passed them again.

"Don't forget! No ice, no..." Zara shouted after them, Julia muffling her mouth with her hands.

Max strode ahead. Alex had to run a few steps to catch up. When they turned the corner out of sight of the girls, they could still hear Zara laughing loudly.

"Do you know the way?"

"I think so," Max said, taking a misstep and stumbling against Alex, appearing drunk. "So you're in love with Julia?"

"I guess I am," Alex answered, unthinkingly.

"Well, you're lucky," Max said. "She seems to be in love with you."

"How can you tell?"

"Let's just say I've met a few potential Mr Rights."

Alex smiled to himself.

"What's the story with Dan?" Alex said.

"He's never got over their one night – it's like a Chekhov play."

"What night?" Alex asked. His heart beat racing, he felt his face redden. "When was this?"

"End of school summer ball. Everyone crashed on the floor of the barn after, that's where it happened, apparently. Julia says she can't really remember it. They weren't even undressed, and by all accounts it was over very quickly.

"After a whole summer of trying to seduce her, Dan thought it was the beginning of something."

"And was it?"

"Not for Julia."

Alex was silent.

"How old are you, Max?"

"Thirty-five. You wouldn't believe it, would you?" Max, with his boyish face and jet-black hair, glanced down at the curve of his stomach and patted it. "Apart from this, I find exercise such a bore."

"How did you know Zara was the one for you?" Alex said.

"We've been knocking about together, and with each other since Oxford," Max said. "I'm not sure anyone else would put up with either of us – well, with me, anyway."

In the mini supermarket on the corner of the high street, Alex picked up one of the last remaining bottles of Pimms from the shelf.

"Damn it." Alex turned, Max was rummaging around the shop's fridge unit. "We're not going back empty handed." Max added.

***

Max was taking them back a different route. When they got to the Horseshoe pub on the edge of the Heath, Max stopped before marching in, Alex following just behind.

"Hot out there," the barman said with an Australian accent.

"Roasting," Max replied, putting his hand on the bar. "We're in a bit of a pickle, my friend. You see, my lady friend simply can't drink her Pimms without ice."

"You tried the shops?"

"Sold out. Ice is a precious commodity today, it seems."

The barman shrugged his shoulders.

"Sorry mate, I'd love to help but we can't give out ice to everyone on a hot day, we wouldn't have any left for our customers."

"But we're customers."

"You haven't ordered anything."

"Two glasses of whisky and a bucket of ice, please."

"I'm afraid I can only give you the appropriate

amount of ice to go with the drinks you order."

Max's face was red and he was breathing heavily, his hand gripping tightly on the bar.

"Max," Alex said. Max relaxed his grip on the bar and smiled.

"If we order champagne, we get a bucket of ice, surely?"

"Yes, of course."

"Then we'll have a bottle of champagne, my good man." Max smiled.

"We've sold out," the barman said. "I mean, we've got a couple of bottles left, but only the ridiculously expensive vintage stuff."

"That's good," Max replied – the barman looking at him confused. "Because I only drink the ridiculously expensive vintage stuff." His hand now full of bank notes, as if by magic. "We'll take both bottles."

"You want a line?" Max said quietly to Alex, while the barman was filling a bag with ice, pulling a tiny silver capsule from his top pocket. "Saves going to the bloody toilet every time. My junior trader bought a job lot from Hong Kong. Brokers love them. Russian birds, too – keep them in their bras, apparently." He unscrewed the capsule and leaned behind a pillar, putting the little spoon attached to the lid to his nose.

***

"You know, I did three million-pound deals this week, but you know what was more satisfying?" Max said. "The ice deal!" he shouted, holding the bag of ice aloft like a trophy as they stepped onto the Heath.

"You could probably have bought a small iceberg for the money you just spent," Alex said.

"I've been on the trading floor ten years. End of my first week on the trading floor, I was sick of running to McDonalds and Starbucks for the traders and they were sick of me begging to make a trade."

"A trade?"

"On Friday minutes before the market closed, the head trader, the big dog of the floor, gathered the whole floor round his desk.

"While they all shouted and screamed at me, he made me get out my knob and press it onto the keyboard to do a trade. I bought a hundred thousand pounds worth of oil futures."

"Was that fun?"

"I work with a bunch of scumbags. Sometimes I leave the building feeling dirty, the way we leech off the system and the obscene banter," Max said. "But that's also why I fucking love it."

"For the money?"

"You don't get it. It's not about the money, Alex. After a certain point, I'd do it for free," Max said.

He stopped – Alex with him – and opened a bottle of the vintage champagne, deftly and decisively, offering it to Alex before taking a swig.

"What's it about then?" Alex said, as they began towards the Heath again.

"It's about the deal, it's about winning, it's about the game.

"It's about screwing over the market, your brokers,

the other banks. It's about doing a deal and walking round the trading floor saying, 'You bunch of pussies, I just made ten million in five seconds. How do you feel about that?'"

"Wow," Alex said. "I'll have a drink now." Max handed Alex the bottle.

Julia and Zara were in high spirits. The lack of ice didn't appear to have stopped them drinking.

"Are we interrupting you girls talking about how big our cocks are?" Max asked.

"How did you know?" Julia replied.

"We were actually talking about success and what it means."

"It looks like this." Max pulled out the ice with his left hand and raised his closed hand to his face, making the motion of a blow job, his tongue pushing against his cheek. "And this!" He pulled the other bottle of champagne from the other bag.

"Hurrah! Champagne!" Zara said, grabbing the bottle from Max. Straddling it, she peeled off the metal covering over the cork.

"She loves having something hard between her legs," Max said.

"Makes a change," Zara said, instantly, giggling.

Alex looked down at her, she was opening the bottle without looking at it. Her thumb slipped at the last moment. The cork shot out of the bottle, missing her face by a fraction.

They all looked up, the cork so high into the air it was almost too small to be seen. Champagne was bubbling out of the bottle, Julia put her head between

Zara's legs and her mouth around the champagne bottle. Zara put her hands on Julia's head and started giggling again.

"What's success then?" Alex asked.

"When I was studying fashion, a girl on my course had a theory," Zara said, catching her breath. "She said success was drunken sex on a Wednesday afternoon'."

"Why?" Julia asked.

"Wednesday is an average weekday. And what could be more indulgent than sex, not in the evening or the morning but, in the afternoon? Combine that with daytime drinking, which always feels decadent, and that's it. Success."

"Interesting theory," Alex said.

"I definitely know what I want to be doing this Wednesday," Julia said.

"You're outrageous," Zara said, the bottle of champagne still between her legs.

"We must be eating in between all this drinking," Julia said. "We have all this lovely food."

***

"I need something sweet to finish me off," Zara said, chuckling.

"Let's have the Madeleines," Julia said. "I've never had champagne and Madeleines." She poured the last of the champagne into their glasses.

Alex offered the Tupperware to Julia and Zara. They took one each, silent for a few moments as they ate.

"I think that's the nicest thing I've had in my mouth for a long time," Zara said. Max was beside her but had fallen asleep, she stroked his hair.

"Are you sure you didn't buy these?" Julia said to Alex, leaning over to kiss him. They looked out together over the London horizon. The sun had peaked in the sky and was beginning its descent.

Chapter Twelve

Without Julia

"I don't like these places," Billy said.

"I don't think I like these places, either," Alex said, looking away from the screen on the wall and screwing up the betting slip in his hand. "Let's get out of here."

"Where are we going?" Billy asked, jumping down from the high, red betting shop stool he was swinging around on.

They walked down Highgate Village to the gates of Highgate Wood and onto its dried mud path.

"Not up another hill," Billy said.

"Down a hill this time," Alex said, as they came to a heavily wooded area. "Let's cut through here."

He picked up a series of sticks, examining and discarding them on the ground before gripping one decisively – Billy mimicking him. Billy led the way along the path, beating away the branches from trees that hung in the path of their faces. At any rustle or snapping branch, Billy would turn to it with his stick poised.

The path ahead was narrowing, the woodland and undergrowth thickening and the overhead canopy making it darker and darker. They reached a dead end.

"Is this the day you try to murder me?" Billy asked, wielding the stick he held above his head, like a sword.

There was a gap in the hedge in front of them.

"Let's try this," Alex said. He went through the gap in the hedge, Billy following.

"A graveyard," Billy announced, with a confused look on his face. They stood in a field of gravestones, of many shapes and sizes.

"This is Highgate Cemetery," Alex said. "Some of the most influential people of the last two centuries are buried here."

"You take me to the strangest places." Billy sighed. "None of the others go traipsing around London for their meet ups."

"Where do they go?"

"McDonald's."

"You can go to McDonald's anytime," Alex replied. "I'm meant to be inspiring you."

"Okay," Billy said slowly, his tone as though he were humouring a child. "By taking me to places where dead people are buried?" Alex smiled.

Billy followed Alex around the graves, Alex pointing out different ones. They stopped at a rectangular stone with a huge bust of a bearded head and shoulders, on top.

"That's Karl Marx, a very important man. He invented communism," Alex said.

"What's communism?"

"It's the opposite of capitalism."

"What's capitalism?"

Alex sat down on a small stone bench and Billy leaned against a nearby gravestone expectantly.

"Capitalism is what we have here and in most of the world. People can own things and make money. There's inequality in financial terms, some people have more and some less, but it drives innovation and everyone's standard of living goes up. That is the idea anyway."

"So what's communism?"

"Communism is where the state owns everything. Everyone shares things according to what they need, and everyone is equal, in theory."

"Communism sounds all right," Billy said.

"The word comes from the Latin *communis...*" Alex said. Billy rolled his eyes. "Which means 'common or shared', communal – like the corridors outside your flat or the lifts," Alex continued.

"The lift always smells of piss."

"That was kind of the problem with communism, at least so far anyway."

Alex bent down to look at the inscription on one of the tombs. "This one is good. Do you want me to read it?"

"I can read," Billy said, pushing out his chest.

Billy bent down beside the grave. He put his hand on the top of it with delicate deference.

"Gordon Bell, 1942 – 1995. 'Tomorrow do thy worst, for I have lived today,'" Billy announced in a clear tone, in contrast to his usual nervous mumble. He smiled to himself.

"Tomorrow do thy worst, for I have lived today," Billy repeated swinging his stick around for dramatic effect.

"The quote," Alex said, "how does it make you feel?"

"How does it make you feel?" Billy said, standing up and puffing out his chest again. "That's the question the social workers always used to ask when they sent me to another family."

"When was this?"

"When my old man got taken away to prison and my mum ended up in the nuthouse."

"I didn't know you'd been in care, Billy. I'm sorry."

"It's not called that anymore. We're called 'looked after children' as in looked after by someone else other than our parents, get it?"

Alex stood up, raising his hands and placing them on his head as he paced around the area they were in.

"I'm sorry," he said. "I don't really know what I'm meant to be doing in these meetings."

Billy shrugged and remained standing, rigid in the same spot.

"How's your homework going?" Alex asked. "I'm crap at maths, but I can help you with other stuff,"

"I don't want your help with my homework."

"What subjects are you struggling in?"

"What subjects are *you* struggling in?"

"What do you want from me, Billy?"

"Nothing," Billy answered. "Because you'll piss off just like everyone else does and forget I existed."

A breeze blew through the cemetery.

"Oscar Wilde said, 'I'm not young enough to know everything'."

"What does Oscar 'know it all' Wilde mean?"

"When you're young you think you know everything but then as you grow up, you realise it's not that simple," Alex replied. "What I am really trying to say is that I'm trying my best..."

"Is he buried here, Oscar?" Billy asked, after a long pause.

"Paris."

"Next week, yeah?" Billy said with a straight face before grinning widely. "Apparently, my mum and dad nearly went to Paris on their honeymoon," he added.

"Nearly went?"

"My uncle says my dad got so drunk on his stag do the night before the wedding, he lost the tickets."

"That's really unfortunate."

"My mum says to my nan sometimes, 'I'd rather have had the trip to Paris than him'."

Billy sat down, finally. The sun was now low in the sky. Alex hadn't noticed the afternoon pass so quickly.

"Is your mum here?"

"My mum?" Alex said.

"I guessed she was dead. You only talk about your dad."

"No. It's mainly just famous or very rich people. She was cremated. Her ashes were scattered down there." Alex gestured into the distance towards the Heath. "She walked over the Heath every morning with my dad and the dog."

"Do you remember her well?"

Alex looked out into the distant Heath as he replied.

"I don't at all… I remember her funeral but nothing before, I suppose I've blocked it out," Alex replied. "That day, I remember lots of people being in the flat, more than I had ever seen – there's even a photo of me with my arm around the dog. Then the flat was completely silent again the next day. The day after, there was this strange woman there."

"A childminder?"

"Yeah, a nanny."

"Was she nice?"

"That first day – it must have been bath time. This grim-faced woman standing over me and there was water running, I remember the sound was so loud it hurt my ears. She left the room and I didn't want her to come back in, so I reached up to the door handle and turned the key."

"What happened?" Billy's chin was in his palms, looking at Alex intently.

"The door handle rattled, then there was banging. I moved to the corner of the room, I tried to hide."

"The door flew open. She must have forced the lock, and she was screaming and shouting at me. 'You wicked child!' she kept saying over and over again."

"Then what?"

"After she'd stopped shouting, I called for my mother. I must have said 'Mummy' or something like that. With no emotion she said, in this cold voice,

'You don't have a mummy anymore'."

Billy looked ahead blankly as if he'd stopped listening, recalling a memory himself, before turning back to Alex.

"You ever tell your dad about it?"

"We don't speak about the past much."

"At least he's not in prison or a smack addict, or both like my mine," Billy said. "You know, you make him out to be some kind of bad guy but he doesn't sound like one to me. You've lost your fancy job and you think your life is shit, but you don't have it bad."

"It just feels like there's this big gap between how my life is now and what I'd like it to be," Alex said.

"Well, what are you going to do about it?" Billy said, raising his stick above his head again.

"You told me that if I focus on the positives, then I will get the best possible outcomes. That I can't control what others do to me, but I can control how I react. That the world can be cruel but if I make the little bit around me better it will spread, like ripples in water."

"Did I really say all that?" Alex said.

Billy lowered the stick down from above his head. The sun had gone down. They walked out of the wood in silence and almost darkness, in the direction of the glow of the lights from the high street.

"What happened to the dog?" Billy asked.

"A man came and took him away the day after the funeral. I never asked my father why?"

***

"So, the beard appears to be a permanent fixture," Alex's father said as Alex stood in the kitchen doorway.

A shadow had fallen on the lake and across to the kitchen floor. His father was seated close to the window, the light muted, his head turned towards Alex. His face had a week's stubble growth.

"You can talk, Dad."

His father smiled, raising his hand to his face. He looked strange to Alex, he'd never seen him not clean shaven – even at weekends he'd shaved.

"In this light, you can see some ginger in your beard," his father said. "I used to get that. It's white now." He was looking out at the dull London horizon over the Heath. "When I was on honeymoon with your mother, I didn't shave. She said she liked it, that it made me look like a sailor."

Alex made tea and sat down slowly opposite his father, putting a mug in front of him. His father nodded his thanks.

"I'll need to shave for all these meetings with recruiters next week," Alex said. Unusually, his father didn't appear to be paying full attention to what he was saying.

"Now I'm retired," his father said as if he hadn't heard Alex, "it doesn't matter anymore."

"Where did you go for your honeymoon, Dad? You never mentioned it before, I assumed you stayed in London."

"We flew into Lisbon. I borrowed a car from a

Portuguese friend I met at law school and we drove down the coast.

"I had to call your grandfather and ask him to wire us money as we ran out; we lived on peaches for two days while waiting for it, camping on the beach in Cascais, a beautiful fishing village.

"To travel like that was quite an adventurous thing to do then."

"You make it sound like it was the eighteenth century, Dad."

"Alex, there was no flying to New York for shopping trips then. Flights were so expensive, people didn't travel."

"Your trip sounded fun," Alex said.

"It was fun. She was fun. She made me fun, too," he said. "I'm sure you'll find that hard to believe."

Alex wondered if his mother would wait for his father at the kitchen table – where they now sat – in the evenings. Whether his father would come through the front door home from work and call her name, in the same way Alex did to his father now. The light dimmed further and shadows danced on the water of the lake as the branches moved in the breeze outside.

Alex saw his father smile and, from the look in his eyes, Alex could tell he was recalling a memory. Perhaps they'd sat here on a day the sky had looked exactly the same. Alex looked outside again and the cloud rolled over before his eyes and cast a huge shadow over the whole lake.

"I've got to go, Dad," Alex said, standing up and starting for the kitchen door.

"Where?" his father asked. At the front door of the flat he heard him say in a louder voice. "Alex, good luck with the recruiters."

"Thanks, Dad. I've got to go," Alex said, calling back from the front door. "I've got to get to the post office before it closes."

* * *

Alex stumbled up West End Lane from Kilburn past West Hampstead station. It was nearly 7 p.m. but people were still coming out of the station in office clothes. He passed a side street on his right, there was a bar on the left with a Brazilian flag in the first floor window.

He took a deep breath and steadied himself – he'd been refused a drink at the last pub. As he tried to walk in a straight line towards the bar, folk music flowed from the open upstairs window.

In the downstairs bar, it appeared an exercise class had taken place earlier in the evening, people were dressed in gym clothes. There were some brightly coloured leaflets with 'Zumba dance' on them scattered around the tables, indicating upstairs was some kind of function room.

He ordered a glass of red wine. The barman, dressed in a black shirt and trousers, poured the wine from an already open bottle into a French, goblet-style wine glass.

When Alex asked, he explained the music from upstairs was Saudade, traditional Portuguese folk music. About sailors leaving their betrothed for the seas and never returning. The sound of bittersweet longing for someone you'd loved but lost.

He climbed the stairs and emerged into a dimly lit room, with black walls and red lampshades. In the near corner, a long-haired man delicately strummed an acoustic guitar. Beside him, a handsome, dark-haired woman, singing in a deep, haunting voice. Alex took a seat on the ledge by the window. He shook with a chill from a passing breeze.

As the singer finished one song and began another, he imagined the anguished goodbyes of the sweethearts as a ship left a Portuguese shore never to return.

He closed his eyes. All he could see was Julia's face and all he could feel was her heartbeat against his chest.

Chapter Twelve

With Julia

Alex's eyes were closed. He could feel Julia's hair on his face, and smell the soft skin of her neck with the faintest hint of perfume from the day before. Their bodies were tangled up under the white duvet of her unfamiliar dark wood sleigh bed.

Julia untwined her arms and legs from his. He thought she was leaving the bed, but she was turning in his arms to face him. Her face appeared in front of him. They were so close their lips brushed and he felt her breathing. She opened her eyes.

"I want to drown in the oceans of your green eyes," Alex whispered.

"Can you do that after you've made me a coffee?" Julia replied.

***

"You know that thing you said to me at the Italian restaurant on our first date?" Julia said.

Alex was standing at the stove in the kitchen of Julia's flat.

"In your ear?" he replied, without turning.

"No, not that," Julia said. "When you said I wasn't real to you yet."

Alex glanced over his shoulder.

"Am I *real* to you now?"

Julia was standing in the doorway in only a white towel around her. Her hand on the door frame.

Alex turned down the heat on the stove and turned around fully to face her.

"Yes," he said, breathing out. Looking Julia up and down intently before turning back to the stove. "Very."

"You've made yourself at home, haven't you?" she said, sitting down at the kitchen table.

"I hope that's okay."

"I'm not complaining," Julia said. "I think it's kind of sexy watching you cook for me."

Alex began beating some eggs. Bacon was frying on the stove in front of him. A half unpacked shopping bag on the counter beside him, an opened carton and a poured glass of apple juice beside it.

He'd crept out of Julia's flat when she went to take a shower. The rest of the flat empty, her flatmate had left for a long weekend at the Glastonbury Festival.

In the mini supermarket round the corner, as he browsed the aisles picking things he hoped Julia would like, it was an exquisite feeling knowing he'd be returning to her, and he savoured it. By the till he'd put a Saturday *Guardian* on the top of his heavily laden basket.

"I wasn't sure what you liked," Alex said, looking over his shoulder again at Julia, and shrugging. "So I got everything."

"Well, I'm starving, so let's have a bit of everything."

"Juice? Coffee?" Alex said. Julia nodded enthusiastically and he put the coffee he'd just made for himself down in front of her and the glass of apple juice he'd poured. "Your phone was beeping while you were in the shower, by the way."

Julia left the room and returned with her phone, looking down at it and checking her messages.

"It's just Dan. He's worried about me working too hard," Julia said. "I promised to message him last night. I totally forgot."

"Must have been the great company," Alex said, Julia tapped away quickly on her phone before a final decisive tap. She threw the phone gently onto the small sofa in the hallway just outside the kitchen. It began to vibrate on the soft surface of the sofa. It went silent and then started to vibrate again before finally stopping.

"Dan likes to keep tabs on you, doesn't he?" Alex said.

"He worries. He's like a brother."

"More like a mum, it sounds like."

Julia sat down at the table. She put her feet up on the nearest chair and cradled the coffee mug in her hands.

"It's sweet you made breakfast," Julia said. "When I came back from my shower, until I saw the note, I thought you'd run off. I'm usually the one who does that."

"Is that right?"

Alex put the plates down.

"Wow, mushrooms," Julia said, eyes widened. "You really pushed the boat out."

"Is mushrooms pushing the boat out?"

"Mushrooms is officially pushing the boat out." Julia nodded in appreciation after her first mouthful. "You've set the bar very high on the breakfast front."

They ate and drank, without speaking. Behind Julia, in magnetic Scrabble letters across the fridge door, spelled in book title puns were – "Pies and Prejudice", "Olive Twist", Alex smiled to himself at "Tequila Mockingbird".

"Leave the plates," Julia said, when Alex went to clear them. He suggested they returned to bed to read the papers – Julia laughed. He protested it was literally what he'd meant. In bed, Julia took a pillow and moved to the opposite end. They were facing each other.

"Where are you going?" Alex asked. "You seem like a long way away."

"I'm going," Julia said, with a smile, "where I can keep an eye on you."

A slight formality had come between them. The spell of the intimacy from last night, which had spilled into breakfast, now broken. With the daylight coming in from the half-opened blind, even the scene of their night's passion seemed mundane to Alex – until he looked over at Julia again. She was sat up opposite him, duvet drawn up to her chest – *the Guardian* magazine, *Weekend*, in her hands.

"Have you heard of the Proust Questionnaire?"

Alex said.

"No," Julia said, looking up from the magazine.

"It's a list of questions about your personality, tastes, beliefs. Marcel Proust famously wrote, or answered, it. The weekly Q&A feature in *Weekend* is a bit like it, a different famous person each week."

Julia flicked through the magazine and held it up at the Q&A page.

"You must say the first answer that comes into your head as that'll be the most honest," she said. "Agreed?"

"Agreed," Alex replied. Julia looked down at the magazine in her hands.

"If you could go back in time, where would you go?" Julia asked.

"Paris in the twenties."

"Who would play you in a film of your life?"

"I've been told I look like the guy from Twilight."

"Robert Pattinson? You wish."

"What is your favourite word?"

Alex rubbed his chin. "Melancholy."

"Are you sure it's not 'pretentious'?" Julia said, rolling her eyes. "What did you think when you first saw me at the bus stop?"

"That's not on the list," Alex said, eyes wide. "You really want an answer?"

"Yeah," Julia said. "You're in my bed, remember?"

"Okay, give me a pen and a bit of paper," Alex said. Julia reached next to her bed to her handbag and then handed Alex a scrap of paper and a pen.

"I can't tell you. How about I write the answer on

this bit of paper and you open it later on your way to work, fair?"

"Fair," Julia replied, nodding her head.

Alex shielded the piece of paper as he wrote on it in the blue Biro she'd given him. He smiled at Julia across from him as he wrote. He folded the piece of paper and held it in the air between them.

"Can I trust you not to look until later?"

"Yes," Julia answered, taking the note from his hand and slipping it into her handbag. She picked up the magazine again.

"Who would you most like to say sorry to and why?"

Alex looked down at the duvet.

"I'm going to pass on that one," he said, after a short pause. "Let's swap. Your turn now, surely?"

"Okay, okay," Julia said, and tossed the magazine down onto the white duvet between them. Alex picked it up.

"What's your greatest fear?" Alex asked.

"I'm terrified of drowning."

"Ophelia, she drowned."

"She did," Julia replied, pulling a sad face.

"If you could edit your past, what would you change?"

"It would be tempting to edit out all the crap stuff but, then would I appreciate the good stuff?"

"What do you most dislike about your appearance?"

"My nose," Julia said, as she touched her nose, which had the slightest kink. "Damn. I've drawn your attention to it now."

"I love your nose, it's mainly what attracted me to you in the first place," Alex said, Julia laughed. He paused.

"What does love feel like?"

"Woah. Great question. You know what, I'm going to pass," Julia said. Alex opened his mouth but Julia continued. "You had a pass."

"Okay. Next one then," Alex said. "What's the worst thing that anyone has ever said to you?"

"This is so unfair. You had fun ones and I get all heavy ones," Julia said, will a little sigh.

"We agreed, you must say the first thing that comes into your head, remember?"

"I'm not ready for this," Julia replied.

"You're not ready for what?"

"No. That's the worst thing anyone's ever said to me."

"Oh." Alex took a breath. "Who was it?"

"My ex," Julia replied. "Ex-fiancé."

"What? You were engaged?" Alex said. "Sorry, I mean, what happened?"

Julia looked away and shifted in the bed, pulling her knees into her chest and the duvet over them.

"He left."

"That's terrible," Alex said.

"It wasn't so terrible," Julia replied. "If it hadn't happened, I wouldn't have quit my job and gone to drama school, something I've always wanted to do."

"You know, I knew he wasn't ready the day we moved in together."

"How?" Alex said, in a quiet tone.

"We were unpacking boxes of books. The flat was a Victorian conversion with these floor-to-ceiling bookshelves either side of the fireplace – which was great, as we both had lots of books. And he wouldn't mix our books together.

"He insisted on keeping them separate, his shelf, my shelf, etc. I remember being upset at the time, but I was so happy we were moving in together, I didn't make a big deal of it – I thought I was being silly.

"It was only after he'd left and I was packing the books again to move, and I thought, I should have known that first day it wasn't going to work out."

Alex put down the magazine on the bed beside him. There was a stillness to the silence that followed, a sense it would last as long as it needed to. After a few minutes, Julia reached over to his side to pick up the magazine.

"Your turn again," Julia said, smiling, but the faraway look that had appeared in her eyes remained. "Who would you invite to your dream dinner party?"

Alex breathed out. "Heavy."

"And my called off engagement confession wasn't?"

There was another silence between them, this time it felt awkward.

"Okay, another time. If there is one, that is," Julia said, and winked.

"My mother," Alex said, before she could speak again. Alex glanced out of the window. Julia put down the magazine.

"You said it was cancer?" Julia asked.

"Breast cancer. It was diagnosed quite late."

206

"She had treatment?"

"Not until it was too late."

"Why?"

"She was pregnant with me."

"Oh."

"She got treatment after I was born. Went into remission for a couple of years, but then it came back," Alex said. "I've always thought, perhaps if she'd decided to start treatment earlier..."

"Whatever happened, it was her choice to make," Julia said.

"Has your dad met anyone since? I mean, it was a long time ago. He would have still been young."

"There was one woman, another lawyer. It got quite serious apparently, I was about seven or eight at the time. I remember even meeting her," Alex said. "As far as I know, he didn't want to marry again, she did, and that was the end of it."

"And that was his choice?"

"I suppose he just couldn't, or can't, forget my mother. He just seems so lonely. I'm worried it will be worse now he's retired."

"He still has you."

Alex glanced out of the window again.

"Who looked after you before you were old enough to go to school?"

"Nannies, when he was at work."

"I imagine you were such a cute child. A real little heartbreaker."

"Apart from the first one, who was a witch." Alex sighed. "I used to get so attached to them. When they left because of other jobs or boyfriends, I'd be the heartbroken one."

"Oh, Alex." Julia patted the duvet over his leg.

"I remember one in particular, Rachel. When she left, I was inconsolable. I wouldn't get out of bed for days. It was the only time my father ever raised his voice to me as a child," Alex said. "His voice sounded so strange, like it was coming from someone else."

"What did he say?"

"'For God's sake, Alex, she's not your mother,' he shouted. I cried. He apologised immediately and then barely spoke for days. In fact, he went away for a business trip soon after."

Alex slipped out of the bed. "I'll be back in a minute. I'm just going to go to the bathroom."

"You know where it is?"

"Yeah."

"Alex," Julia said, and Alex stopped and turned. "Your mum. You weren't to blame. You know that, right?"

***

Alex stood in the bathroom opposite the mirror in his pants and a white towelling robe Julia had given him, which was small on him and only went down to his knees. He washed his hands and face, put some toothpaste on his finger and brushed the inside of his mouth with it.

When he returned, Julia was holding *Weekend* magazine again in both hands.

"We've got time for one last question for you before I go to work," she said.

"I'm ready," he said, smiling.

"Have you ever said 'I love you' and not meant it?"

"It was in Paris, in French, to a French girl. Does that count?"

"Who was she?" Julia asked. Alex, still in the robe, sat in the reclining chair in front of the small desk in her room, and put his feet up on it.

"I was thirteen, it was a school trip," Alex said. "We were paired with this Parisian girls' school. It was our last day and girls from the school were showing us the city."

"There was this one girl. I fell for her, badly. She was beautiful and she smoked, which seemed so cool and sophisticated then."

"What was the name of this French seductress?"

"Celine."

"Oh la la, sexy Celine," Julia said in a French accent, with a little pout.

"I know, right? So picture the scene: all day we're walking around Paris together talking to each other, or trying. I'm carrying her rucksack like an English gentleman and telling her anything I could think of that might impress her. Like I'd had tea with the Queen – literally anything that came into my head."

"So what happened?"

"The day of sightseeing is coming to an end. All I can think about is that I want to kiss Celine more than anything in the world. We're all standing by the Eiffel Tower saying goodbye to each other in turn, the

French way, with kisses on each cheek, and I think, this is my last chance and if I don't say it I'll regret it for the rest of my life."

"I lean in and I say the words, I'd been rehearsing in my head: '*Je t'aime, ma cherie.*' 'I love you, my dear'."

"And what did she do? What did Celine do?" Julia lent forward, her eyes widened, a mischievous smile on her face.

"She kissed me, the French way. It was amazing. It was the first time I'd had a girl's tongue in my mouth and it blew my mind," Alex replied. "She tasted of cigarettes."

"You know, I think that's why I started smoking. Every cigarette I smoked reminded me of her and that kiss, even years later."

"I need to cool down." Julia waved her hand like a fan in her face before breathing in and out deeply, she looked down at her phone in her bag. "Okay, we actually have time for a final one," she said. "As long as we don't get your life story this time."

"What's the most important thing life has taught you?"

"Easy," Alex replied. "Always start conversations with beautiful women at bus stops."

Julia smiled widely, before leaning back in the bed and stretching out like a cat.

***

Julia was getting dressed. Alex stood near the door of her bedroom, looking at a framed black and white map on the wall. The place names were printed in Italian and written in ornate writing below the map, 'Venezia'.

"What are you looking at?" Alex heard Julia's voice behind him.

"Have you been?" Alex asked, without turning.

"No. I picked that up in the local charity shop when I moved in. I've always wanted to go. Venice just seems the most beautiful place in the world," Julia replied. "What about you?"

"It's so beautiful." Alex turned. Julia was now standing directly in front of him. "It's almost overwhelming."

Chapter Thirteen

Without Julia

"A penny for them?" Sal said.

Alex glanced up at her. In the three long days it took for the money to hit his bank account, he'd spent almost all his waking hours staring into space, at Richard's flat or Nico's. Thinking about the race.

He scribbled the name of his horse repeatedly on used betting slips and found himself in conversations with Bob, daily, about its great prospects. It took on an almost mythical quality in his mind.

"Follow the money! Follow the money!" Bob had been saying all week. Lonesome Dude's betting odds coming in from 15/1, the price he'd backed it at, to 9/1.

At the betting shop, Alex'd seen regulars win some days and leave the betting shop 'up' – with more money than they came in with. However, they always ended the week 'down' overall – all except Bob.

Alex found them the morning after Richard's shock confession he'd never seen the *Godfather* films. Sat on the floor of the basement flat surrounded by boxes, amongst his DVDs were the Premium Government Bond certificates his grandparents had given him for his first birthday. The value was £1500 and he'd sent the certificates along with the signed redemption form to the post office the same day, after visiting his father.

If he could get 8/1 or even 7/1 and bet the entire amount and won, he'd win back all the money he'd lost in recent weeks. It was the perfect bet.

There was only one problem with Alex's plan: the horse had to win. Lonesome Dude had to win the 3.30 p.m. race at Newmarket the following day.

***

"What happened to these amazing dinners you promised to cook us every night?" Richard asked, as he set down his bag.

Alex was sprawled on the sofa. It was only six in the evening but he still had the duvet over him. It didn't appear he'd moved all day.

"Sorry, Richard, I forgot to go to the shops again," Alex replied.

"Looks like you forgot to get up," Richard said, but Alex didn't answer this time. He switched the TV channel as if it was some kind of response. "I can smell something, though," Richard continued.

"I had the last can of tomato soup for lunch. I'll replace it." Alex said.

"I didn't realise my offer of accommodation came with free meals, too. But it's fine. I'm going to the Crown with Swanky," Richard said, getting up to leave. "So I can have an actual conversation."

"Wait," Alex said, still staring ahead at the TV. As he spoke he heard the front door slam shut. Alex threw the duvet off himself and rushed to the window. Richard's shoes, and Swanky's cowboy boots, were at eye level. "Richard!"

Richard bent down, his face at the barred window. "What?"

"Come back," Alex said.

He picked up the remote and pressed play – the theme music from *The Godfather* came on. He ran to the kitchen, turned the dial for the electric stove, and took out a huge pan of meatballs in tomato sauce from the unlit oven and placed it on the heat. From the fridge, he pulled out two sticks of garlic bread and a bottle of supermarket brand Cava. Richard and Swanky appeared at the kitchen door.

"Can you open that?" Alex asked Swanky, handing him the bottle of Cava. "Grazie," he added, in an Italian accent.

Richard stood, seemingly fixed to the ground, his mouth wide open but without any words coming out. Alex put his hand on Richard's shoulder.

"Don't look too shocked, Richard. I said I would cook for us." Alex smiled. "I was just waiting to get inspired."

Richard and Swanky parted to let Alex back into the lounge. Swanky was wrestling with the bottle of Cava and Richard was still motionless as Alex pulled a bag from behind the sofa.

"I got these from the Market," he said and tossed a black fedora style hat at Richard, and one at Swanky, before placing another on his head. Richard dropped his, Swanky – with no hands free – moved and caught his on his head the wrong way round.

The Godfather theme music was becoming louder and quicker; on the TV screen was a montage of scenes from the film, Michael and Sonny Corleone in their father's study – Michael sitting in a chair in his arm uniform and Sonny standing in front of him in a white vest.

"If Clemenza can figure out a way to have a weapon planted there for me," Alex, now sitting in the armchair, said. "Then I'll kill them both."

Swanky pumped up his chest, adjusted his hat theatrically.

"Nice college boy didn't want to get mixed up in the family business, now you want to gun down a police captain 'cause he slapped you in the face?" He clenched his fist, making his hand into the shape of a gun.

"You think this is like the army where you shoot 'em from a mile away? No, you gotta get up close like this – bada-bing! – you blow their brains all over your Ivy League suit."

"The sauce!" Alex said, dashing off to the kitchen – the other two following.

***

"Richard tells me you are writing a film script," Swanky said to Alex. They stood in the kitchen drinking. Swanky from the only wine glass, Alex from a glass tumbler, and Richard from a white mug with 'I heart spreadsheets' on it.

"The screenplay's kind of on the backburner. I don't seem to be able to finish it," Alex said. "I don't seem to be able to finish anything."

"Why not?"

"I don't know, I start things but then seem to lose faith halfway through," Alex said. "I think I lost faith in my writing a long time ago."

"When?"

"I won this poetry competition when I was at junior school. Only competition I've ever won," Alex said. "When I told my dad in the car home, he didn't say anything."

"Maybe he didn't hear you, sometimes you mumble, Alex."

"Then he said, 'everything good has been written'."

Swanky picked up an open pad of lined paper lying on the table. "Well, this looks suspiciously like writing."

"It's not writing. They're just daydreams and memories I've been scribbling down."

"I'm out of booze," Swanky said, looking down at his empty glass. The bottle of Cava on the sideboard was also empty. "We're out of booze. This is an emergency situation."

"I'll pop out and get some red wine to go with the dinner," Richard said, heading towards the stairs.

"I can go," Alex said. He then looked down at the pasta sauce bubbling away in front of him. "Actually, I probably shouldn't leave the sauce at this crucial juncture."

Alex lent across to Swanky and whispered in his ear.

"Thanks for lending me the twenty pounds to buy dinner tonight."

"Prego," Swanky replied, gesturing dramatically with his hands.

***

Alex placed the crisp notes, picked up from the bank only minutes earlier, on the counter of the betting shop in front of Erin – the young junior cashier. She gave him a tight half-smile and looked back at Anne-Marie, who was counting out notes into the security box on the side table.

When Anne-Marie looked up, it wasn't with her usual friendly expression. Instead, it was with a look he'd seen her give to regulars – or former regulars. He stepped back, physically recoiling from it. She finished counting the pile of money in front of her, before standing and turning to the counter. Erin stepped aside.

To take the money out, Alex had to go into the bank with his passport as it was more than his withdrawal limit. He told the bank clerk the money was for a car in way of explanation for withdrawing such a large amount. Embarrassed by his unkempt beard and scruffy dress, he also mentioned he was about to go on holiday.

"I'll only ask this once," she said in a low voice

Alex had not heard from her before. Anne-Marie looked him in the eye. "Are you sure?" she said.

Alex nodded slowly, not looking at her, almost in a solemn but silent prayer. A few seconds later and the notes he'd placed on the counter were gone and he had a small pink betting slip in his hand with *Lonesome Dude 7/1* scrawled on it, below was printed the race meeting and time.

"Let's hope it's your lucky day, sunshine," Anne-Marie said. Her usual cheery tone and friendly smile had returned.

"What price d'you get?" Bob asked Alex as they passed each other outside the betting shop as he left.

"Seven to one."

"Sevens – not bad," Bob replied. "Follow the money," he heard Bob repeat as he entered the betting shop behind him, clapping his hands together.

Alex wandered up and down the high street before entering another betting shop at the end of the road. He took a seat in one of its blue chairs. He noticed the chairs were nailed to the floor. Presumably, so that they couldn't be stolen or thrown around by gamblers who'd lost all their money.

Alex breathed in and out slowly, his heart rate seeming to slow. The noise of the shop increasing as more people came in and it filled up, but even the man banging one of the roulette machines nearby didn't disturb him. However, when the commentary for the next race began, adrenalin rushed though his veins as he imagined, an hour later, Lonesome Dude winning his race – he felt for a moment a wave of relief.

Alex yawned widely, involuntarily closing his eyes. He made for the door. Walking to the end of the road, he decided to keep onto Regent's Park. Sitting by the Gothic fountain, he looked at the various paths that led from it: one down to Euston Road; one into the playing fields; another towards Primrose Hill; and finally, the one opposite him that led back into Camden. His stomach ached, he realised he hadn't eaten yet that day. The air was warm, he felt he could barely breathe.

Alex laid down on the grass towards the fields on the left. He felt his watch against his side, a silver Rolex that had been his grandfather's. He slipped it off his wrist and placed it by his left shoulder, where his bedside table used to be, now Richard's coffee table.

***

Alex woke in a cold sweat. He'd dozed off. He stood up quickly, giving himself a head spin, and began walking back towards Camden. Passing the York & Albany pub on his right, he looked down at his wrist to check the time. Realising his watch wasn't there, he turned and ran back towards the park – grasping his naked wrist in disbelief.

He scrambled around on his hands and knees on the patch of grass where he'd slept, running his fingers though the grass. After a few minutes, empty-handed, still on his knees, Alex cried out. He pulled his phone from his pocket to check the time.

Its battery was dead. He'd been forgetting to charge it overnight. At the firm he would have been tormented by his phone battery running out but when it had happened a few days earlier he'd found the isolation almost comforting.

Walking back into town for the second time, he peered into shop windows and glanced at the wrists of some of the people he passed; getting a rebuke from one, a tall thin man with a swagger. In Paradise Dry Cleaners, halfway back into town, he saw he had only a couple of minutes to the race. He stopped at the nearest betting shop, it had familiar red colouring – the same chain as his usual shop.

He sat close to the screen, the horses were warming up at the starting gate. In the final seconds before the race, all the seats around him were filled. It was happening. He could barely lift his arms to rest them on the table in front of him.

"They're off!" The smoke from the starter's gun hung in the air as the horses took their second strides. Lonesome Dude and his jockey, in yellow and purple colours, starting slowly at second from the back.

The beautiful black horse moved up into fifth place. Alex imagined Bob along the road tapping his Racing Post on the table in front of him – trying to hide his excitement. "Not too shabby," he'd be saying to those around him.

Lonesome Dude seemed to change gear as the pack rounded the turn to the finishing straight. He overtook two horses, the movement happening within seconds – only one horse left in front of him. Lonesome Dude was quickening still, his front legs high in the air.

Alex held his breath and gripped the plastic table. Lonesome Dude then went clear at the front of the race. As the horse pulled further out in front with each stride, Alex looked down. He made a promise to himself that after picking up his winnings, he would never step inside a betting shop again.

Sighs and groans came from behind Alex. He didn't look up at first. Finally, he raised his head, then his eyes. A crouched jockey in purple and yellow colours rolled away to safety across the green turf, while the pack flew past a fallen beautiful black horse.

***

"You can have a brew while I finish up. Lock the door behind you," Big Sal said, leaving the set of keys in the door and wandering back into the café. "Dregs, I'm afraid. Last of the pot." She handed him a takeaway cup.

Alex pulled up a chair directly opposite the mural that took up the whole of the wall. A white, Greek-style villa on a hillside with a yellow setting sun on a blue sky and a green and blue sea in the background.

"Do you know where that is?" Alex asked.

"Long way from here, that's for sure," Sal replied, shivering, a gust of cold wind coming through the café's ill fitting door.

"Not so far, could be one of the Greek islands," Alex said. "Could be Nico's house." He pointed towards a small figure of a man sitting on the porch of the villa.

"Yeah, sipping Ouzo and living like a king after making his fortune from this place," she said, laughing. "Sweetheart, you've got quite the imagination."

"I never noticed before but he's all alone," Alex said.

Big Sal had finished cleaning and had put on a big overcoat. She stood beside Alex.

"Thanks, Sal," Alex said, still looking at the mural ahead of him. He followed Nico's eyes to the ocean, its thick green and blue lines, the sound of waves lapping on the beach, the sea swallowing the pale yellow sun – the unknown horizon; he held his breath and felt it pull him in. "For the tea, and everything."

"That sounds like goodbye," Sal said. "You going on your own trip?"

Chapter Thirteen

With Julia

"What are you looking at?" Julia asked.

"You," Alex replied. He was sitting on the bed dressed for work.

Julia was on a stool in front of a long mirror on the wall, brushing her hair. Alex watched the way she unconsciously pushed away the strands of hair that fell in front of her face, the way she had at the bus stop when they'd first met. Their eyes met in the mirror and they both smiled.

"You like to watch me, don't you?" Julia said. "I think I'm living with a crazy person – you're crazy."

"You make me crazy."

In the kitchen, the metal cafetière on the gas stove began to stir and hum satisfyingly behind them.

"I'm not sure which I like more," Alex said.

"Between what?"

"You coming home to me, or finding you here when I get home," Alex said.

They sat facing to each other at the kitchen table. Alex was dressed in his suit and Julia in her coffee shop work uniform, black skirt and white polo shirt.

"You know, it won't be like this all the time," Julia

said.

"Like what?" Alex asked.

"We won't be having sex on kitchen tables every morning."

"No?"

"Things ebb and flow. We won't always feel this passion."

"I will for you."

"If things work out between us, one day, years from now, we'll be in another kitchen. Maybe we'll even have kids. I would have put on some weight, you'll have some grey hairs. The fire won't always burn as bright," Julia said. "That's reality – everyday stuff gets in the way."

"Like what?"

"You'll be sitting here and I'll be over there de-frosting the freezer and it won't be sexy," Julia said, gesturing towards the fridge unit.

"I think you could make even defrosting a freezer sexy," Alex said and, still sitting, reached over for Julia. "Let's try it out now."

"No. Alex, I'm trying to be serious," Julia said, raising her voice.

"Julia, I must have told you a hundred times in the last few weeks that I love you."

"I know that. You really don't get it, do you? Love is the easy bit, Alex," she said, taking her arms off the table and leaning back in the seat. "Although loving you is pretty challenging at times."

They were silent. The only sound was the water in the cafetière bubbling through the layer of coffee.

"Do you remember when we met you said you knew the reason I never finished that screenplay?" Alex asked.

"Haven't you figured it out yet?" Julia replied. "It's the same reason I get nervous before an audition." She leaned back. "I always show up though – you have to, even to fail."

Alex leaned forward, his arms on the table. "Can I take you out for dinner tonight?" he asked. His hands reached out across the table towards Julia.

"You know all this Shakespeare and all these quotes about it by heart, you even tried to write a screenplay about it. But I wonder sometimes if you really know what love means."

Alex leaned back in his seat, both hands around the back of his head. "Is that a yes to dinner?" he said. "Or you'll think about it?"

"I'll think about it," Julia replied, sighing. She stood and left the room, without turning or saying goodbye. Alex watched her until she was out of sight. He thought about the first time he saw her walk away from him, when she stepped onto that bus.

***

"Food and sex," Julia said.

"What do you mean?" Alex asked.

"They're pretty good. I'll give you that."

"I still don't get it."

"Your distractionary tactics – whenever we come close to talking about anything serious," Julia said,

225

as they walked up Junction Road towards the restaurant. "Or to me dumping you."

Alex stopped walking and turned to Julia. She stopped.

"Sometimes I don't know when you're joking," Alex said.

"Neither do I," Julia replied, widening her eyes and giving a little smile.

Julia had changed from her work clothes into a T-shirt and jeans. Alex had also changed into jeans, but was still in his white work shirt – open at the collar and with the sleeves rolled up.

"Julia, I want you to walk up the street ahead of me."

"Why?" Julia said.

"Just do it," Alex said.

Julia began walking up the street ahead of Alex. He watched her move, she seemed to glide. She turned, hand on hip and looked back at Alex.

"Don't think I'll be taking off my underwear in this restaurant tonight."

"No? What about after?"

Alex smiled, he began walking towards her. She turned and continued walking. Alex caught up with her, taking her hand.

"I've never met a woman, so intelligent, witty, thoughtful – or who looks as good in a pair of jeans."

***

The décor of Spaghetti House didn't have a coherent

theme. On the walls were a selection of ornaments and pictures that appeared to have been picked at random from the local charity shops. Alex put down a black plastic bag at the side of one of the tables, containing a bottle of Prosecco and a bottle of red wine – the restaurant didn't have an alcohol license.

An elderly, smartly dressed couple were in the corner of the restaurant. They were eating their food in a leisurely manner, stopping to converse between mouthfuls and small sips of wine. When either of the waiting staff returned from serving tables, they often exchanged a comment or smile with the couple.

The old man had a crutch resting on the side of their table, the old lady sat next to him touched his leg caringly every time he winced in pain. He'd reach for his glass of wine after each wince to take a sip, she would quietly tell him off and he'd put his hands up in mock protest.

Alex turned to Julia, who was studying her menu with a serious concentrated expression.

"I can't decide what to have," she said. Alex smiled. "The sea bass sounds amazing but then I really fancy the steak," Julia continued.

"I don't believe in gender stereotypes, but when deciding what to eat in restaurants I've never known a woman to know what she wants," Alex said. "About almost everything else, but never that."

"I know when I'm hungry," Julia said. "I just don't always know what I want to eat."

"How about you order the seabass and I order the steak," Alex said. "And when the food arrives if you change your mind then you can have my steak, or not, whatever you decide."

"I like that plan."

"I had a feeling you would."

"You're quite charming." Julia reached and rubbed Alex's leg with hers under the table.

"Thanks."

"And frustrating, in equal measure."

The waitress put a jug of tap water on their table and two glass tumblers. Alex picked up Julia's wine glass, which had a washing smear on it and swapped it with his. He dipped one of the paper napkins into his glass of water and wiped it around the glass carefully.

"I like that," Julia said, watching him.

"Like what?"

"That you notice things, little things."

"I don't really think about it."

"I guess that's kind of the point. This morning I noticed I'd run out of rice milk. I was still angry with you when I got home but then I looked in the fridge and you'd got me more – I didn't have to ask you and you didn't say anything about it," Julia said. "You're not like other men."

"Is it a good thing or a bad thing?"

"Both."

Julia leaned over the table and kissed Alex. He smiled.

"You know, that was a good kiss. I feel like I earned it."

The waitress appeared with their food. Julia made them swap plates over twice between them. As they did, Alex saw Julia notice the old couple in the corner.

"So, your dad worked in the City at his law firm and your mother worked from home?" she said.

"Sometimes she went to students' houses, but mainly she taught from home," Alex said. "My aunt told me once that during the week my dad would call her every lunchtime from his office, and then again from a payphone at London Bridge station to tell her he was on his way home – it was, of course, before mobile phones."

"And when he got home, he'd always have a gift for her. On Fridays it might have been a bunch of flowers, but most days it was just small, like a chocolate bar – Turkish Delight was her favourite, apparently. Every day without fail he would do that, or so my aunt says."

"That's lovely," Julia said. She was silent for a few moments. "Do I get to meet your dad?"

"Tomorrow, if you like. Actually, he's been asking to meet you. He'll adore you."

"As much as he did your ex-girlfriend?"

"Did I mention that?" Alex said. Julia laughed.

"I can't wait to meet him," Julia said. "You talk about him so much."

"Really?"

"How did your mum and dad meet? They had very different careers," Julia said.

"On a train. My dad rarely talks about the past but he likes telling that story. I'll let him tell you," Alex said.

"Intriguing. I'll ask him tomorrow."

Julia and Alex finished eating and the waitress cleared their plates away. Alex looked at the old couple again and thought how attentive they were to each other.

The man stood and steadied himself with a hand on the table. His wife stood and tried to help him, but he waved her away. Then she waved him away as he tried to hold up her coat for her to put on, and they stopped to laugh at themselves.

The old man placed his hand on Alex's shoulder as he passed their table on the way out. He was looking down at Alex and Julia. His wife caught up with him and stood by his side.

"It's a beautiful thing to see two people so in love," the old man said.

"You know, I was thinking the same thing about you two," Alex said.

"And such a handsome couple," the old man's wife said. "You're so pretty," she said to Julia, looking into her eyes. "And he's not bad, either." She winked at Alex.

As the old couple left they shouted their thanks to the staff who called back to them. The door closed shut behind them. Alex and Julia were the last people left in the restaurant. Alex's right bare forearm was resting on the table. Julia stroked the inside gently up and down, while they sat in silence.

***

Alex's father was at the kitchen table, waiting, when Alex and Julia came down the corridor. He looked like he could've been there all morning. He stood as they entered.

"I'm terribly sorry, how rude of me not to meet you at the door," he said. He and Julia kissed on both cheeks.

"I've heard so much about you, Mr Wright."

"Ian, please."

"I'm going to go in for a hug – if that's okay?" Julia said, with one of her wide smiles. She gave Alex's father a gentle hug, which he returned.

"It's a pleasure to meet you, I've been so looking forward to it," Mr Wright said. "He's been hiding you away."

"I said exactly the same about you, Mr Wright – sorry – Ian."

Before they'd sat down, Julia and Alex's father began talking about the new play she was auditioning for and the acoustics of various different London theatres. Julia sat next to Alex's father and Alex sat opposite, observing them for the most part, except when Julia would turn to him to tell him something or for his input into whatever they were talking about at that moment. They were on their second cup of tea.

"I hope you don't mind me asking, Alex mentioned that you and Alex's mother met on a train," Julia said.

Alex's father sat back in his chair. Alex couldn't read his expression.

"I was on the sleeper train from Penzance to Paddington, Sunday of the August Bank Holiday weekend. I say sleeper train as there were sleeping carriages, but most people, me included, only had seated tickets."

Alex leaned forward with Julia, he hadn't heard the story for so long, he'd forgotten the detail.

"It was early evening. We'd left Penzance and I was walking down the train to the buffet carriage to get a gin and tonic. I wasn't in the office the next day and, as a trainee lawyer in my first year working long hours, I treasured any time off I had.

"As I made my way down the carriage, I spotted this beautiful woman ahead who was reading. I paused as I passed her, but she didn't look up, even for a moment – she was so engrossed in her book. I continued to the buffet car and while I sipped my gin and tonic, I wondered how I would get the courage to speak to her."

"The gin and tonic was going to help?" Julia said.

"It was," Alex's father replied. "But every minute that passed I got more anxious because the train was getting nearer to St Ives, where she might get off – before the train went non-stop to Paddington."

"So what happened?" Julia said. She had her arms on the table, head turned towards Mr Wright.

"I'd been visiting my parents that weekend. They had this beautiful Victoria plum tree that bore fruit only every two years, and for just a few days each time. As well as the sandwich my mother had made me for my journey back to London, she'd given me a paper bag of plums.

"I walked back down the carriage from the buffet.

232

I stopped beside the beautiful woman and offered her the open bag while mumbling something. Whatever I said, she looked up at me with a big, friendly smile and said she'd love one."

Alex looked at Julia who was looking intently at his father. Alex's father continued.

"My nervousness immediately left me, and then she said the only polite thing would be to ask me to join her, at least for a moment. We got some funny looks from the businessman and the older lady sitting nearby, but they got off at St Ives so we had the whole carriage to ourselves.

"I said I should go back to my seat but after the first few times, she dismissed the idea. So I sat there for the next eight hours and all the way to London."

"You talked all that time?" Julia asked quietly.

"We talked all night. By the time the train pulled into Paddington at 6.07 a.m., I was in love," Mr Wright said. "And so was Madeleine – or so she said afterwards." He looked away and out of the window. The morning fog was beginning to lift off the Heath.

The conversation then turned to practical things, their flat and Alex's new job. His father seemed much more enthusiastic about the job when talking to Julia and seeing it had her endorsement. He also asked after Richard's welfare, as he always did.

Alex and Julia got ready to leave. Julia went to the bathroom and left Alex standing with his father in the hallway of the flat. They stood in silence until the briefest moment before Julia returned.

"I like the way she looks at you," was all his father

said.

After they'd closed the front door behind them, gone up the path and stepped onto the street, Julia said, "I adore your father."

"I think he felt the same about you."

"I'm glad. I'd really like to get to know him better."

"So would I."

"What do you mean?"

They turned down the hill towards Tufnell Park.

"It's just, some of my friends now they're older, have different relationships with their fathers – they talk like friends," Alex said. "Some of them even play golf together."

"You hate golf. Don't you?"

"I do."

"Alex, maybe you'll never be friends with him in that way, but do you really want that?"

Alex and Julia then turned down the hill towards Camden. The fog had now disappeared and they could make out the Roundhouse in the distance.

"He seems a lot of fun. You made him out to be terribly serious," Julia said. They walked past the Hampstead ponds. "Are these the famous ponds I've heard about?"

"He swims there," Alex said. "They're public and open every day of the year."

"Your father doesn't swim there every day, surely?"

"No. He really does. All year round, ever since I can remember. Even when it's frozen over, they break up an area so that people can go in."

"Who does he go with?"

"He goes alone now. It was something he did with my mother after they got married, not that she always went in winter, I understand."

"Growing up, you must have gone with him?"

"He never took me."

***

"Alex, do you know what time it is?" Julia said, rubbing her eyes.

"It's early," Alex replied.

"Why have you woken me up then?"

Alex managed to convince Julia to get dressed only after promising to make a coffee, although she only had time for a few sips before he was rushing them out of the door. He was carrying a blanket and a bottle of Prosecco.

"We don't have long," he said as they walked along a deserted Camden Road.

"The only reasons to be up at this time are because, either you haven't been to bed yet, or you're on your way to the airport to catch an early flight."

They turned the corner and were at the foot of Primrose Hill.

***

"What was she like?" Julia asked.

"I was too young to remember," Alex replied. "Growing up, I'd look at old photos of her for hours, hoping I'd recall some moment we were together.

Nothing ever came, not a single memory."

They were wrapped in a blanket looking over the city from the top of the hill, the sun rising in front of them. They'd run up the hill after seeing the tip of the sun on the skyline. An empty bottle of Prosecco now lay beside them, alone on the hill with only a few dog walkers in the distance.

"What does that feel like?"

"It doesn't feel like anything. Sometimes it just feels like there is this blackness, this void, inside me," Alex said, touching his chest unconsciously.

"The only time I've felt close to her is when I used to play her piano when I was younger. I suppose there was something about sitting in the same spot she would have been in, seeing the same view as she would have done."

"Did she enjoy teaching?" Julia asked.

"Everyone says she was really kind and patient. Even though she'd cut down on teaching while pregnant with me and after she got ill; apparently, her students – present and past – packed the church at her funeral."

"Do you still play?"

"I haven't for years."

"Will you play for me one day?" Julia asked.

"I'll try to play, at least. If you'd like?"

"I'd like that very much."

***

236

Alex and Julia drifted sleepily down Primrose Hill and across through Regent's Park, turning right at the Gothic fountain monument. Walking back into Camden along Parkway, Alex and Julia passed a café with a poster in the window. It read 'Lost Elephant' in large handwritten letters above a hand-drawn picture of an elephant and a phone number.

They went in and ordered coffee from a friendly old man. As he made their coffee, they noticed his hands shook slightly. When he handed them their Styrofoam take-away cups, Julia asked him about the poster. He turned and waved to what looked like his middle-aged son behind him. The man took down a tin box, about the size of a cigar box, from a high shelf behind him and handed it to the old man.

"Well, young lady, I adopted an African elephant in 2004 from an elephant charity. I paid £10 a month by standing order, and for three years they sent me photos and reports of my elephant. I would look forward to the letters. I would find out how well she was doing – it was marvellous."

They sat down at a table opposite the man with their coffees. Some faded photos and letters were beside the open box.

"Until one day, it all stopped. They wrote to tell me my elephant had gone missing. They thought it might be poachers, but they had no way of knowing for sure."

"That's terrible," Julia said. "Did they find her?"

"No. But I've never forgotten her, even after all these years," the old man said. He shook his head and looked past them. When Alex looked into the old man's eyes, he thought the man was imagining his elephant on the plains of Africa.

After their coffees, Alex and Julia turned onto Chalk Farm Road and walked, hand in hand, in the direction of Camden tube station. They passed people heading home from picnics in flip flops and carrying bags and rugs, or dressed up and beginning their nights out.

"I can imagine you like that old man one day," Julia said.

"Why? I'm not crazy about elephants," Alex said. "I actually prefer zebras."

"I hate it when I try and be serious and you make a joke."

"Okay, why am I like the crazy old guy, then?" Alex sighed.

"He's stuck in the past. He's so busy remembering, when he needs to forget."

***

"So what does it feel like?" Richard said.

Alex was sitting at the bar of the Crown and Goose with Richard.

"It feels like I've been hit by a train. I feel different. Everything looks, feels and seems different," Alex said. "Do I seem different?"

"No. You're still a pain in the neck."

"The strange thing about falling in love is, we know what it looks and feels like. But we can't really explain why it occurs and where all the madness it brings with it comes from.

"Or why it just seems to happen like magic between two particular people but not others."

"The appearance of love seems totally irrational, inexplicable and without reason. Yet, when it happens it feels like the only thing that makes any sense. True love, I guess, is when it keeps on making sense after you actually get to know the other person."

"It's a real paradox," Alex continued. "Richard, are you listening?" He could see Richard was now looking in the direction of the door. He thought perhaps Ciara had come in, but Richard mentioned earlier it was her night off.

"I think your paradox has just arrived," said Richard. Julia had walked in and was looking around.

"Julia, meet Richard. Richard, meet Julia."

"So this is where you two hang out," she said as Richard slipped clumsily off his bar stool to greet Julia. She caught him. "So, what are we talking about?"

"So far this evening it's been mainly about how wonderful you are," Richard replied. "He hasn't even asked how I am."

"Alex, how rude. Get Richard another pint of whatever he's drinking, and I'll have a glass of wine," Julia said to Alex before turning back to Richard.

"So, Richard, tell me about your day."

Chapter Fourteen
Without Julia

"What's this game?" Alex said into his phone. He was sitting at the bar of the Crown, his head rested on his free hand, elbow on bar, phone to his ear – the phone attached to a charging lead that went over and under the bartop.

"Under 16s – we're unbeaten in the cup. I'm captain at the weekend," Billy said to Alex, down the phone.

"Captain, really?" Alex asked.

"The regular captain's sprained his ankle and the coach reckons I'm a natural leader," Billy said. "Mum says that's another way of saying I've got a big mouth."

"Well, congratulations."

"Come if you like. It's no big deal."

"It sounds like a big deal," Alex said. "Where are you playing?" Alex asked. The phone felt like a dead weight in his hand.

"Hackney Marshes."

"I'll come."

"Really?" Billy said, sounding surprised. "Like you'll actually turn up?"

"Like I'll actually turn up." Billy grunted positively

and hung up on Alex. Alex put his hand holding the phone down beside the top of his head and left it there. He slumped over the bar.

Alex had not been able to face Bob, or Anne-Marie, for that matter and wandered to the Crown purposely but slowly. He put his hand in his pocket and pulled a crumpled twenty pound note from it – all the money he had in the world.

The image of Lonesome Dude on the ground, fallen, in his eyes. His mouth dry and a nauseous, sick feeling in his stomach. He felt as if he'd cursed the horse by backing it, once its fate had become intertwined with his, it was doomed.

"Are you okay? Alex." Ciara had to say his name a few times before he registered she was in front of him. "Do you want a drink?"

"I think so," Alex replied, putting his hand to his head.

"To being okay or wanting a drink?" Ciara asked, with a concerned expression.

"Both, I think," Alex replied.

He drank the pints she put in front of him at a great rate, thinking about the next one even before he had finished the one he was drinking.

"Whisky?" Alex said.

"You'll have to pay for one of those," Ciara said.

"Double, please." Alex slid seven pounds across the bar – the last of his money.

The door to the toilets wasn't the toilets. There was a staircase there instead. He started up the staircase, slowly, clinging to the railing. A step from the top, he lost his balance, holding on desperately with two hands to the banister, lurching back and forth.

On a landing he saw Ciara coming towards him. Her hair was now worn up. Her arms were on his shoulders. It was the first time anyone had touched him, or he'd had any physical contact with another person in months. He lifted his head, reached his arms around her and went to kiss her.

***

Alex looked up at an unfamiliar ceiling. He turned his head to one side and saw the back of Ciara's head as she left the room. He then heard running water. He pulled aside the duvet and rolled slowly off the sofa bed and stood unsteadily to his feet, finding himself cold, looked down; he was naked. His clothes neatly folded on top on the low table nearby, his shoes on the floor beside it.

His head was pounding, his mouth so dry he could barely swallow. After putting on his clothes, clumsily, he picked up his shoes and crept along the corridor. His heart was beating out of his chest, expecting Ciara to come out of one of the doors he passed at any moment.

Staggering down the staircase at the end of the corridor, he tripped, holding onto the railing to stop himself falling forward. At the bottom of the stairs, a door marked emergency exit, which to his surprise, opened without an alarm.

The sky outside was black-blue – too late to be

night but too early to be morning. He breathed in the cool fresh air calming his sick feeling. An alarm sounded loudly behind him and startled him. It was the door alarm. He walked quickly up the street, away from the door and pub.

**

The flat was empty, but Richard could be back any time that morning – he'd stayed overnight at his parents' place in Barnet after going for dinner there.

Alex took out a cupped handful of cut up plastic pieces from the desk drawer. He sat on the sofa, dropping the pieces on the table in front of him and began putting them together like a jigsaw – into a credit card.

He opened Richard's laptop on the table and typed payment details into the website from the fragmented card in front of him. The flight booking reference popped up, he only had two hours until check in.

He closed the laptop lid. He picked up the plastic carrier bag beside the sofa, first taking out the empty sandwich packet before stuffing a handful of clothes into it from the nearby box. He picked up his own laptop case beside the sofa containing his own laptop within it.

Alex paused on the bottom of the stairs to the front door. He crossed the room, opened Richard's desk and took out the emergency £100 and spare Oyster travel card he kept there. He slammed the drawer shut.

"Just hand luggage?" said the uniformed woman at the airline check-in, looking down at the plastic bag Alex was holding and laptop case under his arm.

"Err. Yes," he replied, handing over his passport. She returned it to him with a printed boarding pass. It read, 'Sofia, Bulgaria.'

Alex continued to airport security and joined a line of people waiting to go through the scanners. Checking his jacket pockets, he felt inside and removed something, holding it out in front of him. He stared in disbelief. It was a fifty pound note. He smiled for the first time that day.

The bright lights of the Duty Free shopping area hurt Alex's eyes and he blinked. In a far corner of the mall-like floor of bars and restaurants, he spotted a dimly lit pub, its name in gold letters: The Britannia.

There were quotes written around the pub on the red walls below the ceiling from W. C. Fields, Ernest Hemingway and F. Scott Fitzgerald. Alex bought a pint of cider and sat down in a faded, red leather armchair. The quote above him, 'I'm not a writer with a drinking problem, I'm a drinker with a writing problem' – Dorothy Parker.

Alex sat back in the sticky chair, propping his now fixed laptop – fixed by the IT person at Richard's work – on his knees. Opening a Word document, he looked back at the white blank page.

He started typing. A flashing power icon came on in the corner of the keyboard. He reached into the main pocket of the laptop bag and pulled out a power cable. It was the one for Richard's laptop. As the laptop started to shut down, he caught the words he'd written on the screen, I am lost, over and over again for half a page.

The last call for his airline's flight to Sofia was announced from the speaker above Alex. He stood, stuffed his laptop into the bag and began to run towards the departure gate.

***

"Excuse me," Alex said to a short-haired male flight attendant, as soon as he finished the safety evacuation demonstration beside Alex's aisle.

"Yes, sir?" the attendant said, turning to Alex and smiling.

"When you start serving, can you bring me a double gin and tonic, please?" Alex asked. The man nodded. Alex then handed him the fifty pound note. "Then one every fifteen minutes until that runs out, or we get there. Thank you."

The plane straightened up and began accelerating rapidly. As it lifted off and Alex felt his stomach lurch, he remembered he was meant to be at Billy's football match the next day.

Chapter Fourteen

With Julia

"What do you really want?"

It was Sunday evening and Alex and Julia were lying together on the sofa.

"To have you again on this sofa."

Julia slapped Alex, softly.

"I read somewhere that happiness is the longing for repetition," Alex said.

"Are you saying you want another slap?"

Julia's phone beeped and she picked it up.

"Dan's coming round."

"Now?"

"I told you yesterday. Don't you remember? He's coming to fix my bike."

"I can fix your bike."

Julia got up and left the room.

"Like you fixed this?" She appeared at the door with a blackened toaster and a threadbare wire plug. "DIY is not one of your strengths and that's fine. You're great at other more important things." She winked at him. "Like cooking."

"Okay, I know you're mates."

"He's always been there for me, Alex."

"I can see that, he always seems to be very available." Alex sat up on the sofa. "After everything I've heard about him, I'm curious to meet him finally."

"I know you're going to get on great."

"I suppose I'd better put some clothes on," Alex said, leaving the lounge.

Alex heard the door buzzer. Julia shouted she'd get the door. When Alex entered the kitchen, Dan was sitting in Alex's usual chair, drinking a cup of tea and in intense conversation with Julia. He was tall and athletic, with blonde hair, but receding badly.

"So, you're Doctor Dan?" Alex said, standing next to Julia. Dan and Julia looked up at him.

"Just *Dan* is fine," Dan replied. He shook Alex's hand with a tight grip. "And you're Alex? Julia was just telling me she took you in like a stray, you were going to be homeless, right?"

"It wasn't quite like that," Alex replied.

"Yeah, Dan, that's not quite what I said," Julia said.

"Anyway, nice to meet you, Dan. I've got to pop to the shop to grab something I need for dinner. I'll leave you both to it."

"See you soon," Julia replied briefly, touching his leg before turning back to Dan.

Sitting on the bottom step of the flat's stairs, putting on his boots, Alex could hear them talking intensely again. Outside, he began walking in the direction of where he thought was the nearest shop was. He pulled his phone from his pocket and pressed Richard's number.

"Don't you think it's weird her best friend is a guy?"

"Does she have girlfriends?"

"Yeah."

"Well then, it's not that weird."

"Julia says he's like a brother."

"The question is, does *he* see it that way too?" Richard asked. "Where are you now anyway?"

Alex looked around. He didn't recognise the street he was on. He kept walking.

"Fuck, I think I'm lost. I think I've lost the flat," he said. "Richard, do you remember the address from when you helped me move in?"

"Can't you just call Julia?"

"What, with Mr Perfect there? They'll both think I'm a total idiot."

"And they'd be right."

"Richard, shut up and look up my address."

"Alex, what's the name of the nearest street?" Richard asked.

"Wait, it's dark," Alex said. He was looking up and down the street before seeing he was in front of a street sign at knee height. "I've got one." He bent down to read the sign. "Dalmeny Road."

"Alex, isn't that your street?"

Alex looked up. The light was on in the kitchen window of the first floor flat. A bicycle upturned on the table with a man leaning over it. A women was observing him, tea mug in hand – it was Julia. They both turned at the same time and looked out of the window at Alex, with bemused expressions.

"Richard, I'll call you tomorrow."

***

"Don't worry, we're rehearsing for a play," Julia said to the older, distinguished looking couple at the table next to them. They'd been looking over anxiously at Alex and Julia after they'd raised their voices.

Alex and Julia were rehearsing lines for Julia's upcoming audition, outside a cafe on Swain's Lane, round the corner from the flat; white coffee cups and glasses of water in front of them. Alex went inside to order another coffee for him and a peppermint tea which Julia had requested.

"I was thinking while you were away," Julia said, when Alex returned and placed the cups on the table.

"What were you thinking about with that inquisitive mind of yours, darling?"

"Why do all these women leave you?" Julia said, smiling. "You're not that terrible in bed."

"It's a mystery."

"Do you know what I think, Alex?"

"What do you think, Julia?"

"Your mum, then all those nannies, left you. Part of you is still that scared little boy who thinks he's going to get hurt," Julia said.

"You sure you're not a psychologist?" Alex said, looking away from Julia.

"No, just an adult. You know what? Let's talk about something else." Alex turned to look at her. "I saw Zara today for coffee. Well, she came to see me at work, I made her coffee and we chatted."

"How is she? And Max?"

"They want us round for dinner. West London, Notting Hill."

"Of course, Notting Hill, where else?" Alex said, with a wry smile. "So I got the thumbs up?"

"From Zara and Max? They loved you, everyone does," Julia said. "Except maybe you sometimes. Dan reckons..."

"I thought he worked in Accident and Emergency, not psychiatry."

"He's my friend, we talk – that's what friends do. I would never talk about anything really personal."

"It sounds like you have."

"Dan only wants the best for me."

"He wants *you*, Julia, can't you see it?"

"You've only known him for five minutes," Julia said. "He's just a dear friend."

"I'm sorry," Alex said. He took a sip of his coffee. "This is cold. Your tea must be too. Do you want another?"

"What do you really want?" Julia asked finally.

"I want you."

"Is it really me you want? Or the idea of me?"

"Everything has just happened so quickly, Julia," Alex said.

"We're not teenagers. You're nearly thirty years old, Alex," Julia said, and sighed. "But maybe you're right, this has happened all so quickly. A few days apart might be a good idea."

"What? Don't say that, Julia."

They both sat back in their chairs.

"Brighton. It was the best day and the worst day of my life," said Julia.

"Why?"

"Because I could see how perfect we could be, and also how you could screw it up."

Alex brought his hands to his head. "How?"

"I understand now why Amy, and the ones before, left you."

Alex now sat forward in his chair, his hands had moved to the side of his head as if he wanted to cover his ears. "Why?" he asked finally.

"You were too scared to give them reason enough to stay."

The woman of the couple on the next table waved her hand at them.

"I just want to say, I don't know what play this is or where it's going to be performed, but I'd love to see it. You were both marvellous," she said. "So real," she repeated, turning to her husband, who nodded in response.

"That bit was real," replied Julia. "You just heard us break up."

The woman muttered something to her husband, while Julia gathered up the loose script pages on the table and shoved them into her Daunt Books tote bag.

"We're not breaking up," Alex said in the direction of the couple. He stood. He went after Julia, who was walking away quickly towards her flat, their flat.

Chapter Fifteen

Without Julia

Alex opened his eyes. He immediately felt his pockets, they were empty. Sitting upright, his right foot felt cold on the hard floor. He looked down, he was only wearing his left shoe, his right foot in only a sock.

While he slept his right foot must have been exposed, the other tucked under his leg. His laptop bag was also gone, although he couldn't remember having it since he'd left the plane. Fortunately, he still had the Bulgarian money he'd changed at Heathrow, he'd slipped it into his jacket pocket after changing it and hadn't transferred it to his wallet.

"My shoe." Alex gestured to his shoeless foot.

The security guard looked at him with a curious expression, gave a small shrug and walked away. He reappeared a few minutes later with a pair of shoes – Alex supposed from the airport's lost property. He looked curiously at the fluorescent, lime green coloured trainers the man had put on the seat beside him.

Alex went into the small, and only, shop by the exit. He picked up some cans of soup and a loaf of bread from the dusty shelves, as well as a can of coke and a lined notepad. It was strangely reassuring to see the familiar Heinz and Coca Cola labels amongst the unfamiliar ones.

He approached the group of taxi drivers standing in a fog of cigarette smoke; all seemed to have stomachs protruding below their shirts. The exception, a short wiry man, telling a seemingly amusing story by his animated manner and the laughter coming from his small audience of other drivers.

Alex pulled a crumpled piece of paper from his pocket and handed it to him. The man took it unceremoniously, glanced at it, then ushered him towards a nearby taxi, shouting something to the other drivers. He could still hear their laughter as he sat down, thinking they'd not yet agreed a fare.

They soon left the industrial outskirts of the city and turned off the main road. Ivan, which Alex established after a few conversational false starts was the driver's name, swung the box-shaped cream car left and right down country lanes like a racing driver.

The back seat was all in one, like a sofa – its springiness combined with Ivan's driving meant Alex was bounced around. He experienced a lurching feeling in his stomach and an acidic taste in his mouth at each turn. Alex closed his eyes, but the nausea returned and he reopened them. Ivan's chain-smoking wasn't helping either.

"Can you open the window?" Alex asked repeatedly, gesturing to Ivan with a winding motion. Ivan would open the window, but as soon as Alex looked away it would be closed again.

There were fewer and fewer houses, or shacks – as the buildings they passed resembled – the further they travelled from the capital. They pulled up abruptly in front of a dirt track that led off the narrow country road they were on. Ivan took the turning and after a few minutes they emerged in front of a particularly decrepit, two-storey chalet-style house.

Ivan switched off the engine and turned to Alex in the back seat. He handed back the crumpled piece of paper Alex had handed him a couple of hours earlier. Alex looked at it and at the house again.

"You have wife?" Ivan said to Alex.

"No," Alex replied.

"You are here for wife?"

"No, this is my... Place," Alex said, after a pause.

The building was on its own at the centre of a desolate field of about half an acre. There were no trees or bushes around it, as if the field had once been scorched. Alex wasn't sure if he should be pleased or a worried to see that there were no immediate neighbours.

"Englishman's home his castle?" Ivan said, nodding.

They both looked at the building. Ivan began to laugh heartily and Alex joined in politely but uneasily.

"The Germans buy places in the mountains for skiing. The Russians on the coast for the beach. The English..." Ivan said, and shrugged. Alex noticed his English was better than it had previously appeared.

"But you see, you like?" Ivan said and shrugged again.

"I haven't actually been here before, to the house, or Bulgaria," Alex said.

"You bought but never seen?"

"I've been busy."

"You're not busy anymore?"

"No."

"It's just as well you have time," Ivan said. "You will need it to make this place nice to get a wife."

"I'm not looking for a wife."

Ivan looked Alex up and down, his eyes lingering on his trainers.

"Yes, just as well."

Alex got out of the taxi and handed Ivan a fifty Lev note, the last of his Bulgarian money. Alex tapped at his jacket pockets to indicate he had no change. Ivan tapped his own pockets to show he was out of change, too. Alex got back in the car and crossed his arms and shook his head. After being robbed at the airport he wasn't going to be ripped off.

A smile spread across Ivan's face as though an idea had just entered his head. He disappeared behind the car and opened the boot, emerging with an un-labelled bottle of clear liquid with a cork protruding from its opening. He placed the bottle in Alex's hand then mimicked a drinking motion.

"Rakia," he said.

Alex nodded slowly before getting out of the car. Ivan nodded back at him before getting in the driver's seat and starting the engine. He glanced briefly out of the car window, a look Alex thought resembled pity, before screeching away up the dirt track.

Alex walked up the path to the house. When he reached the front door, he placed his right hand on the door frame, the rough wood under his fingertips. It was a real place.

An old-fashioned key was in the lock and he turned it. Surprisingly, the door sprung open like a padlock. He pocketed the key. The open door revealed a dark room with a kitchen table and chair. He shivered, feeling the draught – the room as cold as it was becoming outside. He took a seat at the table in the centre of the room.

Alex put the bag of things he'd bought on the table. He pulled the cork from the unlabelled bottle still in his other hand and took a sip from it. His mouth burned. When the liquid hit his stomach there was a stinging sensation. He sat at the table, drinking slowly and tearing off chunks from the loaf of bread and stuffing them into this mouth.

When he imagined Richard coming back to the flat, he reached for the bottle, pouring himself a large measure of the spirit into a dusty tumbler that he'd found in one of the cupboards behind him and took a long sip.

He pulled the notepad and pen he bought from the airport out of the bag. He began writing, filled a page, and turned it over and kept going. His head became heavy. He laid it on the table, his hand still around the glass tumbler.

**

Alex's eyes were open but he couldn't see anything. He kept blinking repeatedly, straining to open his eyes wider. There was only grey. His heart pounded. His throat burned.

A scream erupted from inside him. He wasn't sure if any sound was coming from his mouth or if it was just in his head.

He felt for his phone in his pocket, pulling it out and pressing the call button. A dialling tone rang before everything went black.

Chapter fifteen
With Julia

"You know what they say it means when men go very quiet?" Julia said.

"No, what?"

"They're about to leave or propose."

"I wasn't planning on doing either today."

"That was a shitty thing to say, Alex. Given you know what happened with my ex."

"I know, I'm sorry."

Alex and Julia were in the kitchen of the flat. It was around dusk. They were both still dressed in their work clothes, having only just arrived back.

"Let's have those few days apart we talked about," Julia said.

"I don't want that."

"I don't want that, either."

The phone rang. Julia looked down at the table.

"Get that if you need to," Alex said.

"It's only Dan. I'll call him later."

"Will you?"

"Your jealousy is really unattractive, Alex."

"I'm not jealous of him." Alex looked away, out of the window.

"I just don't like the way he messages you all the time."

"You have female friends that message you," Julia said.

"Okay, I don't like the way he looks at you."

"None of those law students you work with have crushes on you?" Julia said.

"They're all about eighteen, Julia."

"And that's why you haven't made a move on any of them?"

"You know that's not what I mean," Alex said. "I just don't like the way he's always around, picking up the crumbs of affection you give him."

"You're doing a really good job of sounding like you're not jealous."

"I suppose I'm not crazy about the fact you've slept together," Alex said.

"How the hell do you know about that?" Julia asked.

"Max mentioned it, the day we had the picnic on the Heath," Alex replied. "When were you going to mention it?"

"I wasn't. Because it's none of your fucking business who I've slept with," Julia said. "Tell me – have I ever asked you about the women you've slept with?"

Alex walked out of the room, then came back in.

"You know what, Dan needs to get his own life instead of intruding on ours."

"He has his own life," Julia said.

"He's good looking, he's got a successful career, his own flat. He's got everything, everything except what I have: you," Alex replied.

"You won't have that for much longer if you keep acting this way."

It was dark outside now. The light had faded as twilight passed without them noticing, the room falling into darkness. Julia shivered.

"I'm going for a bath," Julia said, getting up to leave. She didn't look back or touch Alex as she left, as she always did when she left a room they were in together. The absence of her touch stung his skin.

***

"And he never saw her again?" Alex asked, incredulous.

"No. She got on the plane to Canada and that was the last they ever saw of each other," one of the volunteers, Alan, a retired civil servant who read thriller novels on his breaks, replied.

"That's the saddest story I've ever head. What am I meant to learn from that?"

Alan shrugged. "Well, that's for you to figure out."

Alex was sitting beside Alan at the back of the empty Citizens Advice office.

"But Alan, there's no beginning, middle or end – it has no message," he said. "Maybe I've watched too many films, but stories need a message in order for them to make sense."

"But that's not life, Alex. In life, there's only a story afterwards."

Alex was silent and looked ahead.

"Shouldn't you be getting home?" Alan asked.

"It's Julia," Alex said. "This is going to sound silly, but I guess I'm waiting for a sign."

"Like in the clouds or something? The sign is you love each other and it works. That's the great thing about life – you don't have to let it happen to you. You get to choose. You get to write the script as you go along."

Alex sat back in his chair.

"So, what should I do then, Alan?" he said.

"Well, the thing that scares you the most is often the best thing to do."

Chapter Sixteen

Without Julia

"Have you got my laptop cable?"

"Your laptop cable?" Alex said.

"Yes, my laptop cable," Richard said. "As well as stealing my money and skipping the country, did you also take that too?" He was tapping the side of the bed gently.

Alex was lying in a hospital bed in a long, grey-walled room. Richard was sitting beside him.

"You don't know how sorry I am about what happened," Alex said. He felt a lump in his throat and a weight settle in his stomach. "About what I did. I deserve to suffer."

"You're alive, that's the main thing." Richard said. "How's your eyesight?"

"It's still a bit blurry." Alex said. "Did the doctor say anything about why I lost it?"

"He said whatever you drank from that bottle on the table of your 'villa mansion' was, chemically, closer to paint stripper than vodka," Richard replied. "Where on earth did you find it?"

"Taxi driver from the airport."

"Why did you drink it?"

"To warm me up. The villa mansion isn't well insulated, it turns out."

"It can't have tasted good."

"It didn't taste great, but I wasn't sure what it was meant to taste like – with no label."

"No label. That should've been a sign not to drink it. The doctor said you could have died, not from the booze but from the pneumonia you caught because of how weak it made you."

"Richard?"

"Yeah."

"I'd murder a cup of tea."

Richard sighed.

"I'll see what I can do?"

* * *

"You have a proper beard. Makes you look older," Richard said, before taking a sip of his tea.

"I feel older." Alex sat up in the bed, glancing around. "Wait a minute. How did I get here?"

"You don't remember calling me?"

* * *

"Let me get this straight. You let me stay with you rent free. I lie to you, steal from you, then run away to another country," Alex said, sitting up in the bed, pausing as he ran out of breath. "You drop everything, fly to Bulgaria and save my life."

"Yes. That's pretty much it."

"Richard, there is something I really need to tell you," Alex said.

"About the whereabouts of my laptop cable?"

"No."

"About Ciara?" Richard said. "Don't worry, you didn't."

"Really?"

"She'd never sleep with you, and no woman would have done the state you were in that night. Her twin sister Rose was staying with her at the pub.

"Apparently, you were wandering around upstairs ridiculously drunk. You tried to suck Rose's neck and then took off all your clothes. Ciara rang me and we all put you to bed."

"I'm so relieved," Alex said, putting his head back onto the pillow and looking up at the ceiling. "And so embarrassed. But mainly relieved."

"We all found it hilarious," Richard said. "They've been calling you the 'naked vampire', actually 'the horny naked vampire' to be precise."

Alex sat up again. He caught a glimpse of a grey and cloudy Sofia sky through the far window.

"What am I going to do, Richard? I've really messed up."

"Not really, you're going to have a gap on your CV, but you're still a qualified lawyer."

"I'm not even sure I want to be one anymore."

Richard got up from his seat beside Alex and went over to the window, looking out of it before turning back to Alex.

"You seem to have a good rapport with that kid,

Billy, isn't it?" he said.

"Yes, Billy," Alex said, sighing, remembering Billy's big match.

"What about teaching? You could retrain," Richard said. "You have all that redundancy money to support you."

"Actually, I don't – it's gone."

"Where?" Richard said, with a confused expression on his face.

"I'm too tired to explain," Alex said. "I'll tell you later."

Richard's phone made a noise. He looked down at it and smiled.

"It's a message from Ciara."

"Oh really?" Alex said.

"She's keeping me updated on the cricket, actually," Richard said, typing into his phone, not looking up. "I can't get wi-fi in here, they don't even have it in the hotel. It's like the internet hasn't made it here yet."

"You know, Richard," Alex said, "you can't hate me more than I hate myself."

"I don't hate you, we're winning the cricket."

Alex picked up the plastic cup beside him. He took a sip of tea. Returning it, his arm shook and Richard steadied it with one hand, while still tapping into his phone with the other.

"You must have one hell of a hangover after drinking that stuff," he said.

"The worst."

"The doctor says you'll be fine to travel tomorrow. I've booked us on a flight back at midday," Richard said, heading for the exit door of the ward. "I'll come and pick you up at ten."

"You're leaving me?" Alex said, leaning forward, nearly falling from the bed.

"You'll be fine. I promise I'll be back in the morning," Richard said.

Alex tried to get out of bed, before a wave of tiredness overcame him and he fell back onto it. "Heathrow, departure lounge, The Britannia pub."

"What?" Richard said, looking surprised.

"The laptop cable," Alex replied. "That's where I left it."

"Marvellous," Richard said, sighing. "See you tomorrow." He walked out of the ward door but reappeared a moment later.

"By the way, nice trainers," he said. "Holiday shopping?"

Alex followed Richard's eyes to the pile of his clothes on the bedside table next to him – the pair of lime trainers resting on top. He opened his mouth to reply, but Richard had already gone.

***

Alex woke. He didn't know how long it had been since Richard had left, but sensed it was the same day. He felt rested, with more energy than earlier. He slid out of the bed and walked to the nearest door in his hospital gown.

The corridor was narrow and the walls seemed to bear down on him after being in the open ward.

When he turned the first corner, the space opened out. He'd entered a modern area of the building that must have been an extension to the old part of the hospital he'd come from.

There was a huge airy circular atrium with a spiral staircase in the middle of it. Around the atrium were the names of famous people from history, some alive but most dead: Gandhi, Mother Theresa and Churchill, amongst others. Above their names, which were written in English, were quotations but written in Bulgarian, with its different alphabet.

Alex began walking round the atrium, stopping in front of a quotation attributed to Albert Camus. He was powerfully drawn to the words, although he didn't know what they meant. He reached out and ran his fingers along the unfamiliar letters of the quotation. He heard gentle breathing behind him.

"You want to know what it says?"

Alex turned. Dressed in overalls was a very old but beautiful lady, with a broom in her hand. She must have been sweeping the atrium but he hadn't noticed her.

"Very much," Alex answered.

The woman stepped forward and stood beside him. They faced the wall together.

"'In the depth of winter, I finally learned that within me there lay an invincible summer'," she said.

Alex turned to thank her but she was gone.

***

"How are you?" Richard asked.

"Better, thanks. I can see properly," Alex replied. "How's Ciara?"

"She fine. She says she hopes you feel better and you're still welcome in the Crown. But upstairs is out of bounds."

"That's nice."

"She said something else."

"What's that?"

"That you're incredibly lucky to have such a good best friend."

Richard picked up the sheet of paper beside Alex – Alex'd asked the nurse for some paper the previous day. It had some words scrawled on it in Alex's handwriting. Richard looked down at it.

"Did you write this?" he said, handing Alex the loose page.

Alex recognised the words as the Albert Camus quote from the hospital wall that he'd transcribed, and he smiled to himself.

"Maybe you really should finish that screenplay." Richard nodded.

***

Richard took the bags out from the back of the cab while Alex climbed out of the back seat onto the curb, in front of the airport. He looked around but couldn't see Ivan amongst the rows of waiting cabs.

He barely recognised the airport when he followed Richard into the departure lounge. It had only been three days but it felt like three weeks since he'd left the UK.

"Have you enjoyed your time in Bulgaria?" the grinning airline attendant asked as she swiped Alex's boarding pass at the departure gate. Alex and Richard looked at each other.

"It's been an experience," Alex said.

"A good experience?" the attendant asked, looking confused.

"Akin to emergency dentistry," Richard said.

"See you again," she said. Alex and Richard looked at each other once more before boarding the plane.

Chapter Sixteen

With Julia

He found a packed bag beside the kitchen table and a note on top. Julia had written 'Alex' on the single folded piece of paper, it looked like a name place at a dinner party for one. Without taking off his jacket, he sat down at the table and opened the note.

She wanted some time apart. She'd gone out and wouldn't be back until late. He should call her in a few days. Alex wasn't sure he'd be able to wait that long, they were usually in contact many times during the day.

Alex stepped out of the flat, bag in hand. He hoped for rain, to reflect the way he felt inside. But it was a perfectly sunny afternoon. He looked back at the flat, wondering when he would be returning and under what circumstances, before turning the street corner.

***

Alex was at the door of his father's flat. He sighed and let himself in before shouting for his father.

"I'll get some more food in," was all his father had said when he'd phoned earlier. Alex had explained as best he could about Julia, that they'd had an argument, and asking if he could stay for a few days. His father seemed unusually sad to hear the news. Alex looked down at his watch, his grandfather's silver Rolex. Julia would be arriving home about now after her lunchtime shift.

Alex hadn't slept over at his father's flat much in recent years. During school and university holidays growing up he'd often stay with friends. Perhaps that was why the flat felt like his father's – rather than his – home.

He found his father unpacking some shopping when he entered the kitchen.

"I'll have to be more civilised now that you're here for more than a cup of tea," he said. "No sardines on toast for dinner."

"I rather like sardines on toast."

"Well, it's a bit early for supper, actually. Did you eat lunch?"

"I drank lunch."

"Alex?"

Alex noticed a bottle of expensive brandy on the kitchen counter and an empty tumbler on the table. He'd never seen his father drink during the day. His father looked at him observing the brandy bottle and empty tumbler.

"Looks like you drank lunch, too," Alex said.

"Do you want one?" his father asked him.

Alex slowly took a glass from the cabinet and poured himself a drink, and his father another. "I didn't think you ever drunk during the day, especially spirits, Dad."

"Well, I don't have to get up in the morning anymore."

His father slowly and carefully made sardines on toast. It was the way his father always cooked and prepared food, not preciously but methodically.

Despite not having eaten that day, Alex had no appetite, but he forced down a few mouthfuls. While he ate, his father looked out of the window, also barely touching the food on his plate.

"Do you want anything else?" he asked him.

"No, thanks," Alex said, topping up his and his father's glasses from the brandy bottle – too drunk to worry about asking his father first. His father barely seemed to notice anyway. Alex was still finding it strange to see his father with a glass of brandy in his hand. It didn't seem natural.

"So, you like this new job?" his father asked.

"There's a fair amount of law. I'm mentoring the volunteers, which I'm enjoying," Alex replied. "I helped save this woman and her disabled kid from losing their flat today, at least for the time being."

"'Love all, trust a few, do wrong to no one,'" his father said.

"I can never remember which one that's from," Alex said.

Silence fell again between them.

"I think I'm going to go to bed, Dad. I'm shattered." Alex stood and reached to clear the plates on the table.

"Leave them. I'll wash up tomorrow."

"Okay. Night, Dad." He was almost out of the kitchen when he heard his father speak.

"All's Well That Ends Well," his father said, and Alex turned back.

"I hope so, Dad. I really do," Alex said immediately, before realising his father was referring to the play and his line from earlier.

Alex lay in the single bed in his old bedroom. He thought about what Julia had said to him the previous day. He reached over to his jacket hanging on the chair beside his bed. He took out the leaflet, the Citizens Advice Bureau logo across the top. *Are you depressed?* said the title in green writing below.

"Are you depressed?" he said aloud to himself.

Alex awoke to ringing. He stuck his hand out and pushed down the top of a small black alarm clock on the bedside table. Its yellow fluorescent hands indicated 7 a.m. – his father must have set it for him. Alex yawned and stretched, his feet protruding from under the duvet. His whole body ached. He took down the small threadbare dressing gown he'd last worn as a teenager from the back of the door and put it on over his boxer shorts. He left his room for the corridor to the kitchen.

Alex felt the coffee pot, it was lukewarm. He poured some into a cup already on the table, drinking it black rather than making it cooler by adding milk. There was a box of cereal on the table and a rack of toast – the options presented on the table made like a kid's breakfast, or a bed and breakfast. Alex didn't have a desire to eat, but he wanted the pain in his stomach to go away. His father walked in and they nodded at each other.

"Thanks for sorting out breakfast, Dad," Alex said. "I haven't had these in a while." He gestured towards an opened box of cereal his father had bought, his favourite as a child.

They ate breakfast in silence. Alex looked over at the radiator. His father's swimming trunks weren't there, as had been the same on his previous visit.

***

"Drinks?" asked Katie, one of the volunteers, who was leading the office staff to drinks. It was 4.15 p.m., the office closed early on Fridays. Alex was still getting used to leaving work whilst there was still daylight.

A lot of the regulars who hadn't been in all week came into the office that day before the weekend. But in between clients, Alex had been checking his phone for messages from Julia. He'd sent a couple of messages, but nothing. He would have to call if he wanted any response from her.

"I've got to go," Alex said. "Have fun." He waved at the party from work as they headed off along the road in the direction of The Grand Union pub.

Alex walked on, up Parkway and across the road into Regent's Park. He walked a few circuits of the park, taking out and checking his phone for messages every few minutes.

He left the tarmac path and cut across the grass

towards Hampstead. As he stepped onto the wet grass, his right foot went from under him, then his left immediately after – he flipped forward, landing heavily on to the ground. His face was damp against the grass, the smell of earth in his nostrils.

He heard his phone beep, and he reached into his pocket as quickly as he could with his muddy hand. It was Richard.

***

"Have you been drinking?" Alex's father said when he looked up from the stove.

"I tripped walking across the park," Alex replied. He was standing in the kitchen doorway barefoot, in a white vest and his work trousers. There were two plates on the kitchen table.

"I wasn't expecting to see you until later, I thought you'd be out with Richard or something. I was going to leave this out for you."

"You didn't need to make me anything."

His father lifted the wooden spoon he was stirring the pot in front of him with to his mouth. The spoon had a cream coloured sauce on it.

"Carbonara," he said.

"Can I do anything?"

"You can have a shower," his father replied. "It won't be ready for fifteen minutes."

Alex wandered out of the kitchen and past the music room, his mother's piano covered with more stacks of books and files. Alex moved the files that were now on the piano lid onto the top of the piano. He sat down on the seat in front of it. He sat for a long time without moving.

He lifted the lid and placed his fingers on the keys. He pushed down as he played three chords very slowly, the opening chords of Nat King Cole's 'Unforgettable'.

He hit a wrong note and stopped.

"I haven't seen you sitting there for a while." His father was at the door. He now had oven gloves on and a faded apron, decorated in a picture of the different types of sailing knots. "You found the piano?"

"Found it? It was more like an archaeological dig," Alex replied.

"I was never very good at filing. It was the thing I hated most when I was a trainee, and I never got better at it." His father put his hand on the top of the piano. "Is it in tune?"

"The piano is," Alex replied. "I'm not sure about my playing."

"Your mother used to play that one. It was her favourite. Our favourite."

"I remember – you told me," Alex said. "I imagine she could actually play it, though."

"She could play anything. Sometimes we'd hear a song at a restaurant and she would come home and play it. Not always perfectly at first, but after a few attempts."

Alex watched his father intently as he spoke about his mother; when his father spoke about her she became more real. Without a single memory of her,

Alex felt sometimes like she'd never existed.

"When did you stop playing?" his father asked. Alex took his hands off the piano keys and turned to him. "When did you stop swimming, Dad?"

"Ah."

"I don't understand. You have more time now you're retired," Alex said. "When was the last time you went?"

"My last day at work," he replied. "The day I retired, I just stopped going. I don't really know why."

His father appeared to be looking through him. Alex wondered whether it was his mother he was looking at in his mind's eye, sitting at the piano. When he spoke, his father didn't hear him at first.

"Well. Let's make a deal. Dad?"

"Sorry, yes." His father's attention returned and he looked at Alex. "A deal? I don't do deals anymore, and neither do you."

"I promise to start playing again if you start swimming again."

"I should get back to dinner. It won't be long," his father said, leaving Alex at the piano. Alex tried playing again. After a few false starts, he managed to play 'Unforgettable' all the way through.

When he put down the piano top, slowly, so it barely made a sound, he thought about where Julia would be at that moment. He pictured Dan turning up at the flat, all smiles and sympathy.

His father at the stove looked around when Alex entered the kitchen, after quickly showering and dressing.

"You didn't sound too bad."

Alex sat down at the table, and made the shapes of the chords with his hands on the table.

"It's funny how the body remembers when the mind forgets."

***

Alex heard a tapping, it took him a few moments to open his eyes as he awoke from a heavy slumber. The taps got louder. His father's head appeared from behind the bedroom door. Alex glanced at his father's face and then across to the alarm clock on the bedside table – it was 6 a.m.

"Huh?" he said, looking at his dad.

"Five minutes. If you're coming?" his father said, and threw a faded, blue ball of coloured material in Alex's direction. It landed on the floor beside his bed.

Alex looked down at it, squinting, sleep still in his eyes. When his father had gone, he realised what it was – a pair of his father's swimming shorts.

Chapter Seventeen
Without Julia

At the front door, Alex automatically put his hand in his pocket for his keys before remembering he didn't have them, they were somewhere in Bulgaria, as good as lost. He rang the doorbell. He could hear music from the inside, jazz, louder than his father would usually have on.

Alex pressed the bell another time before sitting down on the step, his back against the door. He stretched out his legs in front of him. Everything looked different from down there. The geraniums were beginning to flower. He remembered his father saying that it was a late bloomer, flowering during summer rather than spring. The Heath was their real garden his father said, they just shared it with others.

***

"Alex?" He heard his father's voice, and tried to work out where the voice was coming from. Realising he'd fallen asleep against the wall by the door, he turned and looked up.

Alex tried to stand up. His head span and he fell

back. He saw Julia's eyes when he had caught her at the bus stop.

"Julia?" he said. He felt arms under his, supporting him. He turned. "Dad?"

"Alex," his father said again. "Richard should have helped you back."

"He tried to, Dad, I told him I'd be fine and to go and meet Ciara," Alex said. "I feel bad enough about putting him out already." He wondered how much Richard had told his father about what had happened.

"Who's Ciara?"

"His lady friend."

"Ah," his father replied. "So who's Julia?"

"Someone I met a while ago," Alex replied. "I think you would have liked her. She's an actress."

"Let's get you inside," his father said, shutting the front door.

"Dad," Alex said, stopping in the corridor and turning to his father. "You sure it's okay to stay?"

His father ushered him down the corridor to the kitchen, gently, with a hand on his shoulder, Alex unsteady on his feet.

"I can sleep on Richard's sofa."

"This is your home, Alex." His father continued to lead him towards the kitchen, guiding him onto the nearest wooden chair. It was still warm from where his father must have been sitting.

"Do you want a drink?" his father asked, looking at his son, concerned.

"No. I'm okay, thanks," Alex said, his mouth still dry and his stomach still with a constant ache.

"I meant water, or tea."

"Oh. I see." Alex got up and shuffled across the room. "I'll get it." His father took out a glass from the cabinet and placed it on the surface for Alex to use.

Alex filled the glass from the tap slowly, concentrating hard. He forgot the pain in his body until the glass was full and he'd turned off the tap. There was a pot on the stove beside him; the air smelled of onions.

"I'm cooking," his father said.

Alex thought his father wasn't sure what to say. His father then began talking about how the weather had been, as he would on one of Alex's usual visits.

"You're travelling light," his father said. "Do you have a bag?"

"No bag," Alex said. He thought about Ivan for the first time since he'd got back and wondered if he'd meant to poison him, or if it had been an accident. He guessed the quality control for homebrew was unlikely to be very precise.

"I haven't seen those shoes before." Alex followed his father's eyes to his feet, he was still wearing the fluorescent lime green trainers. He opened his mouth but felt too tired to explain, he just nodded in response.

"To be completely honest, you look like you got dressed in the dark," his father said, with an earnest expression.

Alex looked down at himself again. His entire outfit comprised of items from the hospital's lost property. Mustard chinos, a red Chicago Bulls T-shirt and a purple bomber jacket.

"In somebody else's bedroom," his father added.

It was then that his father smiled. Alex smiled back. His father began to laugh, slowly at first and then more. He hadn't heard his father laugh in years, it was such a strange and unusual sound it made him laugh too.

They stopped. Alex caught his father's eye, they both looked down at what he was wearing again, and it started them off until they were crying with laughter. Alex's arms on the table and his dad with his hands on it.

Suddenly his father looked serious and turned quickly back to the stove. He sighed in relief.

"You should have a wash and change into clean clothes before we eat," he said. "It will make you feel better."

Alex didn't have the energy to move, but stood up. When he left the room, his father followed him down the corridor. He pushed open the bathroom door as they passed it.

"Bath?" he asked, as if the idea of a bath was a new concept. "Dinner, well, supper, will be an hour."

Alex stood at the door. His father went in, put the plug in the bath, its metal chain rattling against the back of the old iron tub – the bathroom hadn't changed since he was a child. His father ran the taps before turning to Alex.

"Do you need a hand getting in and out?"

"No, Dad," Alex said, pausing. "But thanks for asking."

His father didn't say anything, leaving the room for the kitchen.

The only physical contact between them when Alex was young had been a brief hug at the end of each term of boarding school. As an adult, it was even less frequent. The last time must have been their awkward embrace at the nearby bus stop when Alex had gone travelling for nine months with Richard after university – he'd insisted on coming to see them off.

Alex kicked off his shoes into a corner of the bathroom and pulled off his clothes. He looked down at his pale naked body. Looking up, he saw his face in the mirror, a stranger – he was still unused to seeing his face with a beard.

Leaving his clothes in a crumpled pile at his feet, he stepped heavily into the bath. The water was scalding hot. After pausing for a moment, he lowered himself into it. His skin below the surface of the water turned from pale white to a bright red – but he didn't move.

As the water cooled slightly his body relaxed and he stretched out to the whole length of the bath. His mind began racing with the memories of the last seventy-two hours.

He brought his hand up to his face, it felt wet to touch. His whole upper body began to shake. When his tears hit the water, he heard a whimpering sound, realising it was coming from his mouth – he turned on the taps.

Water thundered out from the Victorian pipes and into the bath, drowning out his cries.

"Do you feel better after your bath?"

Alex was sitting on a kitchen chair, dressed in one of his father's old work shirts he wore for gardening, it was blue with a white collar. He had on some old black tracksuit bottoms he'd found in his room.

His father was making the thick yellow batter for a toad-in-the-hole, while onion gravy was warming in another pan. He'd made it for Alex when he was a child, when he was home at the weekends, or sick. Alex could already feel it warm him inside.

Alex closed his eyes. He was standing at the hospital wall again, reading the Camus quote, with the help of the mysterious old woman. He hadn't realised at the time but after everything that had happened in the last months, staring at those words, perhaps he'd finally found his 'invincible summer'.

Chapter Seventeen

With Julia

Alex followed his father out onto the jetty. The area around the pond was greener than he'd expected and there was a stillness to the place. At this early hour, it was only them and the man sitting in a lifeguard's room behind them, reading a newspaper.

His father was getting undressed. Seeing his body with its sagging skin and head of thin white hair, Alex noticed how old he'd become – how vulnerable he now seemed. Alex was suddenly overcome with feeling for him. Always there, latent, deep within him, but in that moment it felt something physical that he could not contain inside, as if it could tear his heart.

His father seemed to sense Alex did not know what to do next.

"Jump in, thrash around for five minutes, and then come out," he said. "It's all you need to get your heart going. Watch me." His father walked to the edge of the jetty and fell into the water without jumping, slipping below the surface gracefully and with barely a splash.

Alex followed him in, holding his breath a moment, the water colder than he'd expected. He went in a different direction to his father. As he stretched his arms out in front of him, shallow strokes, he noticed his father watching from the other side.

After some minutes, his father hauled himself up the wooden step ladder out of the water. He followed, copying the way his father shook the water off his legs before he stepped onto the jetty.

In the dressing area, his father was sitting on the bench drying what remained of his hair with his towel, dressed except for his socks and shoes. Alex sat down on the bench, beside him.

"I keep forgetting I'm retired," his father said. I rush when I needn't." He put the towel he'd been drying his hair with down beside him. "I could spend all day here."

"Rather you than me," Alex said, the breeze cooling him.

"January this year was cold. The temperature now is like a bath in comparison."

***

They walked up the mild slope from the pond in silence, his father petting the occasional passing dog – as he'd seen him do many times before on the high street.

"Dad?"

"Yes, Alex?"

He opened his mouth but couldn't say the words.

"Alex?"

"Do you ever wonder what would have happened if

286

Mum had got treatment earlier?"

Alex's father stopped walking. Alex stopping beside him. He felt his stomach buckle, his chest tighten. He was hunched over, tears falling from his eyes. He wept for the disappointment he believed his father felt for him, for all the years without his mother. He wept for his sad, lonely father who stood before him, and because he'd wrecked things with Julia even though he loved her and she was everything he wanted. It was then that his father took him in his arms.

"My son, my dear son," he said, his hand on Alex's head, holding him close. "It wasn't your fault," Alex heard his father saying over and over again, until it was all he could hear.

After a few minutes, without any ceremony, they parted and began walking again, both looking ahead. His father kept his arm around Alex, and squeezed very slightly when the breeze came from time to time and Alex shivered.

They reached the edge of the Heath and turned back for a moment, the deep green land stretching out below them. Alex could see the spire of a church in the distance, the one they could see from the kitchen window when the sky was clear.

***

"Is this situation with Julia very bad?" Alex's father asked.

"I think so. She's been hurt before," Alex said. "Some guy messed her around."

287

"Are you messing her around, too?"

"No. I couldn't be more serious about her."

"Well, maybe you need to show her that you're serious."

"I moved into her flat."

"You're not there now."

Alex and his father were sitting in the kitchen, tea mugs in front of them. Alex looked over to the radiator, his father's swimming trunks were drying, beside them the blue ones he'd worn. Alex breathed in.

"When I was your age, I was already a father, although only just," his father said. "I'd just been made partner at the firm, too, thinking about it."

"If you're trying to make me feel better, Dad, it's not working," Alex said. "I mean, what have I got?"

"You've got a job you like. Okay, it doesn't pay nearly as well as your previous one, but it's a job, you're finding it rewarding and it has a social benefit."

"True."

"You've got Julia."

"But for how long?"

"Well, perhaps you should pick up the phone and stop with all this messaging business."

Alex put his hand on the table and pushed himself up. He picked up his phone from the kitchen worktop – where it'd been charging – and cradled it in his hand. He pressed to call Julia.

"Julia," Alex said into it. "What are you doing?"

"Dan's been round," he heard Julia respond.

"Why?"

"To talk."

"What about?" Alex said, pacing down the corridor towards the front door. "About how he's in love with you?"

"Yeah – sort of."

"You're kidding me?" Alex was now pacing back down the corridor towards the kitchen. "Fucking snake."

"When can I see you?" he asked.

"Let's speak again later, Alex."

Alex stopped pacing. "Okay. I'll call later." He sighed.

He stood in the corridor, imagining the scene at their flat, Dan slagging him off and making himself out to be the big hero.

Alex knew Dan could give her things he couldn't, and he knew Dan could make her happy, or at least some kind of happy. "Believe in me, Julia", Alex whispered to himself as he continued towards the kitchen.

He sat down. He stood again almost immediately, leaning against the wall. His father filled the kettle.

"Dad, I've got something to ask you."

"Should I sit down?" Alex's father looked at him, the kettle still in his hand.

"I think that would be a good idea," Alex replied slowly. He took the kettle gently from his father's hand. "I'll finish making the tea."

Chapter Eighteen

Without Julia

When Alex stepped into the lift, the smell of stale urine hit him.

"Some old dude got stuck in there yesterday and pissed himself," the youth walking past said to Alex, who had turned around. "There's another one down there." He gestured down the hall.

On the lift floor around his feet were empty plastic sandwich packets, cans and bottles; a crumpled pizza box lay in the corner, propped against the side of the lift. Alex stepped out of the lift and watched the doors close and it go up, someone calling it from above. He saw from the panel beside the lift that he needed the ninth and top floor.

He walked up through the stairway. The breeze got stronger each level he went higher. He felt sweat on his forehead as he climbed the last set of steps to the ninth floor. Pausing at the top, looking out, the building was surrounded by four tall concrete high-rise blocks, identical to the one he stood in.

He'd looked down at the address Mary had given him over the phone and then up at the door. His shirt was sticking to him uncomfortably. He pressed the buzzer twice but there was only a dull thud in the buzzer socket. He heard a shouting inside and a dog barking. He knocked on the door.

The woman who opened it looked tired. She was wearing a thin shirt with a logo, he recognised it as the budget supermarket he passed on the way there. She had the same red hair as Billy, worn simply with a hair band at the back. She looked him up and down.

"You from the school? Or the social?" she asked.

"I've come to see Billy. I'm his..." Alex paused.

The woman was tapping her foot against the door frame.

"...Friend," Alex said, after another pause.

"You're the posh guy? Didn't show up to his big match?" she said.

"I guess that's me," Alex replied, quieter than before.

"I told him you'd let him down. All men do in the end, even the ones with fancy accents," she said, without any emotion.

Alex could see puppies wandering around dozily behind her. A small blonde girl in yellow track-suit bottoms and a grey-white vest was holding and stroking one of them. A large bulldog, appeared behind the girl, with what looked like a half shredded take-away menu in its mouth. The dog rubbed its head against one of the puppies before moving off, muscular body swaying from side to side.

"It's Sarah, isn't it?" Alex said to Billy's mother.

Billy appeared from the back of the flat, stopping for a moment, looking directly at Alex, his expression changing from surprise to disgust.

"He's a wanker," Billy said, before wandering out of sight.

Sarah shrugged at Alex. "Don't speak like that, Billy," she said in a raised voice over her shoulder.

She turned around and let the door swing shut behind her. Alex faced a closed door. He reached down, taking out an envelope from his pocket. He was about to slip it under the door when he heard a growl from inside. He put the envelope back in his pocket and stood.

***

Alex sat on the ledge by the stairwell along from the door to the flat, looking out over the cloudy, grey skyline. He heard a door open. Billy was idling along the corridor towards him.

He sat on the adjoining ledge facing Alex, knees under his chin, in his faded Arsenal top and grey tracksuit bottoms. He was barefoot.

"Woman from the place said you had some kind of breakdown," Billy said.

"Well, I wouldn't put it quite like that," Alex said. "I got kind of lost for a while. But in the end, I found some perspective."

"Like from the top of that hill?"

"Exactly. I just had to go a little further."

"They're not going to lock you away, like they did to my mum?" Billy asked, looking concerned.

"No," Alex replied. "I'm fine now."

"You don't look it," Billy said, with a chuckle. Alex looked down at his loose jeans, he hadn't recovered the weight he'd lost in hospital.

"Did you win the match?"

"Five-nil." Billy pushed his chest out, unconsciously.

"That's good, right? You beat them."

"Yeah, we smashed them."

"Congratulations," Alex said. "I'm so sorry I didn't make it."

The wind blew down the concrete corridor from the open stairwell, the nearby lift shaft clunking as the lift passed down it.

"Shame there's nowhere here to kick a ball around," Alex said. "No outside space."

"Do you have a garden?" Billy asked.

"Not at Richard's, no. My dad's flat is next to a kind of park, though, Hampstead Heath – we saw it from the cemetery, remember?" Alex replied. "What about you? Before you lived here."

"Nah. My nan had a garden. Looked more like a building site, though. Granddad left her for the barmaid at The Grapes, halfway through building her a rockery."

"Did she get the rockery finished?"

"She never wanted a rockery in the first place. Do you know what she used to say?"

"What was that?"

"There was only one thing worse than having a rockery, and that was having half a rockery."

"I suppose we don't always get what we want in

life."

"She called it an eyesore. I never really knew what that meant."

"It means to look at it makes your eyes sore. Not literally, it's a metaphor."

Alex took out the white envelope from his pocket and slipped it across the ledge towards Billy. It was open, and two tickets with the red Arsenal Football club badge were visible inside.

"It's a special match, I'm told." Billy looked down at the envelope.

"Champions League," Alex continued, smiling.

The breeze picked up. Billy jumped down off the ledge, grabbing the envelope as the wind lifted it into the air.

"You dickhead," he said to Alex, holding the envelope into his chest. "Do I have to give you one?" he added, his head at an angle.

"It would be wasted on me."

Billy was smiling, the tickets still held tightly in his hand.

"You're still a wanker. And that's literally and metaphorically."

***

When Alex finally scored a goal, they both dropped their games controllers onto the cream carpet, jumped off the black leather sofa, and cheered – fists high in the air.

Alex looked at his watch. "Sorry, I've really got to

go."

"We're in the middle of a game." Billy sighed.

Alex walked to the door, followed by Billy.

"We've got one meeting left. If you still want to do it?" Alex asked.

Billy put his arm against the wall. "Well, there's a big game on Saturday," he said, smiling to himself.

"You sure?" Alex said after a pause.

Billy turned back to the flat and shouted towards the Kitchen, "Mum, Alex is taking me to the match on Saturday."

"I'll see you then. Please say goodbye to your mother for me."

Billy closed the door and Alex walked towards the stairwell. He took a step down.

"Hold on!" he heard Billy shout behind him. He turned.

Billy was now standing in front of him, one of the puppies in his arms.

"We can't afford to feed them all. Going to keep one, flog the rest down the market,"

"I can't have a dog, I've no idea what to do with it," Alex said.

"It's not for you," Billy said, rolling his eyes. "It's for your dad. Sounds like he could do with another friend."

Billy placed the tiny brown puppy in Alex's arms like he was handing over a baby.

Yesterday
With Julia

"I'm starting to think I've been asking the wrong questions, Richard." Alex and Richard were sitting at one of the tables at the Crown, it was particularly busy.

"What do you mean?" said Richard.

"I'm always asking, 'This woman or that woman? Lawyer or writer? Chance or fate?' Etc, etc."

"These are the wrong questions?"

"Yes, I think so now, because there are no answers, we can never know the right thing to do for sure," Alex replied. "Life, I've realised, is always a leap of faith."

"'To be, or not to be, that is the question'," Richard said.

"Exactly. Gold star to you." Alex tapped Richard's shoulder. "To know when to leap and when not to – that's the only bit I haven't figured out yet."

"I think I know one question you should be asking," Richard said.

"What's that?" Alex asked, turning to Richard.

"'Richard, can I get you a pint?'" Richard continued.

Later, Alex stood opposite the pub's bathroom mirror, surrounded by the dark green tiles that covered the walls. He wondered what turning points had occurred, what life resolutions had been made in between the four walls of the Crown toilets – most of them forgotten by the morning, he imagined.

"So, are you ready to leap?" Richard said, when Alex returned. "Sounds like if you don't, this Dan guy is definitely going to, if he hasn't already."

"I need to make a call," Alex said, and took out his phone and left the pub, holding it to his ear.

* * *

"You'll need your passport," Alex said. "Yes, I'm not joking. And could you bring me some clean socks? No. That is a joke."

"You're definitely going to be there, Julia, right?" He leaned against the side of the pub. "Are you still there? Okay. You think so." Alex took a deep breath. "Is that the best I'm going to get?"

* * *

Alex walked back into the pub, picked up his pint and downed it.

"She said yes?" Richard asked.

"She said maybe, after a very long pause."

"She'll be there."

"What happens if she doesn't come?"

"I'm not helping you move again." Richard smiled.

"She'll give you this chance. Just don't fuck up again or it sounds like you'll lose her for good."

"I've got to go." Alex downed his pint and rushed for the door. Out of the corner of his eye, he saw Ciara place her hand over the bar onto Richard's arm.

***

Alex entered the CAB office. The main office light was off and Raman was at one of the desks with the lamp on, reading some papers.

"Missing me?" Raman said, when he looked up and smiled.

"I need a favour."

"What, no 'Good evening'?" Raman laughed.

"Oh God, sorry, Raman. Good evening. I need to book some holiday."

"That's fine. You have fourteen days in your contract."

"I know Friday's our busiest day but..."

"You want tomorrow?"

"I'll be back on Tuesday."

"We'll survive without you for a few days."

"You sure?"

"Lock up with me."

While Alex looked on, Raman pulled the back door twice. He imagined Raman had closed the place in the same methodical way for years.

"You know, when you first walked in here, I wasn't sure about you."

"Neither was I."

"But you've made a real difference in your short time here."

***

Alex took out his phone after he'd left Raman at the street corner. He dialled Mrs Jacobs's number.

"Mrs Jacobs? Yes, sorry – I'll speak up," Alex said, talking slowly and loudly. "I can't speak for long but I think I've found someone for your dog, Bobby."

"Yes – they do live locally. They've kept dogs before, although not for a while. Yes – they'll have time to pop by and see you with Bobby."

***

"So, this cricket match you've been so obsessed with," Alex said, "has it ended yet?" He put his overnight bag down beside him.

"How many times have I explained this? It's not a match. It's a series called The Ashes and it's the greatest and most long-running sporting rivalry in the world," Richard replied. "But yes, it's over and we were victorious."

"So you really weren't just here all the time to chat up Ciara?"

"Well, I suppose there have been two games going on," Richard said. Alex looked at his watch.

"Richard, you know Plato valued the love between friends above romantic love?"

"I guess Plato didn't get out a lot."

299

"Richard, I'm being serious, you've been a great friend to me."

"I know," Richard said, and headed off in the direction of the toilets.

"Richard, I'm not joking," Alex said. Richard didn't stop and disappeared through the toilet doors. Alex pulled a wooden cricket bat carefully out of his bag.

"Ciara, can you keep an eye on this until he gets back?"

"What is it?" Ciara said. "It looks like one of those things they've been swinging about on the TV for what seems like all summer." She winked at Alex.

Alex smiled. "You're right, it is," he said. "A very special one, though."

"Why special?" Ciara asked.

"This cricket match Richard and half the country has been glued to," Alex replied. "It's to do with that."

"How did you get it?"

"One of the former partners from the law firm phoned me a few weeks ago. Heard I'd been let go. Asked if he could do anything to help me," Alex said. "He's left law to do something important in cricket."

Alex placed the bat on top of the bar. The open face of it was covered in blue and black signature scrawls.

"It's signed by the players of both teams: England and Australia."

"He's going to love this."

"I hope so."

When Alex got to the door of the Crown, Richard was returning from the toilets and approaching the bar and Ciara. Richard and Ciara's eyes met, the gaze held, they were the only people in the room. Richard lent over the bar, Ciara towards him; a kiss.

Alex smiled, turned, and walked out of the Crown and into the warm summer evening.

***

Standing at the door, Alex saw there was a small box in the centre of the kitchen table. He smiled to himself. He pulled out a chair and sat down at the table.

He picked up the box and opened it slowly. Inside was a diamond engagement ring, the one his mother was wearing in the wedding photograph on top of the piano.

He closed the box and slipped it into the pocket of his biker-style leather jacket, zipping up the pocket. He stood, picked up his overnight bag and stepped towards the corridor. He didn't have much time.

Glancing back at the table, he saw there'd been a folded page of yellow legal notepaper under the box. He picked it up and opened the note. In pencil was scrawled in his father's handwriting.

Faint heart never won fair lady – love, Dad

Yesterday

Without Julia

Alex let himself into the flat with the spare key his father had given him. He set the puppy down onto the floor from his spare arm. It struggled to its feet, trotting off quickly towards the kitchen before he could grab it.

When Alex entered the kitchen, his father was stroking the puppy and gently playing with its ears,

"Who is she?" his father asked.

"She?" Alex replied.

"She's a bitch."

"Oh, right."

"Whose is she?" his father asked.

Alex explained what had happened. His father nodded.

"She's no oil painting, this one," his father said.

"You should've seen her mother. She looked like a killer."

"We can take it – sorry, her – to an animal shelter, dad," Alex said. His father didn't answer.

Alex made tea for them, after he'd filled a bowl of water for the dog, as instructed by his father. They sat at the kitchen table. He watched his father stroking the puppy, which now lay sleeping in his lap.

"Kent," his father said.

"Kent?"

"I'm just thinking about what to call her."

"The Earl of Kent?"

"Yes," his father said, and tapped him on the shoulder proudly. "King Lear's Kent, the most loyal of all Shakespearean characters."

"I always thought the Shakespeare you made me learn might help me get a girlfriend one day," Alex said.

"The whole of the human experience is in Shakespeare," his father replied. "It's not for chatting up girls."

"That's just as well."

It was now dark outside.

"I have a favour to ask, Dad."

His father stopped stroking Kent and looked up at him.

"I'm thinking about a change in direction. I'll need somewhere to live while I do the course, I thought maybe I could stay here," Alex said. His father stopped stroking the dog. "I know it's a lot to ask." Alex added.

"It's not a lot to ask." His father began stroking the dog again. "You don't need to ask, and you never need to ask again – this is your home."

Alex put his hand on his father's shoulder and stroked the puppy his father was gazing down at.

"I'll make us some more tea," Alex said finally. "It looks like she's got you occupied."

He put the kettle on and turned back to his father. He looked different, but Alex couldn't put his finger on what it was.

"Dad, when did you last go to the cinema?"

"When did we see that film about the Second World War? I think it had Tom Hanks in it. Five years ago?"

"The one you fell asleep in? More like fifteen years ago."

"Why don't we go next week. Do you remember that Italian place we always used to go to after?" Alex asked.

"I remember. "

"Dad, seriously though, now you're retired, if you don't have anything to keep you busy, you'll get bored, or worse."

Alex looked at his father and followed his father's eyes down to the puppy.

"Perhaps, some human interaction too," Alex said. "Charities always need volunteers, and with your legal background..."

"Alex, are you going to keep me in suspense all evening?" His father said, smiling. "Tell me about this course of yours."

Today

With & Without Julia

Tick tock, tick tock, tick tock... Alex felt the regular, rhythmic click of St Pancras station's huge, ornate brass clock above him, the minute vibrations running through him with each of the long hand's clockwise movements. His heartbeat seemed to fall in line with the mechanism's perpetual forward motion, counting out the passing seconds. The seconds that would make up the minutes, hours, days, weeks and, eventually, years, of the rest of his life.

A pigeon swooped into the station, passing over his head. Sensing its containment, Alex watched as, squawking loudly, it threw itself at the glass ceiling again and again in its desperation to escape.

For as long as Alex could remember, he'd woken up each morning anxious. With the sense, after falling asleep in the middle of the day, of waking suddenly and disorientated – lost, not knowing the time or the place. He'd stood waiting with that feeling six months ago, weighed down by it. Today was different, he felt a lightness of spirit and a relentless optimism for the future.

How did I end up here, Alex thought, remembering

all the decisions he'd made in the past six months, the handful of big ones and the hundreds of small ones. When faced with the decision to follow Julia onto that bus or not, he now knew he'd made the right choice. *Whatever was going to happen next was inevitable.*

Looking up at the clock again, he wondered how many moments of his life he'd really lived, rather than just sleepwalked through. He knew, however hard it might be, or how terrified he was, he didn't want to be afraid any more. He didn't want to waste any more time, any more of these precious seconds.

There was a rushing sound above. Alex looked up to see the trapped bird in flight again, heading straight for the exit but too high. It dipped at the last moment and he glimpsed it once again fly free into open sky.

Today
With Julia

Only fifteen minutes remained until the train left. Julia was late and she was always on time. Alex was standing in black jeans, a white T-shirt and his biker jacket, an overnight bag at his feet. He glanced anxiously at the faces of people passing. Looking for one particular face in the crowd. Her face. *What if she didn't turn up?*

A smartly dressed old man in a tweed suit, an old-fashioned camera around his neck, stopped beside Alex. He heard the click of the man's camera, the mechanical sound so clean, almost exotic, after the sound of digital cameras. Alex looked round at the photographer's subject – The Meeting Place statue behind him. Unusually, the statue's figures were dressed in modern clothes, they could've been one of the couples he'd seen walk by it.

There was a familiar tapping sound of heels on the hard station floor in the distance. Alex knew it was her without even looking. When he turned around, Julia had a serious expression on her face, like she was going into battle. She hadn't seen him yet.

"Julia!" Alex called. "You came."

"How could I not come?" Julia said. She had an unreadable expression on her face. "You saved my life once, remember?" It was then that Julia smiled.

"You save me every day," Alex whispered to himself. They kissed tentatively at first, like nervous lovers, and then passionately.

He looked at Julia. She was wearing a sky blue dress with a thin red belt and had on her black leather jacket.

"I've missed you." Alex said.

"How much?"

"Endlessly, infinitely, eternally."

"Is that all?"

A clattering sound came from above, they looked up. Rain was hitting the roof of the station. Alex noticed a large group of people of mixed ages pass by; they had matching rucksacks with, 'Cardiff Community Choir' printed on them.

"Alex, it's been less than a week."

"It's been the longest less-than-a-week of my life."

"Sometimes I think you should be the actor." Julia said, rolling her eyes.

"Passport?" Alex asked.

"Yes." Julia patted her handbag. "And yours." She had a black canvas overnight bag over her other shoulder. "When I was packing earlier, I realised that surprise weekends away can be a contradiction for women."

"Why?" Alex asked.

"Because women love their men to be spontaneous," Julia said. "But they also like to know what to pack."

They walked down the stairs towards the train platforms.

"Did you worry I wouldn't turn up?" Julia asked.

"I was starting to worry," Alex said. "You've never been late before."

"You've never taken me for granted before," Julia said.

They stopped walking for a moment and locked eyes before continuing. They walked past the parade of shops; a piano appeared ahead of them with a sign hanging from it that read: 'Pianos In Public Places: Play Me.'

"Are you going to play for me? Or was that only when you were trying to woo me?" Julia asked. "I should be clear, I expect the wooing to be a continual phase."

"We really don't have time," Alex said, a pained expression on his face.

"But you promised," Julia said, and pulled a sad face. Alex stopped walking and Julia did the same.

"I've been thinking about what you said in Brighton, on the pier," Alex said. "Whether it's chance or fate or something else, it doesn't matter, I choose you, Julia – always. The only question is..."

Alex knelt down and reached down into his bag. When he looked up at Julia, she was standing still, eyes wide and mouth slightly open.

"Alex. Not now," she said finally, in a quiet tone that Alex could barely hear.

Alex sighed.

"Wait until we get to wherever we're going," Julia said. She winked at Alex, flashed him her smile and sat down on the piano seat.

"I promise to play this piano for you as soon as we arrive back," Alex said. "But we must go." He reached out his hand to Julia, she reached out and took it. They picked up their bags and continued down the station.

"Back from where?" Julia asked. "You still haven't told me where we're going." They passed the large signs overhead for the Eurostar. "The last time I went to Paris was on a school exchange when I was fourteen. I snogged a boy called Jean-Pierre outside the Louvre. It was a huge scandal at school when we got back."

"Well, we could have looked him up, but we're not going to be in Paris very long," Alex said.

"We're not?" Julia stopped walking. Alex went on until he saw she wasn't beside him and turned around.

"Julia, we've only got five minutes until our train," Alex said. "We're going to miss it, please."

"Not 'til you tell me where we're going," Julia said, standing still with one hand on her hip.

"How's your Italian?"

"Italian?"

"Yes. We change trains at Paris – we'll be in Venice in eighteen hours," he said.

Julia smiled, her beautiful smile with her eyes and Alex knew then everything was going to be okay. That day, the day after and, perhaps, every day for the rest of his life.

The rain shower had stopped and the sun was now shining through the roof into the station. When Alex and Julia passed through the check-in desk they glanced back, the choir from earlier had broken into song and began to sway. 'I Can See Clearly Now' by Johnny Nash echoed around the station.

Today

Without Julia

"You're as beautiful as I remember," Alex said without thinking, to the woman walking past – her eyes on the train departure board above him. He was in shock. He could reach out and touch her, but part of him didn't believe she was really there in front of him. It was Julia.

"The beautiful actress from the bus stop," Alex said. "Remember me?"

Julia stopped. She was wearing a sky blue dress, red belt and a small leather jacket – on its lapel, a small white badge with 'Sisterhood' on it in black letters. She turned and looked directly at him and smiled, with her eyes – the same way she'd done when he'd made her laugh six months earlier at the bus stop.

"How could I forget?" she said. "The handsome lawyer who saved me from certain death."

"Handsome still, I hope," Alex said. "Not a lawyer anymore, though. And I'm not sure I can take the credit for saving your life but I'm glad you remember it that way."

They stood looking at each other. Julia glanced up at the clock behind Alex.

"Would you like to get a coffee?" Alex asked.

"I haven't got much time before my train, but you can walk me to my platform," Julia said. "If you'd like?"

They walked side by side, Alex glancing at her often, as if to make sure he hadn't imagined her.

"Did you get that part?" Alex asked.

"No," Julia replied. "I was so nervous I screwed up, forgot my lines."

"I'm so sorry," Alex said. "Are you on the way to an audition now?"

"Rehearsals," Julia replied. "I got another part."

"Where?"

"At the Hampstead Theatre."

"Really? That's close to where my dad lives," Alex said. "And where I'm moving back, for a while."

"How come?"

"It's kind of embarrassing at my age," Alex answered. "I'm going to study full-time."

"Really? What?"

"English and Drama, at Goldsmiths. I'm on my way to enrol. I'm training as a teacher," Alex said. "I've got an English degree as well as a Law one – it'll take me a year."

"You're brave, but I'm really so glad. Your heart didn't seem to be into law."

"It wasn't."

"I'm sure it will be nice to spend time with your father, too," Julia said. "I'd love to live with my family right now, but they don't live in London."

Alex stopped walking and she also stopped beside

him.

"You know, Julia, you made quite an impression on me, after you got on that bus," Alex said, looking into her eyes. "I thought about you."

"I thought about you too," Julia said and smiled coyly. "For about five minutes."

"I never thought I'd see you again," Alex continued. "I regretted not asking for your number."

"I'm afraid you're too late."

Julia looked down. Alex's eyes were drawn to where she was looking. On her left hand was a very shiny, large diamond ring.

"You're engaged?" Alex asked, taking a deep breath.

"Yes," Julia said. "But only in the play." She smiled mischievously. "I've been wearing the ring all the time so I don't lose it."

Alex breathed out. "In that case, can I have your number before you get on your train, or another bus?" he asked. "That is if you don't mind going out for dinner with a student?"

"I'd like to, I really would," Julia said. "But I have barely anytime to see my friends, let alone go on dates." She lifted her leg, with one foot pointed to the ground – as she'd done at the bus stop – like a ballerina, her head slightly to one side. "I'm sorry." Alex breathed in.

She looked up at the clock and down at her phone.

"I should really get my train."

They continued walking in the direction of the platforms. *Time was running out.* They walked past an old wooden piano with a sign that read: 'Pianos In Public Places: Play Me.'

"What's this?" Julia said.

"They've got them all over London this year. It's some kind of public art thing."

"Do you play?"

Alex looked over her to the clock above The Meeting Place statue. He sat down at the piano. He played the first few notes of Nat King Cole's 'Unforgettable', then stopped and looked up at Julia.

"Is that all I get?" Julia asked.

"Come and sit beside me." Alex gestured for Julia to join him on the small piano seat. She rested her bag on the top of the piano and sat beside him. She was close and Alex thought he could feel the beating of her heart.

"I'm not sure I remember it the whole way through."

"No excuses."

Alex began to play "Unforgettable" again, slowly and haltingly at first.

"It's an old song," he said, over the sound of him playing. "Do you know it?"

"I think so," Julia said. "Do I get singing, too? That would help me remember."

Alex glanced at the statue of the two lovers in the distance and began to sing along quietly, playing until the end of the song.

An elderly couple, in matching rain jackets, who'd stopped to listen, quietly applauded. A tourist with a large SLR camera took a photo of the scene. Alex turned to Julia.

"You were great," Julia said.

"I wasn't, but thanks anyway," Alex said.

They got up to leave as the small crowd around the piano dispersed.

"Do I get your number now?" Alex asked.

"Maybe you should give me yours," Julia replied, with a smile. "Just in case an audition gets cancelled one day and I end up with some free time."

The Lost Elephant Café

by Alex Bendrix Wright

I could still taste her kiss on my lips as I walked along a deserted Chalk Farm Road at sunrise.

Camden was quietly stirring, a bright sun emerging from behind smoky white clouds, a ghostly presence in the morning sky. Rising in the East, above St Luke's majestic red brick tower, it would descend to sunset behind Camden Stables, in the West, travelling in a perfect arc. Signalling the day from beginning to end, its events yet unknown.

I passed the Lost Elephant Café – now closed and shuttered – and thought of the old owner and his lost elephant. I was certain we'd return one day with another. I even imagined him standing unsteadily on a wooden chair of the café, taking down the faded lost elephant poster from the window. Rolling it up delicately in his shaking hands and slipping an elastic band around it, in case it was needed again.

It was then that I realised the old man didn't want a new elephant. He only wanted his elephant to return, and no other could take its place.

Perhaps we all have our own lost elephants: things, or people we've loved – will always love – but which

317

we've lost. And however hard we search and however great our longing, we can't find them again, but also can't ever forget.

I turned away and continued towards the metal bridge over Camden Road, 'Camden Lock' painted in huge yellow letters against black across its side. The lush green mound of Primrose Hill in the distance.

I looked down. I stood at the foot of a rainbow-coloured tree drawn across the pavement in coloured chalk. The swirling branches, scuffed and faded from the passing steps, now blurred. Only the lines of the tree's brown trunk and green roots remained strong and clear. Vital almost, as if holding the ground beneath me together.

There was an unexpected break in the clouds and I closed my eyes as the warm London sunshine hit my face. In the few precious seconds before the spring sun disappeared again, I felt inside me a sudden rush of an unstoppable sense of fun and infinite possibility. I opened my eyes and looked up in wonder at a sky, so very clear and so impossibly blue.

Thank you
from my heart
to you who helped me
believed in me
loved me